Jackson Pollock (1912–1956), *Number 5, 1948.*
Oil, enamel and aluminum paint on fiberboard, 96 x 48 ins.
Private collection.

Image courtesy Pollock-Krasner House and Study Center, East Hampton, NY

In 2006, a Jackson Pollock painting purportedly sold for one hundred and forty million dollars. The private sale was never confirmed and the precise whereabouts of the Pollock remains shrouded in mystery.

ACKNOWLEDGMENTS

I'd like to thank all my friends and family for their help and early criticism of this book. Many of the places and events are real. [See the Disclaimer Sample at the beginning of the book] Some individuals have been fictionalized in the book (and any resemblance to their real character is coincidental). Importantly, the information regarding Mount Sinai Hospital is entirely fictional, and was written long before I had any affiliation with the hospital or medical staff. A few local proprietors in the Hamptons or San Francisco are themselves in their actual locales (Evelyn from Jackson Court and Theresa from the Hamptons Coffee Company). There really is a Simon from Beach Bakery Café in Westhampton Beach. Dr. Mirowski invented the implantable defibrillator and actually said "The bumps in the road are not bumps, they are the road." Some other characters in the book are loosely based on real people but have been fictionalized. Any resemblance to a real person is coincidental. The timing and the sequence of events are real. The Transcatheter Cardiovascular Therapeutics conference occurred where and when it did, as did Sandy. And David Brubeck unfortunately died when he did also. I'll miss him. Other places also actually exist, but likewise have been fictionalized for the purposes of creating a good story. This includes Ghost Motorcycle, a myriad of restaurants, etc. And yes, you do have to bring your bottle of wine to Farm Country Kitchen in Riverhead, NY. Otherwise, the story is entirely fictional. I would also like to thank my copyeditor, Margarett Harrell, as well as friends, family, defense and exoneration attorneys, an actor, and even a Krav Maga expert for their input and feedback with respect to Pollock No. 5!

POLLOCK NO. 5

Todd J. Cohen, M.D.

A Black Opal Books Publication

GENRE: MYSTERY, ART THEFT/ROMANCE

POLLOCK NO. 5
Copyright © 2021 by Todd J. Cohen, M.D.
Cover Design by Transformational Concepts
Cover photo used with permission: Image courtesy Pollock-Krasner House and Study Center, East Hampton, NY
All cover art copyright ©2021
All Rights Reserved
Print ISBN: 9781644372616

First Publication: MAY 2021

Published by Black Opal Books **http://www.blackopalbooks.com**

DEDICATION

To the memories of my art-loving mom and my New York Yankee-loving dad, both reincarnated as the main character's parents in Pollock No. 5.

PROLOGUE
July 2012

I looked at the wall at the framed letter sitting next to an image of a beautiful Mark Rothko painting. It was one of those museum four-panel cards with a separate inner space for writing. The card was cut in half with the front Rothko image on the left, and the inside writing component on the right. I didn't read the letter often, but I knew what it said. It was there. It always seemed to make sense:

What do we strive for?
What do we need in life?
What things do we as human beings yearn for?
Success? Contentment? A Job? Art? Family? Love?

Chapter 1

BAM!" I felt a fist hit me in the jaw and fell to the ground. Lucky for me, I was with my compadre Dr. Alexiev Shaw, former Israeli defense engineer and master of Krav Maga. Or should I say, unlucky for the three goons who thought they were going to make out like bandits right outside of the Red Rooster—Harlem's latest trendy home-cooking restaurant. I never quite understood how Shaw got tied up with the Israeli Ministry of Defense, but he was always a bit of a mystery. In his grey Armani suit and blue Ferragamo tie, the six-foot-two-inch tall, olive-skinned Shaw looked somewhat subdued. We were about to present our latest startup venture—MATAL Inc.—to one of the hottest VCs in the world, but now that meeting was seriously in jeopardy.

"Guys, I will give you one chance to step back and leave as quickly as you came," said Shaw with a very calm, French-accented voice. The goons just laughed!

"What the fuck you gonna do?" said an over-tattooed bandana-wearing goon wielding a switchblade.

"Yea!" said another equally tattooed goon holding a crowbar.

"Alex, just leave him alone." I cringed. I did not want him to do what he did the last time. By *the last time*, I was referring to when "the gang of twelve" jumped him last spring. Each gang member wound up with permanent injuries, only Shaw was left unscathed.

"This fucker can't do anything to us," said a chuckling third goon. This third guy pulled out an even bigger, badder knife and began to move ever so slightly towards Alex.

Within a nanosecond, Alex moved opposite the third's lunge, spun, and grabbed him from behind in a headlock, and with one rapid jerk broke the sucker's neck, then twisted his arm. The blade clanged to the ground, falling alongside the now motionless assailant. The two other goons surrounded their fellow gang member, both simultaneously raised their weapons, one to his left, and the other to his right.

"You've got a problem, motherfucker. You're gonna pay for that," grunted the overly-tattooed first goon.

"Yes," snarled the second, "you can't do that to us!" as he proceeded to raise his blade.

"By us, are you referring to both of you? I think you underestimate your opponent," said Alex. With what looked like two twists, one lunge, and a kick, both goons were doubled over in pain—one flat on his face, the other fully supine.

"Matt, are you okay?" asked a concerned Alex.

I looked back at Shaw standing there after this ordeal, and it came to me. Perhaps it was the combination of his martial arts with his large muscular stature. No, it was the addition of his recently changed hairdo. Shaw had always parted his dark black hair and combed it behind his ears. Not now. He had let it grow, and now he combed his near-shoulder-length hair straight back in a ponytail. Yet his body, underneath the jacket and tie, was Schwarzenegger-esque. The entire package was more like Steven Seagal in *Under Siege*.

Seagal played a former Navy Seal serving as a cook on

a military ship attacked by terrorists. Seagal—with his aikido jabs, kicks, twists, and spins—made chop suey out of the terrorists. And Shaw was the spitting image of Seagal. Perhaps the only difference in appearance when compared side by side to Seagal was a very slight twist to Shaw's nose from some sort of brawl he preferred not to talk about. He originally told me he was into "jujutsu" to stay fit. But finally, after five years of our friendship, he confessed. It was not jujutsu at all. It was Krav Maga, the Israeli ancient art of self-defense. But those Israelis really didn't play around. Krav Maga was not for fun, it was for survival. It was life or death, and Shaw knew how to survive, better than anyone I had ever met.

"I'm okay. How about you?" I responded. I knew Alex was fine, but I just had to ask. I also knew the three goons who attacked us were not okay, to put it mildly. But we had a meeting to go to, one that *could* change everything. Alex extended a hand and helped me to my feet. We both walked to the door, and he proceeded to open it as I made my way unobtrusively towards the bathroom in the far left-hand corner of the restaurant. I looked at him and said it.

"Has anyone ever told you that you bear a striking resemblance to Steven Seagal?"

"I have heard that once or twice," Alex smugly responded.

I chuckled and then I said it: "Seagal for Shaw!" I was always poking fun at his last name. Substituting "Shaw" for *sure*. Now I had something else to poke fun at. I opened the door marked MEN, walked in, and looked in the mirror. My jaw was starting to swell, and my hair was disheveled. I cupped the water from the sink and splashed it on my face.

"MD," I said to myself. "You have an important meeting to go to." Again, I poured more water all over my face, then my hair, using my fingers to brush my drenched hair backwards in some semblance of what I thought would be a cool, entrepreneurial look.

"That's better," I thought. I proceeded to dry my face and my dripping wet hair with a paper towel, then straightened my black Saks Fifth Avenue V-neck T-shirt and fixed the collar on my Brooks Brothers herringbone blazer.

"Ready," I said to myself as I made my way back toward Alex standing at the front with the maître d'.

Chapter 2

D r. Dawson, this is Mr. Fredrick Morgan." Alex made the introductions. Morgan was a tall, slender grey-haired gentleman, wearing a blue pinstripe suit. He must have been in his mid-seventies, and his demeanor was cool. Morgan Capital Associates was the largest venture capital fund on the West Coast. Morgan's last four investments all had returns of greater than $5 billion. And I mean billions with a capital B. If you scored a deal with Morgan, success was almost always assured.

"Nice to meet you, Mr. Morgan," I replied. "I've heard so much about you." He was the senior partner and founder of Morgan Capital Associates. The VC firm itself had a net worth of over $50 billion. Everybody knew Morgan Capital, but for every one-hundred proposals they looked at, only one received funding. "What a lucky one percent," I thought. Just about every startup Morgan invested in turned into gold. I knew that if our MATAL, Inc., did a deal with him we would be fully funded, and our novel artificial valve implantation system would become a reality.

"The pleasure is mine, Dr. Dawson," said Mr. Morgan. "I've heard so much about you as well."

The hostess proceeded to seat us in the back corner, a quiet table as requested. We each began to look over the menu.

"Dr. Dawson, please tell me how you got started down this road," said Morgan.

I was certain, Mr. Morgan already knew a fair amount about my partner and me. One Google search of "Matthew Dawson, MD, New York" would tell it all, and I was not good at talking about myself. This kind of stuff always made me uncomfortable.

"Let me tell you about Dr. Dawson," proudly said Alex. "Dr. Dawson, or shall I say MD, is one of the most humble guys I know. So, let me give you his dossier. He was born and bred on the North Shore of Long Island and attended Johns Hopkins, where he received his PhD in biomedical engineering as well as his MD degree. He trained in cardiology at Stanford under the world-renowned interventionalist Dr. Arthur Smillar. He began his inventing career during his training at Stanford, working on several areas of coronary artery interventions, three of which were acquired by Johnson and Johnson, Abbott Labs, and Boston Scientific. From there he started working on applying little metal springs—which he removed from the inside of ballpoint pens—into blocked coronary arteries to keep them open. This was the predecessor of the "coronary stent." His most recent breakthrough came together with my assistance, when we applied magnetized wires to form the stent and compared it to the standard bare-metal variety. His magnetic version worked much better! A patent was filed and the rest is history. Magnetostent, Inc., was acquired by J&J for an undisclosed amount, but I can tell you that "undisclosed amount" was north of a 'C-note.'" Alex chuckled.

Alex was clearly trying to make a joke. A C-note was slang for $100, and that wouldn't pay for a halfway decent bottle of wine on this menu. In reality, Magnetostent was sold for over $500 million, of which I received 10 percent. Not too bad a payday for that simple idea. "Too bad I didn't just stash the cash under my mattress," I muttered inside my head. Then I had to open my mouth before I was entirely embarrassed.

"Alex, that's enough. Please don't bore our guest," I interjected.

"Drs. Dawson and Shaw, I am well aware of both your achievements. In fact, I may know more than you think. Number one in your class at Hopkins, right, Dawson? Finished cardiology and interventional cardiology training in half the time at Stanford. Isn't that correct? Met your wife, Shari, during your internship at New York Hospital. Have two kids, Jason and Bridgette. Isn't that also correct?

"Hey, how the hell do you know all that? Who are you, the FBI?" I said in a somewhat irritated tone.

"Sorry, Dr. Dawson, but I have to know everything about anyone I may be contemplating doing business with. And you, Dr. Alexiev Shaw—your mother was Russian and your father of French and Scottish descent. You grew up in Marseille and immigrated to Haifa, where you worked in Professor Saul Bodnick's research laboratory at the Technion. Your project on molecular clues to atherosclerosis won you a full scholarship to MIT. You are also a member of the elite operative unit of the Israel Defense Forces known as the Sayeret Matkal. The same unit that was part of the July 1976 Operation Thunderbolt, better known as Operation Entebbe, that rescued over one hundred Air France passengers hijacked to Uganda by Palestinian terrorists. I know you are not just any ordinary doctor, but a magna cum laude graduate from MIT, where you not only achieved your bachelor's in engineering but your PhD in the combined fields of nanotechnology, robotics, and reparative cardiology. Once you met Dawson, that's when the real chemistry started."

I did not respond, just paused for a minute and thought to myself that Morgan was right on the money. Alex and I are a perfect pair. I have the crazy ideas, he makes them a reality. If my concepts don't work, he makes them work. And if they do work, he makes them work better.

"The area of structural heart is my primary focus, and your artificial valve implant system is genius!" said Morgan. "This will revolutionize aortic valve replacements. That is, or course, if it works."

Transcutaneous aortic valve replacement, or TAVR, is a procedure that allows a patient the ability to get an aortic valve replacement without open-heart surgery. My system is the answer to the problem of how to safely access the heart. Not by going around the aorta, as was first performed, nor by going directly through the ventricle, as it is currently being done, but by something completely different. Safer, simpler, and different—always the way to make a better mouse trap! I proceeded to reach into my left pants pocket and pulled out what to the outside observer would have been a jumbled-up set of wires and plastic, but to me was my latest and greatest innovation. I had the concepts and Alex made it a reality, tooling everything according to specifications.

"Voilà!" I said. "This is it. The MATAL system." I proceeded to unravel the system in order to demonstrate. "MATAL stands for Mechanical Aortic Transvalvular Axial Longitudinal system, or MATAL for short! The system consists of a long, soft, flexible guide wire, which traverses the patient's malfunctioning valve. The guide wire incorporates my patented rotational outer coating, together with the 'launchable,' low-profile transcutaneous valve." As I opened it, I pointed to the valve that traversed the wire and rotated in my hand. I simulated a tight, or stenotic, diseased-aortic valve by curling my left-hand's index finger together with the hand's thumb. "Once in position, all you have to do is advance this proximal lever, and, voilà, the valve springs open and is deployed!" I said emphatically as the valve sprung open into its full position between my tightened thumb and my index finger. It was like magic. As the prosthetic valve proceeded to open, it pushed the small space between my forefinger and thumb wider and wider until the valve was completely open. "Deployed" if you wish. The valve now was in place, and I easily released the guide wire.

"Two voilàs in one short presentation? Must be making Dr. Shaw proud with my française," I joked to myself.

"Very impressive, Dr. Dawson! But I thought MATAL stood for your two first names—*Mat*thew and *Al*exiev! I've never seen anything quite like it. Current TAVR systems are so big and difficult to deploy. This puts those systems to shame. You've sold me!" Mr. Morgan concluded with a smile.

"Well, let's make it happen," said Alex.

"Not so fast," Morgan proclaimed, raising his right hand like a cop stopping traffic. "We have a little issue over the IP. You see, my patent attorney found two significant prior art patents that read on your invention, the Brooks patent and the Fairfield patent. Each references a method and system for placing aortic valves using a 'launch-able' platform that appears very similar to yours, at least according to Sid Fox, our IP expert."

"I beg your pardon, Mr. Morgan, but we are well aware of the Brooks and Fairfield patents," Alex abruptly protested. "Neither uses our rotating screw mechanism to deliver the valve, nor its access point. I feel confident that you will come to the same conclusion, once your Mr. Fox talks with our Mr. Lippert. I will email you his number and he will be happy to clarify any and all IP issues. Let's just enjoy our meal."

Alex knew how to change gears. At that precise moment the waitress brought out my Rooster Noodles, a mixture of "pork belly, crab, head-on shrimp, and teff ramen." Alex devoured the Blackened Catfish, while Morgan feasted on Helga's Meatballs. After our feast, we shared one order of Sweet Potato Doughnuts, and sipped our "Illy Blend dark roast coffee" and then all got up to leave.

"Goodbye, Dr. Dawson and Dr. Shaw. You will be hearing from me this week." Morgan extended his hand and gave both Alex and me a firm handshake.

"Goodbye, Mr. Morgan," I said as I wrapped up the MATAL system and slipped it back into my pocket.

"Great meeting you," replied Alex with his usual confident smile.

Chapter 3

The livery service had a Lincoln Town Car waiting in front of Red Rooster. Alex and I hopped in and headed across the Triboro and then to the Grand Central Parkway. The driver pulled to a stop at Alex's stately mansion in Plandome, a North Shore Long Island treasure of a town. Unlike me with my unlucky investments, Alex was smart enough to hold onto his "just desserts" from our ventures, and his seven bedroom, four-car garage, three-acre compound put my place to shame.

"Bye, Alex, thanks for saving my ass from those goons," I said, almost teary eyed. I realized that without Alex's protection, I would not only be wallet-less, but possibly even lifeless.

"No thanks needed. What are friends for?" He shut the door, and I looked back at him and thought of Seagal

The livery driver headed further north, back up Stonytown Road and then up Port Washington Boulevard to the much larger, more populated, adjacent town of Port Washington. Three short turns and we were at my more modest abode in the village of Beacon Hill.

"Here we are," said the driver. "That'll be two hundred dollars."

"Credit okay?" I asked.

"Fine," he said.

I gave him my Platinum AMEX and left him a forty-dollar tip and walked through my side door. I had forgotten my keys but tested the door, it was open. It was almost midnight and the lights were still on downstairs. On the kitchen counter I saw an open bottle of Caymus Cabernet almost completely finished. The cork was still in the opener, and dirty dishes remained on the counter. I went upstairs and looked at my daughter's bedroom. It was dark and shut. My bedroom door was ajar, the lights on, and there was Shari, sitting up in bed, finishing what looked to be the last bit of the Caymus. She was still wearing her clothes and her eyes were slightly glassy.

"Shari, are you okay?" I asked. I had seen her like this before.

"Yes. Why do you ask?" she said somewhat sluggishly.

"Did anything happen tonight? Are the kids okay? Did you have any company? Did my mom call?"

"All is well," she said in a monotone, without making eye contact. "The kids are fine. Your mom did not call. Just sat home and had dinner with our daughter and watched TV."

She did not seem fine. She was a little more than buzzed. In the old days we would refer to this as "shit-faced." My wife was quite petite, and a full bottle of wine would make anyone that size "shit-faced." She started looking ashen grey and then blurted, "I have to go to the bathroom."

Chapter 4

S he scurried to the bathroom and then I heard a disgusting puking sound. I ran to the door and watched as she spewed into the toilet bowl.

"Oh, shit," I rebuked her. "Again? You can't keep drinking like this." I came home and wanted to share the evening's events, but there was no point. Even if I did tell her the news, she wouldn't remember. Not in her inebriated state. After she spewed her guts out, she collapsed on the bathroom floor, apparently unresponsive. I checked her pulse, watching her breathing. I bent over, picked her up, and carried her into bed.

"Shari, what am I going to do with you?" I said. She was out like a light. I was so damn frustrated, that I could not talk with my wife, I just went downstairs, turned on the TV, and switched to Fox. It was a football game. Not college, not the NFL, but an old TV rerun of M*A*S*H called "The Army-Navy Game."

The next morning, I awoke at my usual time: five-thirty a.m. Shari was still out cold, but Bridgette was up early, getting ready for the FIRST Robotics competition. The Schreiber High School bus was set to leave at six-thirty a.m. for Stony Brook University. Shari was supposed to give her a lift, but it was now up to me.

"Bridge, are you ready?" I asked.

"Okay, Dad," she replied. "Let me just throw in some cucumbers and a yogurt and I'll meet you in the garage."

I hopped in the car, started the engine, and within no time Bridgette was in the passenger seat. In less than two minutes we were at Schreiber.

"Bye, Bridge. Good luck!"

"Thanks, Dad. I'll be home by six. Will call you later for a ride. Love you."

She was always the ultimate optimist. Yes, she had her sarcastic moments, but not before a test or a robotics competition. As a senior, this was her opportunity to shine. This was her moment. Four years on the Robotics team, and now she was the team captain—she loved every minute of it! Imagine, the only girl on the Robotics team. "Her pick of the nerdy litter," I thought.

When I returned back, I crept upstairs; Shari was making a loud snoring sound. To say that she was cutting wood was putting it mildly. Her repeated alcohol binges and the ensuing problems to our marriage totally obliterated any attraction in our relationship. It had been years without any romance or intimacy, if you get my drift. All that remained was hanging on a thread with the hope of keeping our marriage going for the sake of our kids, at least until they were all grown-up and out of the house.

I went next door to a small, quiet alcove, which I call my office. It consisted of a black Pottery Barn desk, a series of horizontal files, and some bookshelves. The room was filled with little trinkets from my previous trials and tribulations: a trophy for placing first in the Collegiate Inventor's Competition, a bottle of Perrier Jouet champagne from my lawyer after the Magnetostent deal, an early prototype of the MATAL system, along with a collection of art books picked up from second-hand bookstores over the years. This was my "man cave," the place where I made it all happen, my respite from society, where I could let out all my creative juices.

Chapter 5

I was working on my MacBook Air till midnight every evening this past week. Not rounding on my patients or doing procedures as I used to do. But working on a research paper for our upcoming Twenty-fourth Annual TCT Meeting in Miami, Florida—TCT 2012. TCT stands for "Transcatheter Cardiovascular Therapeutics." My presentation is on "The Effects of Magnetic Stenting on Endothelialization." I am still amazed that I was lucky enough to think of applying magnetism to stents. I have this romantic fascination with those little metal contraptions that I place in a patient's coronary arteries to keep them open to prevent a heart attack. It never ceases to amaze me that these little gizmos work the way I imagined they would. I felt like the luckiest man alive when I learned that the addition of the magnets made the stents more effective, and as a byproduct made me millions. Millions that led to a lifestyle that consisted of a brownstone apartment on the Upper East Side of Manhattan, a mansion in the suburbs in a little town called Port Washington, and a place on the water out in the Hamptons.

That was at least up until five years ago and the downturn in the stock market. You'd think an established doctor would be set—that is, at least financially. But like many other folks, I put my trust in a big New York name and invested all my money with him. Unfortunately, that BIG NAME *made-off* with all my money! My money was caught up in the largest Ponzi scheme of the modern era. Like many wealthy New Yorkers, I lost almost everything.

Just to escape the overwhelming burden of an enormous mortgage on the house in Port Washington and out east, my wife and I had to sell our place in "the City." A beautiful Manhattan turn-of-the-century brownstone on a southern-oriented park block on East Eighty-Ninth Street. And not far from where I worked. Classic stoop, first-floor kitchen and large living room, which led to sliding-glass doors out back, that opened up to a New York paradise. Our own private backyard surrounded by other glorious townhomes. All gone!

But we still have our large brick colonial house in Port Washington! Nearly 6,000 square feet, and lots of wall space to display our art collection. The art we had consisted of very collectible prints, typically of American contemporary artists. And some were from the Bay Area, where I received my cardiology training. Like Richard Diebenkorn, who created masterful abstract landscapes called *Ocean Parks*, colored in whites, blues, yellows, and greens to reflect Northern California. Or Wayne Thiebaud, with delicious chocolate cakes and imaginary San Francisco scenes, with steep streets and tall buildings, all with the greens and blue hues similar to Diebenkorn's.

And we had our majestic place out on the East End of Long Island!

Chapter 6

T hings have not been the same between my wife and me! Last night's drinking episode was just one of many that occurred over the past few years. Easter, at the Breakfast Egg Fest at St. Peter's of Alcantara, hit me like a brick wall. I remember, as clear as day, being pulled aside after Father Bob had scooped scrambled eggs and bacon onto my wife's plate.

"Hey, MD, can I talk to you a second?"

"Sure, Father Bob," I replied. He motioned to me to come into his private library. I followed him. *"MD, I have to talk to you about something personal. I hope it's okay."*

"Sure, Father Bob."

"It's about Shari. While serving her, I detected a heavy alcohol odor on her breath. First, I thought it might have been her perfume, but after we talked for about a minute, I was convinced it was alcohol. For me, this is quite unusual in the morning. I just wanted to bring it to your attention."

"Father, I know Shari has been drinking more than usual. But I was not aware of her drinking so early morning. I'll talk to her about it."

"Maybe you should get some help from AA. We have weekly meetings right here at St. Peters every Thursday

evening. Always confidential! You would be surprised by our regular clientele, well-respected members of our community. Most importantly, AA works. "One day at a time!"

"Thanks for the advice," I realized Father Bob was just trying to help. But this helpful suggestion hit me like a ton of bricks.

I left that breakfast, disturbed. The distance between Shari and me had increased gradually. Perhaps I was in denial, or in my own little world of research and medicine. What began as a spark and developed into a loving relationship was now an emotionally devoid, depressing situation. Did I have something to do with this? Every night, when I came home late from the hospital, I observed her finishing off a bottle of wine, or maybe a few glasses of Dewar's on the rocks, alone. Our relationship suffered more and more. Over the years she became withdrawn and incommunicative. I couldn't seem to reach her.

Fortunately, I thought, our kids were old enough that they would both be out of the house, and we'd lick this problem together. At least, that's what I had hoped! The hope of turning back time, and restoring our spark, and eventually relocating and downsizing to one place. Albeit a much smaller place. And if it had to be one place, it would certainly be *the one* that beacons out onto Quantuck Bay just southeast of the village of Westhampton Beach! Maybe this was just my fantasy world. Or maybe not?

Chapter 7

Thank God for research. The act of identifying a problem, testing a hypothesis, discovering the results, and coming up with sound conclusions. Sounds exciting? Well, not really. It is tedious and boring. I am sitting in my hospital-based office, staring over the park—Central Park, that is—reminiscing about the way things were and "the way we were." Sounds like an old Barbara Streisand flick, doesn't it? Just a few years ago, my wife and I had an active social life. At least one night a week out to dinner in the city. Taking in a show or maybe Lincoln Center on the weekends. And medicine? Just a few years back I had a booming practice, and very little time for research, writing papers, and presentations. Boy, has the world changed! You think that health care has changed due to the reelection of President Obama? Well, perhaps. But the Affordable Care Act of 2010 evoked a whole lot of other changes to us members of the medical field. Changes made for the survival of Big Pharma, medical-device companies, health insurance companies, and, lastly, medical institutions like the one I am currently working for—the Mount Sinai Medical Center. The physicians themselves were left holding the bag. I was fortunate, because I always worked for a hospital. But the physicians in private practice all were scurrying to join with a big institution just to survive. Doctors survive? Yes, survive! It takes a lot of money to cover malpractice insurance, office overhead, and staff (as well as their own health insurance coverage).

Why did I go into medicine in the first place, you might ask? The answer was, to take care of patients. I enjoyed every aspect of the job. And the term "job" is a misnomer. It was more than a job. It was a lifestyle, which included talking to the patients and their families, diagnosing their problems, explaining their treatments, answering their questions, and most of all performing procedures to help unclog blockages in their coronary arteries. As a Stanford-trained cardiologist, *my heart*, no pun intended, was always in taking care of my patients.

The problem is, I don't really have very many patients anymore. At least, not like I used to. Not an in-house consult in over one month, and my medical clinic has almost come to a complete halt. With the competing hospitals' acquisitions of almost all my referrals, I have been relegated to spending more and more hours on research. Hospital rounds have now been reduced to the ritual of grabbing coffee in the doctors' lounge and making social calls to the various administrators.

But they too must realize what has happened! They get my numbers—kind of like the Dow in 2008, falling off a cliff.

Thank God for research!

Chapter 8

Finally, vacation! I have had it up to here with all my work preparing for my speaking engagement at the TCT meeting in Miami. My presentation is almost complete, and a draft paper has been circulated to the other investigators. I had not been spending much time with my wife—hopefully you can understand why—and I rarely get to see my son or daughter. They're almost all grown up, and their friends take priority, plus my late nights and weekends at work don't help the matter. I'm so looking forward to this quality family time with them out east.

But before going out to Westhampton Beach, first a little detour. Besides being my startup partner on all my medical-device ventures, including Magnetostent, Alexiev Shaw, aka Steven Seagal, is also my best friend in the whole wide world. Alex lives with his family in the neighboring town of Plandome. Plandome is a more subdued version of Port Washington, with bigger homes than Port—except for the Sands Point area, that is—but no downtown. Alex speaks quite eloquently and is fluent in at least ten languages. And that doesn't even include his mastery of the computer languages such as arduino, java, and python, to name a few. You can call him Dr. Shaw, Alexiev, or Alex, but please don't call him Al. When I first met him at a meeting up at the Marriott Copley Plaza in Boston, I called him Al and I will not ever forget it.

"Dr. Dawson, do I look like I work at a gas station or a diner? Please, if you may, call me Alex, but NEVER call me Al," he said with a snarl.

To an outsider, Dr. Shaw, with his olive-skinned complexion, may have looked Eastern European or maybe even Middle Eastern. Shaw, however, considered himself only a Frenchman.

A typical ritual of mine was to stop at Alex's place before coming home or before going out east to decompress and unwind. I pulled down Port Washington Boulevard, veered right onto Stonytown Road, left on to Manhasset Woods Road, and then up Alex's winding driveway.

I knocked on the door. "Hello, come right in," Alex said.

"Good to see you." I paused for a moment. "Just going out east for the week. How's it going?" I asked.

"Well, the business plan is done, our corporate papers have been filed, and our latest project is almost complete." Alex always referred to our startup venture as a project. "How's the hospital treating you?" he asked.

"Time for a break. At last, I get a chance to reconnect with Shari and the kids," I replied. "And maybe, just maybe, I could turn this thing around with her!"

Alex then proceeded with his usual ritual, which was more like magic than a ritual. It happened without a request, almost instinctually. It included grinding fresh roasted coffee beans, always deep dark French Roast, putting the delicious ground beans into the holder, pressing them down, and pulling a single espresso shot. At the same time, he pulled a frozen steel container from the freezer and filled the container with whole milk. He then proceeded to steam it to perfection into a frothy delight. The espresso was poured into a classic, rounded, oversized mug, followed by the frothy milk, until the foam created the perfect white heart shape on top of the rich brown espresso. And presto—the "fiesta resistance." The perfect cappuccino à la Shaw.

"Alex, I don't know how you do it, but you put Starbucks to shame," I applauded.

"Old family secret," Alex replied. "Oh, by the way, Bill Lippert called me and filled me in on his meeting with Sid Fox. The meeting went well. By the time it was over, Fox conceded that our patent claims are solid, and he was going to convey that information to Mr. Morgan.

"I knew it," I exclaimed. "Lippert's a great patent attorney. A real gem! How long before we hear back from Morgan Capital?"

"Be patient. It should take them some time to confirm our business plan and come up with a decent term sheet. MATAL will be a reality, especially if we play our cards right." Alex was very confident. At least he made me feel more at ease and less antsy.

"*Patients* is my best virtue. Bad English included. Perhaps that's why I am a DOCTOR!" I joked. I may be good as an inventor, but I was bad with the puns.

After thoroughly enjoying the cappuccino, I bid farewell the best way I knew how.

"*Au revoir*, Alexiev. *À tout à l'heure. Un autre jour.* Oh, and I'm 'Shaw' going to miss you! And give a big goodbye to Steven Seagal, will you please?" I joked.

So, I began to drive from Alex's place out to our vacation home in Westhampton Beach to meet my family. For me the drive has always been short and sweet, only a little more than an hour, and seldom any traffic. No traffic out in the Hamptons, you wonder? Perhaps you are thinking of

East Hampton, Amagansett, or Montauk. Those places are further out than Westhampton Beach, and after you hit Southampton there is only a single lane road that leads to those destinations. Traffic after Southampton typically moves at a snail's pace.

But Westhampton has multiple highways to get you there. The highways themselves are nothing special. They all look the same. There is the LIE, also called the Long Island Expressway (or *Distressway* to some), the Northern State Parkway (this doesn't fully get you there but is a big help), the Southern State Parkway, and even the Sunrise Highway. As John said to Mary, "All roads lead to Rome," or should I say, Westhampton Beach.

Chapter 9

I set my BMW 650i convertible on cruise control and turned on one of my favorite SiriusXM stations, 067, and listened to "Real Jazz" all the way to exit 63 on the Sunrise Highway. The first song was Alex Bugnon's "107 in the Shade." What irony, after just having left Alex's place. "Just don't call him Al," I thought. The piece was syncopated Bugnon piano jazz with a soothing occasional background vocal. A cacophony of bounce and beat. "What an upbeat way to start my vacation," I said to myself. This car and its music were one of my last pleasures, of the good life, from a successful medical practice and an invention gig. Unfortunately, I was at the tail end of an expensive car lease. A lease I was not going to be able to renew, and I was not going to be able to buy the car off lease. I had bigger fish to fry, with one kid in college and the other about to go.

As I passed exit 44 of the Southern State, I veered onto the Sunrise Highway. I was bopping and bouncing to the New York Trio's "Cheek to Cheek." *My heart beat so that I could hardly speak.* That jazzed-up mix of piano and drums was like a second shot of Alex's espresso.

I traveled down past Gabreski Airport and crossed over the railroad tracks, and around the circle past the movie theater on my left, Hamptons Coffee on my right, and then passed the stately brick façade known as the Westhampton Police Station. Then I made a left on Main Street and crossed Turkey Bridge into the little Hamlet of Quiogue (or little Quogue). I tell everybody I'm going to Westhampton Beach because most people don't know of Quiogue. But in reality, I'm just over the border in this little nest egg of a place. Wedged between Westhampton Beach and Quogue. The latter is where Michael J. Fox vacations. My place is just over Turkey Bridge on the right on a beautiful hedged street called Homans Avenue. Or, as my son refers to it, "No Man's Avenue." As he would say, "No Man's, because no man's ever been there."

I have no idea why they even call it an avenue. If anything, the street is narrow and only one car can pass at a time. Tall privet hedges flank most of the road that is, of course, unless you arrive at my place, which is flanked by a small split-rail fence on one side and a stock wood fence across the street.

Our neighborhood, with tall hedges surrounding large, private estates facing the water, is the closest Hampton to NYC, with all the grandeur of Southampton and East Hampton. My place is not like the others. When I first bought it, I called our local plumber, Hal Stanton, and told him the address, and he replied with his craggy voice, "So you bought the shed on the block."

Shed to him, perhaps compared to the ten thousand-plus square-foot mansions. But my three thousand square foot house still stood on luscious wetlands, smack between two mansions, and facing directly out onto Quantuck Bay. And the three thousand square feet were still plenty big for me—four bedrooms, four baths. Who needed all that space anyway? Billy Joel? Jerry Seinfeld? Charley Weisberg? Not MD.

Chapter 10

MD? Was it a curse? My fucking initials. My name. My full name is Matthew Dawson. No middle initials. Hey, I guess I could have been like Cher or Madonna and had only one name—Dawson, perhaps. Or maybe just plain MD. Most people called me one or the other. "Hey, Dawson," "Yo, MD!" One or the other. But others played with the name as if it were a double entendre—"Hey, CLG"—even called me M-2-da-D. The name, or should I say the initials, were both a blessing and a curse.

But not now. Out here I was somewhere else. Reborn if you wish. I remember the first time I set eyes on our place. Like usual:

I was biking through the different neighborhoods in Westhampton beach and stopped for coffee at the Beach Bakery. I wandered back up Main Street to the Prudential office and started looking at the real estate photos of the local spots for sale.

"Can I help you with something?" said the burly dark-haired man sitting on the step with his golden retriever.

"Not really," I replied. I was never serious, but in many respects always serious. "Hey, what the heck. Have anything interesting in the area? Maybe off the beaten path

but near the water and near town, but definitely south of the highway?"

By that, everybody knew that anything of value was south of the highway, Old Montauk Highway, that is.

"Got a few minutes?" he responded.

"Shaw thing," I said, and I must have had Alexiev on the brain.

He went inside, grabbed some keys, and hopped in his black Land Rover. "Goldie," as his dog was called, jumped in the back.

"Hop in. Name's Hadley. Hadley Ferguson."

"Mine's Dawson, Matt Dawson."

Ferguson proceeded down Main Street and over a little bridge, what he called Turkey Bridge. I had thought I had been all around Westhampton but hadn't been here. Very private, hedged, small roads, and some of them were right there on the bay, Quantuck Bay. He pulled down Homans, made a left on Shepard Street.

"Here you have it. This place has six bedrooms, five and a half baths, a pool, and a tennis court, is a brand-spanking new Shinnecock estate, and the owner is eager to sell."

As I looked it over, I knew it would not motivate Shari to move from our little bungalow in the village. Our present vacation spot was perfect in location, but north of the "highway."

"No, thanks," I said.

"Don't you even want to go in?"

"No." As he pulled away, he circled the small peninsula. As we went around the small loop, I saw a FOR SALE sign on a cedar-shingled older home that looked beaten up and worn by its age and the weathered cedar shakes. But the view was to die for!

"Now, this is something that would get Shari's heart pumping," I said. "When can we see it?"

"I'll call and make an appointment," said the realtor.

The next day we both went and saw the weathered place. Water-stained hardwoods, '70s wallpaper and curtains. "Vintage" was not the word: "dated" was the word. But Shari and I could see right past that.

"Place has been on the market nearly three years," said Ferguson. Only this past spring did they get a catwalk installed to give them access to the bay."

"Are the terms negotiable?" I asked.

"Doesn't hurt to try," he said. "Market's been dead as a doornail."

I looked at Shari and she looked at me. We both smiled.

We went for breakfast at Bun and Burger. Shari ordered the flapjacks, and I ordered the oatmeal with banana, with two coffees. "Nothing special," I thought. "But all under twenty bucks including tip, and in the Hamptons no less."

"That place is a real gem," said Shari.

"The view is priceless," I said.

"We can have so much fun out on the back deck," she said. "Breakfast, lunch, and dinner."

"We have to put a dock on the water—that's where we'll hang out!" I warmed up to the idea. "Imagine twilight dinner out on a dock on Quantuck, looking at the Seafield Estate. I can picture the sun setting right now!"

We looked at each other and I got partially up across the bench and bent over across the table, almost knocking over her glass of water. And I kissed her.

"I love you," I said.

"I love you too," Shari said.

Those were the days. Not just buying the house but doing things together with Shari. We met in my residency!

Love at first sight. Shari was a nurse in the coronary care unit, and I was a resident, drawing cardiac enzymes every six hours, titrating pressors, floating swans. Her warmth and companionship helped me survive being on call every other night. And then when I went to the West Coast to specialize in cardiology, it was too painful. We had to get married and seal our bond.

Oh, yes, the letter. Our special moment! Would it be signed, and sealed, and delivered? Well, it was. Our love grew, and so did our family. First came Jason, then Bridgette, and finally we relocated to New York. All for the opportunity at the Mount! We were like-minded for many years and shared the same interests: art, the outdoors, biking, our kids, Thursday nights out in "the City" and even *sex*!

Then the drinking started. I went with her to AA, and I thought it was working, but then a relapse, and then another, and then another. You don't know what pain is until you experience this firsthand. But now, she seemed to be on the mend. Sober again. That was until the night of my NYC meeting. I started thinking of that Streisand song, "Maybe This Time." But I remembered that it was first a Liza Minnelli song from the musical *Cabaret*, written by Ebb and Kander. My mom used to croon this one, never directing it to any of my relationships. I started to reflect to my mom's crooning…

Maybe this time, I'll be lucky

Wishful thinking, I thought to myself. I could hear my mom finishing the number.

It's got to happen, happen sometime
Maybe this time, maybe this time, I'll win

Chapter 11

Ah, yes, "this time!" Back to vacation! Our Hamptons place is an aging cedar-shingled Cape Cod facing directly onto Quantuck Bay and looking innocently out towards the Seafield Estate. This vacation, Shari had invited her sister, Jackie, and Jackie's two kids, David and Frank. Both kids got along great with Jason and Bridgette. Jason was in his second year at Pace University in the city, and Bridgette was in the midst of applying to colleges. As I said earlier, I don't see either of my kids very much anymore. Maybe it's their friends, their interests—or whatever it is, they no longer want to hang with their dad. Perhaps this could change with this vacation?

After a big family meal, I went to our family room and fell asleep on the couch.

"Uncle Matthew, I need help!" called David.

I ran over to Dave, he was in the first-floor bathroom.

"Toilet's overflowing," he said.

"I can see that," I calmly responded.

I am an expert at unclogging the arteries of people but not toilets. I went on the web and searched for home remedies. I did have a plunger, but it failed to do the job. Water started pouring onto the floor, eventually flooding the bathroom. On the floor below, water seeping in between the tile and the molding hit the circuit breaker. Then the power went out.

Shari went to grab for some flashlights. I still had my computer but lost the web service. Luckily, I found a few home remedies for unclogging the bowl that remained on the computer screen even without Internet service. It advised using liquid soap and hot water. The combination thereof led to a bubbling concoction, but no relief for the nonfunctional toilet.

I ran down to the basement and looked at the circuit breaker with my flashlight. One circuit was shut off and when switched on nothing happened.

"No power," shouted Shari.

I tried it again, to no avail. The switch appeared to be a 60-amp circuit breaker. Square D was the manufacturer, to be precise. The whole side of the house had no electricity. No electricity, no TV, no Internet. Only the kitchen on the other side had power. Just when I thought I was going to relax.

Rather than call a plumber and an electrician, like I would have in my earlier years, I ran out to the local Westhampton Beach True Value hardware store. Why should the store be open at ten p.m.? Of course, it wasn't, but I had met the proprietor a year ago and knew he lived upstairs. Fred Levy made a reputation by being inviting, and hopefully now he would live up to his promise. Last time I saw him, he told me his wife was deceased and he lived above the store all alone. He specifically said, "Dr. Dawson, if you ever need anything from me or my store and the store is closed, just ring the doorbell and I'll come down and give you a hand." I thought this very generous, and I also was sure I would never do it. I saw a dim light upstairs and hit the doorbell.

Ring, ring!
No answer.

Chapter 12

After a minute, I saw a slender, elderly grey-haired man in a white tank-top shirt and blue and white boxers. It was Mr. Levy. He opened the screen door and said, "What's all the racket?"

"It's me, Fred, Dr. Matt Dawson. I need some help."

"What seems to be the problem?"

"A shorted-out circuit breaker, and a toilet clog that you wouldn't believe!" I replied as I passed him the dead breaker.

"Ah, a Square D. You'll need a 60-amp breaker. Come with me." He exited through the side door that led to his upstairs home, and then he went with me, briefs and all, to the front of his store. He put on his reading glasses and fished through his ring of keys until he found the one labeled STORE. Inserting the key into the slot, he opened up the dark store and flipped on the lights.

"We're in business," he said.

"Also need to unclog my toilet. What do you recommend?" I asked.

"Good old reliable Mr. Cobra." he said.

"Cobra?" I questioned.

"Cobra, it's my way of saying 'snake' to you, you New Yorkers," he joked. He pulled out a six-foot-long screwing device and then explained, "This spring-like metal hose needs to be inserted into the toilet bowl and shoved down its drain. Once it's inserted, you rotate the red handle around and around and drive the metal snake, or shall I say cobra, further down the drain. You continue this motion until the cobra is down as far as it can go, and then you will have successfully unclogged your toilet." Or, as we say in the heart biz, removed "the occlusion." He also gave me instructions on how to safely handle the circuit breaker. "What a lifesaver," I said to myself. "No wonder everybody, and I mean everybody, goes to Westhampton Hardware rather than travel to Home Depot in Riverhead."

When I got back, I went again down to the basement with my flashlight and did exactly what Fred had told me. I shut off the main and then attached the new breaker and snapped it into the box. I then switched back on the main, and switched the breaker back on and then the lights, and as Alex would say, "Voilà."

Electricity! Electricity had returned to the first floor. Within three minutes I heard my son shout from upstairs.

"I got Internet service," Jason yelled.

"TV's back on," shouted back Bridgette.

"We're back in business," I loudly announced.

Back upstairs, I took the long, snaking device and proceeded to work my upper body around a large rotating handle in a circular motion in order to snake the "cobra" device through the clogged toilet. After a few twists and turns, it easily bypassed the occlusion and freed up the blockage. No stent needed! "Cobra," I thought, "good name for a device that could unclog the coronaries." Maybe I could use this in some way to break up or "Roto-Rooter" heart occlusions? I pondered to myself.

I thought about Andreas Gruentzig, the originator of the angioplasty procedure developed in the late 1970s. Dr.

Gruentzig was a German cardiologist, who in 1977 was the first to pass a balloon catheter, or thin flexible medical device with an inflatable balloon at its end, to a blockage within someone's coronary artery. Once the device "crossed" the blockage, he would blow up a balloon and compress the blockage flat against the wall of the artery, to "unclog" the blood vessel. Dr. Gruentzig's crude device was improved by Stanford's own Dr. John Simpson, who developed the "over-the-wire technique," in which a thin wire, a guide wire, was essentially snaked or "cobra-ed" across the blockage and a balloon catheter or device slid "over the wire" through the blockage. The balloon was then inflated for thirty seconds by a pump until the blockage remained completely open. The Simpson device made the "angioplasty" procedure much easier and more effective. The procedure became widely accepted and used in every cath lab across the country, and the world for that matter. Simpson's invention while at Stanford was legendary and gave me a huge inspiration. His company, Advanced Cardiovascular Systems, Inc., was acquired by Guidant Corporation.

Other "Roto-Rooter" type devices were developed, using mechanical or diamond-cutting techniques and even lasers to break up hardened blockages. But no real large-scale breakthrough came with heart blockage-treating medical devices until the invention of the stent. That tiny little expandable piece of metal that would revolutionize my business and expand my practice and the Cath Lab at Mount Sinai. "Hey, I thought I was supposed to get my mind off of work!" I screamed in my head as I slammed my palm against my temple.

We then mopped the bathroom floor. We haven't had this much togetherness in a long time. Bridget, Jason, and their cousins all helped clean the floor and we all washed up. Then sat in our living room and relaxed to some Seinfeld reruns on our fifty-inch HDTV. A fifty-inch TV that hung like a painting above the fireplace.

Hanging out on our L-shaped sofa, munching on popcorn and laughing to a Seinfeld classic, "Junior Mint!"

Chapter 13

The sun gleamed through the window, awakening me at seven a.m. the next morning. Normally I might pull out a pedal kayak and go out on the bay towards Quogue. Or head out on my trek over the Ponquogue Bridge to Southampton and back. But now I was on a mission.

In order to relieve my mind of the pressures of my job, I headed back to Fred at True Value. Fred was the most sympathetic man I knew, and I was forever grateful for his help last night. Unlike most owners of hardware stores, he was always the consummate gentleman. "Must have been a disgruntled attorney or a former Wall Street guy," I said sarcastically to myself. But now he was truly interested in helping his customers. I brought him two bottles of Pindar Winter White wine from the North Fork and gave them to him to show my appreciation.

"Fred, what do I need to repair my washer drain? Do you have three 100-foot hosing sections? How about a Kohler showerhead? How do I remove the existing old head and put the new one on, etc. etc.?" I asked.

Fred always had the answer. "You need this roll of plumber's tape!" "Don't forget a 12-mm wrench." "Oh, and by the way, if you have any problems you can call me at 631-288-7777. And don't hesitate to buzz me after hours if you need anything. You know where I live."

With my summer vacation at hand, I switched into a more productive mode to get my mind off medicine and our financial struggles. First, I fixed the washer drain, then attached a string of hoses from our house all the way out onto the "T" end of our dock, and finally, I installed a new showerhead in our master bathroom.

With each and every task I felt a new sense of accomplishment!

Chapter 14

Solitude. That's why I got the place out east in the first place. I seldom see any life in the neighborhood. Most of my neighbors are rarely there, even during the peak summer season. One of the neighbors is a famous African American TV personality whose name I am not at liberty to disclose. "Oh," but a little hint—she lives in Chicago. I have only seen her house vibrant with life once in the past two years other than with the maintenance crew.

I had just completed my hose hook-up, at the end of my dock, and set up the kayak rack and jumped off the end into the bay to cool off. As I mounted my ladder I looked back at my place and glanced around the bay.

To my right was a six-foot-tall, balding, somewhat-overweight man waving and shouting, "Hey, Doc, can you give me a hand?" It was Charley Weisberg, senior partner at Goldman Sachs. The same guy I'd seen in appearances on *Fast Money*, *Squawk Box*, and *Morning Joe*. But instead of a dark suit and tie, he was wearing Bermuda shorts and a Yale T-shirt, with an orange juice in one hand and a cigar in the other.

I had met Mr. Weisberg a total of four times, including this morning's encounter. All except one was out back, shouting dock to dock or from my kayak to his dock.

လွလ

One evening last summer, I had to deliver an errant package to their front door. I walked from my humble abode a short distance down the road, past their front-hedged property and though their driveway's gate, up their elegant, lit driveway, and rang the door. The door opened, but it was not Mr. Weisberg. No! It was a stylishly dressed woman reminiscent of Princess Grace Kelly, or Audrey Hepburn in the movie Breakfast at Tiffany's. *She had voluptuous blond hair and was wearing a luxurious black evening gown, a pearl necklace, and Christian Louboutin black pumps, with their characteristic red soles.*

"Thank you," she said. "What is your name?"

"Dawson, Matthew Dawson. We moved here a year ago."

"Sorry, Mr. Dawson, but I have to get back to Charley. Thanks again." She closed the door without much ado.

She didn't tell me her name, and I was unsure who she was and what her exact relationship was to Mr. Weisberg. I didn't even get an invite inside their grand palace! There was no introduction, no "get to know your neighbors," and especially no "why don't you and the missus come over for cocktails or wine and cheese?"

Mr. Weisberg was a world traveler for Goldman, working on M&A: that's mergers and acquisitions, he told me. When Google bought YouTube, I thought that must have been Charley. When Facebook bought Instagram, I also thought of Charley. But I really didn't know for sure. M&A biz was always so secretive.

And there he was, belly hanging out, in flip-flops and a T-shirt! Waving me down from his immense waterside deck on the back of his massive white-shingled estate.

"Shaw thing," I replied, while giggling internally from my Alexiev humor. Like a southern accent or an OCD compulsion. "What do you need?"

"I've tried my contractor, but I didn't get a response. I have to get our pool heater started, leaks fixed from the spa as well as the faucet out on the deck—the list is endless! I see you're having fun out there on your dock, and I thought you might want to give it a try over here?"

"That's what happens when you only use a place three times a year," I thought. He had lots of things to fix. I guess that big old maintenance crew he had out there just made the place look well kept. Their estate seemed to be falling apart. That's at least how he made it seem.

Next thing you know Charley had me helping him out back with all sorts of projects. And boy did I enjoy it. The best distraction ever! Got my mind off medicine. Not a thought of my medical practice or TCT presentation. I was able to mend his Vanderbilt-style Hampton Estate's back-yard woes the same way I used to fix my cardiac patients. After a week of this, I start to wonder:

"Do I return to a dying practice in Manhattan?"

Chapter 15

Back from vacation, I returned to that Mecca of a hospital that towers over Central Park on the Upper East Side of Manhattan in New York City— Mount Sinai Hospital. Typically, I feel refreshed after going to the local beach or kayaking on Quantuck Bay out in the Hamptons. But not this time! My recent break was not a vacation in the usual sense. I wasn't at all tired from the hard work, lifting, hauling, fixing, and plumbing. I was invigorated. Not my typical vacation, more a retreat for a *Home Improvement* aficionado. In other words, a boot camp for the home handyman, or maybe perhaps a plumber's apprentice. But even though I did not do the usual lounging out on our dock or read the latest *New York Times* best seller, I felt re-energized. I had regained that giddy-up in my step—something that had been missing for quite some time.

I went down to the doctor's lounge and grabbed a pod of Tully's French Roast and ran it through the hospital's Keurig coffee maker. With coffee in hand, I raced up to the Cath Lab to check the schedule. I've been the lab director for the past twelve years, during which time I turned a dying program into a bustling cath lab. Not just any cath lab but the biggest and busiest in all New York City. A cath lab is where we "interventionalists" get to unclog blocked arteries and keep them open with those stents that I described earlier. And "stenting" has been a way of life for me, taking care of patients from all over the city and beyond. At least, that was the way it was up until the time hospitals starting buying doctors' practices.

Let me explain. As a specialized interventional cardiologist, I get my patients, or as we say, referrals, from other more general cardiologists. At least, that is the way it was until my referring-doctor medical practices were acquired by the other competing hospitals—Columbia Presbyterian and NYU. First, it was the Goldberg group, then, the Sachs practice, followed by Terry Waxman's entire heart center, and almost all the rest went elsewhere. "Business, just business," I thought.

Chapter 16

Mount Sinai's Cath Lab consisted of six procedural rooms where all the stenting and complicated heart plumbing procedures took place. There were two additional electrophysiology (EP) rooms where our electrician counterparts implanted their pacemakers and defibrillators. A large, twenty-bed recovery room handled the patients prior to and after their procedures. The lab was staffed with a unique cast of characters. Characters that ran the place, and ran it like a finely tuned machine. Each of the characters had a nickname.

Our coordinator was a tall, stern, somewhat muscular, black-haired Russian nurse named Nina. Her real name was Ninotchka Sangamore. *Ninotchka*, she told me, was an old Greta Garbo comedy from the late '30s that was later, in the mid-'50s, made into a Broadway musical called *Silk Stockings*. Nina was the name of the main character. Neither the film nor the play I had ever heard of. But then Nina proceeded to belt out the show's hit song: "I love the look of you, the lure of you . . . I'd love to gain complete control of you."

Ironically, Nina had a surprisingly good voice and was not bashful in showing it off. Had she not been the coordinator of our lab, she might have had a shot at Broadway.

"All of you?" I said back to Nina.

"Yes," she replied. "Cole Porter and Ella Fitzgerald."

"I know it from Ol' Blue Eyes," I said.

"Sinatra did it well after the show," she agreed.

As the coordinator, she organized and supervised all the patients' scheduling, including each and every one of the Mount Sinai Cath Lab nurses. Patient safety was her motto!

"Every patient, every procedure," Nina would say firmly.

She went from procedural room to procedural room, all inside our complex, repeating this often, each and every day, as she inspected procedural time-outs in which the correct patient and procedure were identified prior to any cath lab procedure. This was a hospital Joint Commission requirement, like a pilot's checklist before flying an airplane. The transporters were Gabe and Senior. Senior's son Junior worked in the operating room upstairs. Senior, or "Senior Moment," was the "real" Jamaican, who always called me the "real Ja-Fakin." But I thought "Senior" was quite a cruel name because Senior was near retirement age!

Our cardiovascular techs, or CVTs, were the guys and gals who operated our lab's equipment, including the X-ray equipment used to photograph blockages. The CVTs were headed by none other than Cath Lab Gene. His name was stolen from his sister "EP Jean," who worked over in a busy EP Lab out on the Island. Cath Lab Gene used to joke about his sister having almost the same name. I thought it humorous when he recounted that her boss used to say, "We worked hard to finally isolate 'the EP Jean.'" But true to Cath Lab Gene's name, he was definitely part of the DNA of our lab, if you know what I mean. He was a well-built, former New York City police officer, who had created law and order in midtown Manhattan—the Grand Central Terminal area precinct, to be precise. And for almost the past decade, he has created the same "law and order" in our Cath Lab, along with Nina. His job was also organizing lab staff and equipment, and assuring rapid lab turnover.

The list of name parodies went on and on and on. Fifty folks to run six cath rooms, and all were cranking—stent procedures in two labs, TAVRs (transcutaneous valve replacements) in two, a garden-variety cath procedure in one, and a LARIAT procedure in another. The LARIAT was the lab's latest procedure. The doctor would tie off a part of the heart where clots can form. The procedure was alleged to prevent strokes. At least, that's what the manufacturer purported.

As you would have guessed, NONE of these procedures were mine! I couldn't imagine losing each and every cardiology-referring group to the competition, but that's the way it went. Yes, Mount Sinai bought some other practices, but their patients went to other large Mount Sinai cardiology groups. Not to me! But I still was the Cath Lab Director, at least for the foreseen future. But how long could I survive with a dwindling patient base? A year, maybe two, tops?

I used to have seven-to-twelve "cath procedures" scheduled daily. Now I was down to one or two a day, max. On my clinic day I used to see up to fifty patients, but now I rarely see as many as fifteen. Talk about depressing. I'm holding on to Mr. Jones, who comes just to tell me about his place in the Heights on Shelter Island, and Mrs. Windsor, who just likes to talk about her cats up in Rye! I am more a psychologist than an invasive cardiologist. How depressing! Was that what I was destined to do? With a Johns Hopkins medical degree and cardiology training at

Stanford? I'm playing Freud to a bunch of psychos, not fixing broken hearts as I was trained to.

At least I have my research, I thought. A thought that gave me solace!

Chapter 17

It was October 22, and my presentation was complete. At last, TCT 2012 was here! Just a reminder, TCT stands for "Transcatheter Cardiovascular Therapeutics," the annual interventional cardiology conference. I grabbed a cab from my home in Port Washington and headed to LaGuardia for a three-hour flight to Miami. I've been totally self-absorbed with work leading up to this meeting. I guess it is this perseverance that made me what I am today. But it is not without a cost. At times I've lost touch with my family life. This is one of my major flaws. When I get like this, it's as if they are totally out of my life.

Many years ago, before things totally deteriorated in our marriage, we saw Mary Ann Hanley, the local marriage therapist. Shari put it this way to Mary Ann:

"There can be all this chaos going on at home, and you are totally oblivious to it. MD, I am at my wit's end and you are so self-absorbed. I was left to deal with the kids, the home, and all our problems. And you would get annoyed if I tried to interrupt your train of thought or your work! I was so irritated with you!"

There has been a cost to my prosperity. In the cab, I pulled myself out of MD-ville and pressed the speed dial on my cell. The phone rang, followed by our answering machine message and a beep.

"Hey guys, just leaving for my meeting. Thinking of you. Love you guys!"

LaGuardia was a bit of a pit, at least compared to Miami International. When I hit Miami, I folded my sport jacket and threw it into my briefcase alongside my MacBook Air. I walked out of the airport through baggage claim towards ground transportation. There was a middle-aged man of medium build with curly grey hair sporting a captain's hat, holding a sign that read, "Dawson."

As I walked toward him, we locked eyes.

"Dr. Dawson?" he said in a slightly high-pitched voice with a Spanish accent.

"Yes," I responded.

"I am Eli from South Beach Livery. Dr. Smillar arranged for me to take you to the convention."

"Eli, very nice to meet you."

The conference organizer was kind enough to arrange a car service to pick me up and take me over to the Miami Convention Center. Unlike New York, which was grey and cloudy and 48 degrees Fahrenheit, Miami was sunny, without a cloud in the sky, and 72 degrees.

"Dr. Dawson, where's your home?"

"Near New York City. On Long Island." I was still perplexed by his accent. Central or South America perhaps?

"Where, Doc?" Now with his high-pitched voice, he sounded a little like Mel Blanc's Bugs Bunny. Especially with adding the *Doc!*

"A little town called Port Washington," I retorted.

"You're kidding." Eli chuckled.

"What do you mean?" I inquired.

"My family still lives in Port; wife and kids, that is. I relocated to Florida while my wife is trying to sell my house in Salem."

Salem was a nice, quiet area in Port Washington. Modest homes, but a great place to raise a family.

"Port's just too expensive, Doc. Hard to get by even with two incomes with those property taxes. I had to find a place down here. Much cheaper real estate and no property taxes.

"I agree." Eli was right on the money, so to speak. Long Island in general was much more expensive than the rest of the country.

"Maybe you know my wife? She is a schoolteacher in Schreiber? Vicky Sephardic. She teaches English."

"My daughter had an English teacher named Vicky. Loved her!" Must have been the one, I thought.

Eli took my briefcase and threw it in the back of his black Lincoln Town Car. I hopped in the back and then we proceeded to drive due eastward.

"Hey, by the way, where are you from originally?" I just had to ask.

"Venezuela. Though I spent some time in Israel as well. Perhaps you hear some of that in my voice as well? Been driving in this great country for many years."

"You have a unique twang. I just couldn't piece it together. Where are you from precisely? Caracas?" That was the only place I knew in Venezuala. Closest I've ever been was Aruba, where I fished off the Venezuelan coast and felt their strong trade winds. I knew it was the capital, but did not know any place else in that Commie country. Also knew it was a third world place. Poor as hell!

"Yes, Doc. I left Caracas nearly twenty years ago, to find a better life. That I did, in the good old U-S-of-A. And yes, your home town."

"What a coincidence!" Imagine, six degrees of separation always at play.

"Nice weather we're having. Florida has much better weather than Long Island, especially in the winter. I dread our winters."

"Yes, but not for long," said Eli. "Looks like we're not quite over hurricane season. Forecast shows there may be something brewing!"

"A hurricane? I don't see a cloud in sight."

"Down here, there is always a storm." He paused. "Around the corner. But most of the time, they are not much. Occasionally, we get an Irene like you guys did last year. I was up in Port working during that one."

He was referring to Hurricane Irene. Last year, it was supposed to blow through. But instead, it wreaked havoc on the Eastern Seaboard, including Long Island. My basement flooded out east at Westhampton Beach and the dock was mangled. But not too bad, for all that media hype. I was one of the lucky ones. Fortunately, Irene was not as destructive as it was billed.

"Help yourself to the paper and please feel free to drink the bottled water I left in back," he said.

"Thank you, Eli. I will." I grabbed the water bottle. Twisted off the cap and took a few swigs.

Within no time we were cruising across the MacArthur Causeway. The water was a luscious turquoise. Quite different than the olive green, almost brownish waters up in New York. And the multitude of palm trees made the place look like a Caribbean resort. Eli turned down to Alton Road and then made a right onto Seventeenth Street. The large modern edifice known as the Miami Convention Center was perched there on our left.

"We're here," said Eli.

Chapter 18

The car stopped right in front of the center, and the driver went out to the trunk to retrieve my briefcase, and then opened my door. I handed him a twenty, which he quickly pushed aside.

"No need to, Dr. Dawson. Tab and tip are covered," he said.

"No, keep it," I replied, insisting.

"Thanks, Dr. Dawson," Eli responded.

I walked briskly into the convention center and met Dr. Smillar at the door.

"Your session is in fifteen minutes," he said. "The Speaker Ready Room is on your right."

Dr. Smillar was a thin, grey-haired, six-foot-tall, aging man, probably in his mid-seventies, if not older. He was my mentor, the man who helped start my career. He also was the moderator for the late-morning session where I was giving my presentation.

The title for the session was "Novel Platforms Enhancing Percutaneous Coronary Interventions." My talk was the first of the session: "The Effects of Magnetic Stenting on Endothelialization." I was able to ride the so-called wave of magnetic fields as they were applied to stents, but this time my talk was quite different.

The room could fit only 5,000, and it was standing room only.

Dr. Smillar made the usual introductions.

"Our first speaker is a well-known cardiologist from Mount Sinai. He got his start with me at Stanford and went for bigger and better things in New York. He's got a *magnetic* personality and is none other than Dr. Matthew Dawson."

The audience gave a strong round of applause, one I never took for granted. I always opened my talk with a famous painting by a contemporary artist. The slide this time was of a mostly black-and-white image that looked like a large black moth on white canvas, with a few blotches of yellow ochre and a line of green. Two of the large black bands went from top to bottom, with a black egg shape in between. There were two more large black eggs on the right side of the second band.

"Who knows the artist?" I asked.

"Motherwell!" shouted someone from the audience.

"That's right," I responded. "I hope your *Mother's well*. Yes, this is entitled *Elegy to the Spanish Republic, 108*, painted between 1965 and 1967. It is an oil on canvas, part of the permanent collection of the MoMA. The American-born artist Robert Motherwell painted it. Motherwell was a member of the New York School of Abstract Expressionist artists in the 1950s and 1960s, along with Jackson Pollock, Mark Rothko, and others."

I threw this image up on the screen, almost as a joke to break the ice. The audience might be smart enough to recognize this artist, but most surely would not understand the symbolism. Motherwell used black blotches and color in his *Elegy to the Spanish Republic* pieces, and they were supposed to represent the testicles under a dead bull. I guess you could say I had a lot of balls to put such an image up at a major medical meeting. Truth be told, this little bit of internal humor helped take the stress out of my plenary talks.

"He married another famous Abstract Expressionist artist. Do you know her name?"

Silence.

"Helen Frankenthaler. Born in 1928, Helen recently passed away, at the age of eighty-three, after a long illness. She remained active, painting almost to the very end. As cardiologists, our job is to keep our patients vibrant and active as long as possible. And that is why we do what we do. *Frankly* speaking."

I then went into magnetic theory—our early trials and their results—and by the end of the talk I heard a roar from the crowd.

"Any questions?" asked Dr. Smillar.

After I fended off two, I was greeted by a couple of my former colleagues from Stanford and then went outside the lecture hall. And there he was.

Chapter 19

I had only met him once. This meeting was entirely un-expected. I thought I recognized the same pinstriped blue suit as last time. There he was, with his slender, tall figure and grey hair, waiting in the wings to talk to me. It was Frederick Morgan.

"Dr. Dawson, how are you doing? Long time no see!" he said to break the ice.

"Fine. Any progress?" I calmly questioned.

"Morgan Capital is prepared to make MATAL an offer. I've reviewed the details with Sid and we have a term sheet we'd like to prepare for you. I wanted to make sure that I connected in person and let you know we will be moving forward."

I knew that this was good news, but I also knew that nothing is a done deal until the papers are signed. I had to keep my cool.

"Good, "I responded. "Just shoot it over to Dr. Shaw and Mr. Lippert when you're ready. I look forward to working out this deal," I said with a somewhat subdued affect.

"Will do. You should hear from me in the next few weeks. Take care, now." He showed the enthusiasm of a stone. Not even a smile. But the meeting was not by chance. He made the trip down south in all likelihood to convey this personal message. I meandered to a quiet place next to a large picture frame window, just outside the auditorium, and pulled out my phone and within seconds I got him.

"Dr. Shaw, how may I be of service?"

"Alex, good news! I just ran into Fred Morgan. They're going to prepare a term sheet. Hopefully they will work out the details and shoot something to us in the next few weeks." It was hard to control my excitement. But Alex always put a damper on my expectations.

"MD, keep your cool! Let's see what they send. You know they will try to get MATAL for a song and a dance. Please, keep your patience."

"I will, Shaw! See you soon."

I left the convention center, and there was a much more familiar face just outside. Like Morgan, this gentleman was tall and slender and was also not a doctor. But unlike Morgan he was much younger, in his late forties, with a receding hairline. He was dressed a little more flamboyantly, with a yellow Yves Saint Laurent suit, white dress shirt, and pink tie.

Christian Larosse was an art dealer, one of three principal owners of the Freedman Park Larosse Art Gallery. His name was added to those of the other two senior partners, Freedman and Park, just this past month. Christian flew down to Miami for two reasons: one was to celebrate his recent appointment as a partner in the gallery, and the other was to meet up with me. Freedman Park Larosse was one of the oldest established dealers in New York City. They were originally located on Fifty-Seventh Street on the Upper East Side and recently moved to Chelsea like so many blue-chip art galleries in the last twenty years. Freedman Park, as they were still known to most of their clientele, had an impressive array of contemporary art. Most of it, however, too recent for my taste: artists like Jeff Koons and Damien Hirst. But they still had my favorites: Hans Hofmann, Helen Frankenthaler, Robert Motherwell, Morris Louis, Kenneth Noland, Wolf Kahn, Jasper Johns, David Hockney, Alex Katz, Richard Diebenkorn and Wayne Thiebaud. Christian got me started with my print collection when I first arrived in New York. He was down here scouting out spaces for a private venue alongside the upcoming Art Miami meeting slated for the beginning of December.

We jumped in a cab and headed to where all the action is, namely, South Beach. We pulled up to Joe's Stone Crab restaurant, where one of Christian's art associates had saved us a table. Joe's does not take reservations, but it would have been worth the wait. That is, unless you were pressed for time, as I was. We sat down and ordered the Stone Crab appetizer, and I ordered a Caesar Salad with shrimp. It was delicious.

"MD, I would like to get you more involved in the art scene in Miami. Freedman Park is holding a hotel room for you in the beginning of December at Art Miami. The hotel is on me."

Art Miami is the world's second largest art event, just behind Art Basel in Switzerland. In fact, it is officially called Art Basel-Miami. This event even dwarfs the large art fairs in New York City held simultaneously at the Armory, Pier 92, and Pier 94, as well as the other contemporaneous fairs. Christian was hoping I would take the next step in the art world and actually acquire a significant painting such as a Diebenkorn work on paper or small Thiebaud oil.

I was afraid to tell Christian I had no money to buy such a work. I just listened and enjoyed the lunch, shocked by Christian's generosity and even more shocked that it included a complimentary suite at the very chic W South Beach Hotel on Collins Avenue for three nights in December, including a flight for Shari and myself. I savored every bite of my salad and finished it off with a sparkling Perrier with a twist of lime. Bidding Christian a fine adieu—"See you in December"—I grabbed a cab to the airport and flew back to LaGuardia and was home back lying in bed next to Shari by midnight.

Fresh from my trip, and my revelation regarding my own contribution to my marriage's demise, I hopped into bed with renewed hope.

"I'm back," I whispered softly in Shari's ear. I awoke her from a sound sleep.

"Welcome back," she said.

This night she did not smell of alcohol. Something was different. I rolled over and snuggled next to her. I even thought that she might have spooned back into me. I can't remember the last time she did that.

Chapter 20

The rest of the week was a wash—not many patients, and just the finishing touches to my latest magnetic stent research paper. Finally, I completed the cover letter and the online journal submission. It took till Sunday until I could breathe a sigh of relief.

The next day I drove in early. The LIE was a breeze before six a.m. The ride into the city went too smoothly. I made the usual trip to the doctor's lounge and then up to the Cath Lab. Not much to do for me personally, although the lab was beginning to heat up.

Suddenly, 4400 showed on my pager. I knew that number, administration. Specifically, I knew it as the extension that led to the hospital CEO's office. The CEO of Mount Sinai was none other than James Anderson. Everybody knew Mr. Anderson. He did radio and television commercials promoting the hospital. I called the number and got his secretary, Arlene.

"Dr. Dawson, are you available to meet with Mr. Anderson at eleven a.m.?" she asked.

Whenever I got a call from Mr. Anderson, I knew there was not much option, other than adjusting my schedule to accommodate him. In the past, I may have been involved in a very complicated procedure and would really be unable to meet him. This time, I was not so lucky.

At eleven a.m. I walked inside the administrative office. The secretaries to the CEO, CFO, and COO each had their own desk. Arlene sat to the right.

"Want a cup of coffee, Dr. Dawson?" she said.

"Please," I replied.

She walked over. "What would you like—French Vanilla, Hazelnut, Dark Roast?"

"Dark Roast is fine, with a little bit of skim milk." I said. She prepared the cup, gave it to me, and then said, "Mr. Anderson is ready to see you now."

I walked around her desk, then into the CEO's office. Much larger than any other office in the hospital, it had the traditional large wooden desk flanked by chairs, but another area was off to the side and consisted of two couches facing each other, spilt by a square, centered table, not unlike our family room. Instead of sitting on the couches like we usually did, he chose to stay behind the desk, directing me to "take a seat."

I sat down. "So, what's up?" Anderson proceeded to get up and walk over to where I was sitting. He never took a seat but just kept standing.

"Matt, Mount Sinai has been very fortunate to have you here. You have done some great things for our hospital. But the time has come to let someone else take the helm. I'm sorry, but I am going to have to let you go. The hospital can no longer afford a director that isn't bringing in the bacon."

Did I hear him right? Going to have to let *me* go—is that what he said? Not *me*. Doesn't he know what the lab was like before I got here? What I was able to accomplish?

"But, Mr. Anderson, my lack of patients is directly related to the hospital's decisions not to purchase any of my large cardiology referral practices. This had nothing to do with me," I quibbled.

"I know that, Matt, but that's just the way it is. You'll have three months' severance, and of course collect your pension when you reach sixty-five. But your job is finished effective immediately. Would you please give me the key to your office?" he asked, but it was no question.

I gave him the key and walked out, much like a dog with his head drooping between his front paws. Squirming out the back door of the hospital into the doctors' parking lot, I gave one look back towards "the Mount," and drove home.

Chapter 21

I drove through the Midtown Tunnel back to Port Washington. None of this made any sense. I did not turn on the radio, and I did not call anyone. I just felt like shit! When I reached my house, I pulled my car into the garage port and opened the side door. Shari was not expecting me. "How often am I home at one p.m.? How would she take the news?" I thought. "She's not going to be happy about this!"

In the kitchen, I threw my car keys on the hook in the mudroom and tossed my wallet into the drawer on the kitchen island. The place seemed deserted until I heard a pounding sound coming from upstairs. First, I thought it was someone beating a carpet out the window to get rid of dirt. But the sound continued and just kept getting louder and louder as I approached. As I walked to the stairs, I heard a noise that had more of a spring type sound. A "bo-inging" followed by a female groan.

"OH! Fuck me! Fuck me harder! Harder!"

"Ah, shit! That was my wife," I screamed to myself as I felt a pain as sharp as a knife jabbing me right in the middle of my chest.

"This couldn't be," I thought.

I ran up to the bedroom, and there she was, curled up, banging some young blond motherfucker! Must have been half my age. He was on top of her, with his blue jeans down to his ankles. She was on the bottom, with some skimpy black erotic outfit and spiked heels. An outfit I had never EVER seen before!

"What the fuck is going on here?" I screamed in disbelief.

That blond motherfucker pulled himself out of my wife and threw on his jeans, grabbed his shirt, and ran like a bat out of hell out the door.

"Ah, shit!" Shari screamed.

"What the hell! I shouted back. I was beet red, steaming with anger. My heart was racing, and sweat pouring down my face and across my chest. The medical term was diaphoretic. There was nothing to discuss! I just needed to get away. I grabbed my keys from the mudroom, hopped in my car, and raced crosstown to my oldest and dearest friend.

Chapter 22

I've known Alex almost as long as I have known my wife. For all these years, I thought that his non-American accent plus olive skin might have gotten him mistaken for a terrorist, though he'd been a United States citizen for nearly twenty years. But now I saw Shaw in a different light. He could have easily made a living as a celebrity look-a-like for Steven Seagal. But that aside, he just looked plain dangerous, but he was hardly so. That is, of course, unless you messed with him. Like Seagal, he spoke softly, which masked the martial arts mayhem within. Shaw, however, was also a brilliant and skilled scientist, with Israeli defense expertise. But what's a middle-aged man doing with a slicked-back black pony-tail? Who are you kidding, Shaw?

I used to joke with him about his religion.

"Question: What kind of money do you spend?"

"Answer: Jew dough."

"Question: How do you make bread on the Hebrew holiday of Passover?"

"Answer: With Jew dough." The all-purpose answer, I thought.

"Question: What kind of martial arts do you practice?"

"Answer: Judo!"

Oh, no, not again. He laughed.

And lastly:

"Question: Do you know Puerto Rican Judo?"

"Answer: Jew got a knife. Jew got a gun."

I was with Alex when a gang of hoodlums, in East New York, attacked us. He made a number of moves that could only be described as Bruce Lee-like, and within three minutes all seven were reeling in pain on the ground. His Krav Maga skills and language fluency were just a part of it. Although he never told me where he worked, I could only guess that it was in some top-secret military or security service. But for, and with whom, I did not know. There seemed to be nothing he didn't know or wasn't an expert in. But most importantly, especially after today, Alex was my closest friend, and that was what I needed.

Alex had a loving wife, Joanna, and three adorable little kids. He was on his third marriage, and this one turned out to be a real doozy. "Maybe I'll have better luck like Alex the second time around," I said to myself.

"Alex, I need your help." I gave a big man hug to him with my weepy eyes. Alex knew everything about me. "First, I lost my money, and today I lost my job, and now my wife! I was literally fired from Mount Sinai and came home early to find Shari screwing someone half my age."

He just hugged me back and said, "The living room couch is all yours. I'm there for you, man." He said it with all his heart. *"C'est la vie, c'est la guerre!"* There was no way I was going to sleep at home, and Alex's was the only place I could go.

Oh, and by the way, news predicted a Frankenstorm called Sandy, a confluence of a tropical storm, coming up from the Caribbean, meeting with a Nor'easter. It was supposed to hit New York!

"Never will happen," I thought. "Just another over-hyped media blitz!"

Chapter 23

Unlike almost every other storm, Sandy did hit New York on that Monday night. I was at Alex's place, on the living room couch. Windows rattled all night, and at seven a.m. a tree crashed onto the roof. Water started pouring into the dining room. Alex grabbed a bucket and put it under the roof leak. The bucket quickly flooded, and the water cascaded over their floor. I grabbed some bathroom towels and Alex emptied the bucket and brought it back. We were fighting a losing battle; the floor would soon buckle from our failed efforts.

And then I got the call!

If I had any doubts about where I was headed with my life, Sandy helped solidify the issue. Hurricane Sandy, that is. Yup, the big one that hit New Jersey and New York at the end of October! Like Hurricane Carter, this one delivered a knockout punch to Long Island, with massive power outages and flooded basements and floors.

Then it happened!

My cell phone rang.

Charley called me in a panic. "Dr. D., I'm in Asia and my house watcher phoned me and gave me the news. First floor is under water. Corbusier, Knoll, Eames, all the stuff under water. And the basement—submerged. Hot water heater, burner all replaced after Irene, and now this! You gotta help me out!"

"But, Charley, I have to check out my patients," I said.

After this knee jerk response, I realized: I don't have any patients. What was once a flourishing medical career is now over. Ended! *Finito*! Gone! And my marriage—another *finito*, gone as well! I wasn't even thinking of my place. What if that was gone?

"Charley," I backtracked, "I can be out at your house in an hour!"

Alex had a spare generator and leant me his Honda Pilot. He always had a bunch of gadgets and gizmos to make things happen. He threw a Generac 5500 generator in the back of the Pilot as if it was nothing. Then he placed a couple of filled gas cans, blowers, a water pump, a fire hose, and a few heavy-duty extension lines in the back. "Nice to have friends like you," I thought.

Chapter 24

One hour later, I zipped past the Bridgehampton Bank and went to grab a cup of Joe at Hampton's Coffee. I was surprised to see it open, but it was running fine on their back-up generator. Hampton's Coffee was where locals regained some sense of normality, plus there was an added bonus. Outside the shop there was a large handwritten cardboard sign that read:

WE SURVIVED SANDY, PLEASE ENJOY A FREE BEVERAGE AND PASTRY ON HAMPTON'S COFFEE

"MD, back so soon?" said Terry, the store's owner. She was a true Westhampton gem who made everybody feel like family. Every summer she would house exchange students and give them a summer job in her café. She was always quite benevolent, and this time was no exception. Here's your decaf Hazelnut latte with steamed skim milk and one Splenda. Just the way you like it!" said Terry. "Hey, how'd you make out in the storm?"

"Not so good back home. Power still out, and trees destroyed my pool and spa. I'm out here to check out both my place and the Weisbergs'. Lucky for Mr. G," I said.

"Hey, who is that, your house guy?" she said.

"No, that's the portable generator I borrowed from my friend. It's a lifesaver. Bailed me out with Irene, and got my sump pump going. Other neighbor has a 100,000-watt industrial-sized generator, dwarfing this little 5,500-watt guy, but it does the job. About time I put in a fixed generator, but I just don't have the cash. I'm here to help out Mr. Weisberg. His place is a mess I hear."

"Good luck, and here's your sugar-free corn muffin," she said.

Her sugar-free corns are a local legend. Apple juice for flavor, not the refined glucose that leads to diabetes.

Chapter 25

I headed down Mill Road, past the Seafield Estate. That one survived the Great Hurricane of 1938 and the Perfect Storm of 1991 and is still standing. Their dock was way up on their ten acres of lawn, but otherwise no worse for the wear. Like the majestic East Egg mansion from the *Great Gatsby* stared out upon the Long Island Sound, the Seafield Estate stared out on Quantuck Bay. But now it was all boarded up with plywood.

"Nice to have a crew to put that up all over that sixteen thousand-square-foot monster," I thought. Still, the cedar-shingle facade looked unfazed by this disaster. "Yup, the Seafield lives and breathes for another day," I surmised.

I turned, right past Turkey Bridge, then down Homans Avenue. What was normally a well-hedged Hampton's lane had multiple downed trees cut in half to allow cars to pass. The flooded road had sea debris, but the water had receded back to the bay, and I was easily able to pass. There was still no power in the neighborhood. Only occasional candlelight flickering in the window or a dim generator-driven house light could be seen, but almost all the houses were pitch black. Black, partially from the storm but partially from the fact that they were second-home toys for the rich and famous. I first pulled into my driveway and quickly looked at my home, the so-called "shed on the block" the sea debris had not reached the first floor. One downed tree and some minor basement flooding, but not much to speak of, given the circumstances. The worst of it was the mangled dock, which broke apart and wedged against the wetlands. My house was okay. I grabbed my cell phone out of my pocket to take a snapshot to send to my kids. I saw a text from Jason:

"House in Port is okay, just no power. We're staying warm in front of our gas fireplace. Have hot water. Great for showers, and we're cooking on gas stove. Bridgette says Hi as well. Mom's been acting weird. Crying a lot! Do you have a clue, Dad?"

I snapped a picture of our vacation house and sent it back to Jason with the following text:

"Glad to hear from you. Here's our place. It survived. No power out here. Let everyone know I'm okay." I wasn't going to get into any of the crap that happened between their mother and me.

I drove next door to Mr. Weisberg's compound. His place was also hedged. "Must have been his yearly bonus at Goldman Sachs," I thought. To me, his place was enormous. Unlike "my shed," it sat lower on the property and was a total washout.

Moving past the hedges into his private retreat, past broken branches, dock remnants, even half a dingy, I parked on the side. I had never been past the entryway of the Weisberg compound.

Now I would finally see what was inside.

As I walked up to the door, I reached beneath the mat to retrieve the key. The mat was damp, but the key was still there. I took the key and opened the door. What was once an opulent Vanderbilt-style interior with contemporary furniture was now a complete wreck! Large puddles flooded the oak floors. The furniture was still wet, and there was sea muck everywhere.

I opened all the doors and windows to air out the foul smell.

"Imagine, a guy of Mr. Weisberg's stature without a backup generator," I thought.

Chapter 26

I was so upset by the scene I forgot to look at the wall. And there it was, staring right at me, the pure example of the wealth of the Hamptons, hanging right above the fireplace.

It was an 8 by 4 foot Jackson Pollock drip painting.

Not even out of kilter. And across from the Pollock was a characteristic Lee Krasner work from the same period, sitting over a large, open breakfront. Pollock and Krasner were husband and wife, and like me, Krasner had to endure the hardship of her spouse's drinking and infidelity. "Could my marriage survive the same?" I thought. "Fuck, no!" I shouted, even though there was no one to hear me. This couple comparison was not helping my mental status. Better focus in on the job ahead, and more precisely, what was up on the wall, right in front of me.

Two masterpieces! Priceless treasures from two of the greatest artists ever to be seen in the East End of Long Island, or the world, for that matter. Who would imagine putting these pieces on the wall of a waterfront home? I remembered a number years ago in the *New York Times* a write-up of a similar Pollock painting selling at Sotheby's for $140 million.

Pollock No. 5. The actual name was *No. 5, 1948*. I had an uncanny memory when it came to numbers. I did this by linking an image to the number. Visualization was the trick. The image here was of my Pollock-esque Uncle Billy creating the Pollock painting. You see, Uncle Billy's birthday was July 5, 1948. And he always had us down for a Fourth of July party down at his White Meadow Lake house. Just seeing the painting unleashed the specifics stored within my cerebral cortex. *Pollock No. 5, 1948*.

Weisberg could have bought a dozen Hamptons waterfront estate compounds with the price of just that painting. And there it was, staring out with its brown and white drips, built upon black and yellow drips, with greys and oranges. I think there were even a few red splatters and what appeared to be two cigarette butts right on the canvas. You probably couldn't tell the difference if seaweed and salt water hit this drip painting—maybe it would even have added to the effect.

The Krasner painting was four by seven feet and like the Pollock was also an abstraction. But Krasner's abstract curvilinear and triangular shapes built upon raw canvas were far less recognizable even to a seasoned art lover than the Pollock. Lucky for me, while attending a cardiology meeting in the late 1990s, I went to the Krasner retrospective at Los Angeles County Museum of Art. Krasner was more than just Pollock's wife. Her collages were from the early 1950s. She used her color field paintings from the Betty Parsons Gallery and applied torn shapes on top of the surface. This one had curved black collage elements placed over a green, blue, and orange color field painting. At the bottom, I could make out the initials L.K. blending in with the oval figures. She was the only woman in the so-called New York School, and her art stood on its own.

Much more geometric than the Pollock, her piece was heavily impastoed and seemed to be playing with the Pollock across the room.

I pulled out my iPhone and snapped two photos of the Pollock, one in ambient light, the other with the flash. I proceeded to take two shots of the Krasner and then a dozen more of the damage to show Mr. Weisberg. I left the paintings on the wall, not wanting to try to lift them off, fearing more damage. Plus, where would I put them, on the sea-soaked ground? These paintings did not even shift one inch. They were both securely coupled to the wall. And that was the safest place for them for now.

Heading past a black, yellow, and red metal hanger-like contraption that was twisted on the floor, I remembered it greeting me when I first met the Weisbergs in their entryway. A classic black, white, and red Calder mobile, now twisted beyond recognition, swimming amongst the muck on the floor. I plucked it out of the debris and wiped the painted coat hanger-like metal on my shirt, then placed the mangled stabile on the granite island in the kitchen. What was a perfectly balanced mobile was now a bent, colored mess.

The next job was to pull each piece of furniture onto their deck and some of it onto the driveway. Then I trekked down to the basement. The flood came halfway up the stairwell. I unraveled my three-inch-thick fire hose, placing one end deep underwater, and fed it up the stairwell to my pump out back. Once connected, the water pumped briskly onto their lawn.

As I walked out the front door, I heard a scream from across the street!

Chapter 27

Get help. Mr. Vicks is down—he's not breathing!" shouted a voice from across the street.

Samuel Vicks was a senior statesman. The Vicks once owned the whole entire peninsula but eventually sold off lots to developers, leaving their Tudor estate as the central domicile of the neighborhood. Blessed by being off the water for this storm, but cursed perhaps by the stress of the disaster and the blackout.

I ran out the Weisbergs' gate, across the road, past a century-old wooden barn on their property, to their Tudor-style estate. The door was open. There lay Mr. Vicks, ashen grey and shaking. Their two tall, lanky sons, Maxwell and Jared, were by his side in a panic. They worked in some form of "high finance" according to Samuel, whatever that meant!

"Were they smoking crack and blowing their investors' money like other swindling hedge fund managers?" I humored myself.

Who knows, but it definitely meant they were not in the medical field.

"You've got to do something!" Max pleaded. Max was the older and taller of the two. He was flanked by his petrified younger brother, who just stood there in shock like a deer in the headlights. Both brothers were not spring chickens. Max must have been in his mid-to-late sixties, and Jared in his early to mid-sixties. And you could only guess where that put our senior statesman's age.

I checked his breathing and his pulse—there was neither. So, I promptly began CPR, but not via the ordinary method. I had a bad back after wearing lead year after year at Mount Sinai, and after all the hauling at the Weisbergs' I needed a mechanical advantage. Immediately I thought about a novel invention I learned from doctors at the University of California San Francisco. Those doctors applied a plunger to the chest, what was first called "Plunger CPR" and eventually became Active Compression-Decompression CPR. This method sucked more blood into the chest and pumped more to the rest of the body. And like many a great Bay Area idea, it also became a great Bay Area story.

"The plunger," I thought. "Guys, can you get me a toilet plunger?" I asked. Within seconds, Max handed me a brown plumber's helper, which I quickly applied to the middle of his father's breastbone. Then I proceeded to plunge him, the way I had my clogged toilet the past summer. But this time I plunged his chest at a hundred plunges per minute up and down. Still no pulse! Then I proceeded with another maneuver that was also not a part of any current American Heart Association, or American Red Cross, recommendation. One that had been removed from the American Heart Association Basic Cardiac Life Support CPR course, but I had seen it work time and time again, the "Precordial Thump!" In yesteryear we would make a fist and punch (i.e. "thump") the breastbone, hoping to reset the heart rhythm, but most studies showed that this did not work. Miraculously, the thump followed by two minutes of "*plunger* CPR" got Mr. Vicks going again.

There it was, his pulse and breathing had returned, and so did his color.

I picked up my cell. One bar, but enough to call the Sons of the Beach, the official nickname of the Westhampton 911 Rescue Squad, which was plastered on each of the village's fire engines. They came within minutes and brought Mr. Vicks to the Southampton Medical Center. Both *sons* left with him.

As a cardiologist, I'm well aware of what you as the reader are thinking. Another heart attack? Hell, no! Most people when they collapse have a heart rhythm problem in which the lower chambers of the heart beat very fast. The technical term is ventricular tachycardia or ventricular fibrillation. Ninety-nine times out of a hundred you need to shock or paddle that person to get them out of the *bad* rhythm. But not Mr. Vicks. He was the one in a hundred that made it without being shocked. The good old "toilet plunger" and the good old "Precordial Thump." Hey, what do I know? Just an old-time cardiologist in the new-fangled world of medicine. And like the Seafield Estate weathered the storm, Mr. Vicks lives and breathes another day.

As I walked back to the Weisberg estate, I saw two local men going door to door, looking for work. These two were approaching the Weisbergs' front door.

"May I help you?" I called to two rather large dark-complexioned men walking up the driveway. Each man was over six feet tall and weighed over two hundred fifty pounds. Both had black hair. One had a black elongated mustache!

"Looking for some work. Do you need a hand?" asked Mustache Man with a Spanish accent.

"Sure can. Need some hauling help and some muscle. Two hundred bucks each for the rest of the day," I said.

"Deal," said Mustache Man's sidekick.

The rest of the afternoon we hauled, pumped, scrubbed, hosed, and dried anything and everything we could except their wall hangings. The blowers helped dry the floors and the rest we toweled down. By the end of the day we pulled everything into the garage. There was still no power. I closed up the house and left with the two along my side.

There was no way I could have cleaned and dried up the Weisbergs' place without their help. We turned a tattered mess into a reasonably dry, clean place, though I was uncertain that any of the rugs or furniture would be salvageable. The floor itself was beginning to buckle, and many of the mechanicals in the basement were beyond repair. Nonetheless, Weisberg would be appreciative of my help, and I was pleased by the help of Mustache Man and his sidekick.

I went to look for the money to pay them, but something was missing. My wallet.

Ah, shit. I checked all my pockets and then ran over to my car and checked the driver-side door slot and the compartment between the driver and passenger. All likely places.

"Maybe it slid to the side," I thought. I bent over and looked on the sides, but no luck. No wallet to be found. Racing over to my place, I checked my warm-up jacket and any other logical places. Then it hit me. After witnessing that terrible fucked-up sight with my wife and "that asshole," I had left my wallet in the kitchen drawer. I went over and over the sequence of events: down the stairs, grabbed the keys from the mudroom, and then out the door to Alex's. "I left the damn wallet in the kitchen drawer." I smiled internally. I went upstairs to my bedroom closet, opened the door, reached in the back behind the shelf where I kept my socks, and found a large wad of money rolled up, held together with a thick rubber band. I counted out the necessary amount and, putting some extra in my pocket, went back to my two patient helpers.

"Here it is, two hundred bucks apiece plus a fifty-dollar tip each. Thanks for the help," I said, somewhat out of breath from that fiasco.

Mustache Man and his sidekick walked down the block. "Much appreciated," I heard the sidekick say.

Chapter 28

Mr. G was still cranking out front on the Weisbergs' driveway. After a full day of menial labor, I almost didn't notice its lawn mower-type roar. The loud roar was indistinguishable from the sound of the ocean in the distance after a punishing day of heaving and hauling. Hardly even noticed it. All it did was drown out background noise. But what kind of background noise was there in the Hamptons—especially well off the beaten pathway, on a private peninsula after a major hurricane or at least hurricane-force winds? AND WITH NO POWER TO BOOT! No background noise whatsoever. Could have used Mr. G at my place back in the burbs in Port Washington.

Speaking of Port Washington, Jason just sent me a text:

"Dad, still no power. Mom and Bridgette are playing Bananas in front of our gas fireplace in the living room. Lucky our stove and hot water heater also run on gas. Trees on the bluff downed the power lines. Looks like it will be two weeks before we get power back. We'll get by. How's 'the shed'? J"

I thought my family in Port was lucky to have so many things running on gas. "Imagine a hot shower." I thought. Not here. Not in Quiogue. There was no gas in our neighborhood. If you were lucky you had propane. But all I had in the Hamptons was nada, Zip!

I typed into my phone: "House still okay. Neighbor's place a mess. Please keep warm. Let me know if you need me. Just trying to salvage our next-door neighbor's disaster. Love to all, Dad." I pressed send and off it went.

The kids knew nothing about what happened between Shari and me. That was, unless Shari had said something. To them things were "same old same old." I did not have the courage to tell them. I also did not tell them about my job!

I looked at Mr. G's gasoline gauge and the red arrow was on empty. I shut off the generator and grabbed another five-gallon tank from the back of the Honda Pilot and filled it back up. Ah, Peace and Quiet. I pulled the generator out to the road and onto my property.

Even though this was considered a lightweight generator, it still took a bit of work to get it back over to my place. I needed it to drive my sump pump in order to dry out my basement and give me some light. Perhaps run a few appliances. Grabbing a long, heavy-duty extension cord, I waddled through the water in the basement to the pump. I disconnected the pump's plug from the basement outlet, attached the orange cord, and extended it out the small back window. Once it was attached to the generator, I gave a quick pull to restart the machine. The lawn mower-type engine sound was back, and within seconds the pump was shooting out water through white PVC tubing towards the wetlands. As I glanced towards the bay, I could see my damaged dock, torn apart, and hoped at least some of it was salvageable. The tide was the highest I'd ever seen—

to the point that the wetland grasses themselves were fully submerged.

"If only I had a working generator," I thought, "there would be no water in my basement." Fortunately, the burner had been off before the storm. I was not prepared to fire it up now. Who knew whether it would even work, and if it did, perhaps it would short out immediately. The weather was still mild enough that I could live without heat.

What I really needed was a hot shower. I examined the hot water heater. It had a separate electrical outlet, which I connected to the generator extension cord. The bottom coils of the heater were badly damaged. Nonfunctional, but the upper part was unfazed and seemed to be working. After one hour, the water was pleasantly warm. I waited another hour and by then, the water was hot enough for a soothing shower.

The shower relaxed my aching body. I was in pretty good shape but had not been prepared for all the heavy hauling. The physical labor was much more than a full day at the hospital—even with our intensive cardiac procedures, plus the strain of wearing twenty pounds of lead-radiation protection (vest plus skirt) that was required during each case.

"Ah, that felt good," I said to myself as I left the shower. I went over to my oversized square Carrara marble coffee table in my living room and pulled out an old book I had purchased at a garage sale.

Chapter 29

The book was entitled *Jackson Pollock,* a relatively small paperback authored by Frank O'Hara. O'Hara was a well-known assistant curator and poet who worked at the MoMA, and it is conceivable that he may have had something to do with the art selection for the 1972 MoMA show, where I first was introduced to Pollock, his close friend. Yes, O'Hara was a Pollock expert. The cover of the book had a small photo of Pollock with a furrowed brow and a wrinkled forehead, with his left hand supporting his tilted head and a cigarette butt between his index and middle finger. He looked perplexed. It was next to another more colorful Pollock painting with swirls of whites and greens, orange and yellows. The book had its price on the cover: $1.50. "Those were the days," I thought. The cover said that the book contained "over 80 reproductions, 16 in full color."

Maybe the one from the Weisbergs' house was reproduced inside?

I looked inside and found that the book was published in 1959 by George Braziller, Inc., from New York. Searching for the painting, I thumbed through the pages. I could not find the Weisberg painting. Maybe I missed it. It certainly was not a complete catalogue raisonné of his works, but showed many with different styles, particularly as they related to color, swirls, and curves. I went through the book one more time, page by page, until I came to plate 34 in black and white.

"34. *Nr. 5, 1948.* Oil on composition board. 96 x 48. Collection of Alfonso Ossorio."

To me this painting seemed nice, but not anything out of the Pollock ordinary. In fact, the author did not even discuss it separately, and it wasn't even chosen as a color plate.

How could this be one of the world's most expensive paintings?

I read on about Pollock's classical period with a little digression on page twenty-three about his first "numbered" painting. *Number 1*—that digression said it all.

> *Digression on* Number 1, 1948 *(plate 32)*
>
> *I am ill today but I am not*
> *too ill. I am not ill at all.*
> *It is a perfect day, warm*
> *for winter, cold for fall.*
>
> *A fine day for seeing. I see*
> *ceramics, during lunch hour by*
> *Miro and I see the sea by Leger;*
> *Light, complicated Mezingers*
> *and a rude awakening by Brauner,*
> *a little table by Picasso, pink.*
>
> *I am tired today but I am not too*
> *tired. I am not tired at all.*
> *There is the Pollock, white, harm*

will not fall, his perfect hand

and the many short voyages. They'll
never fence the silver range.
Stars are out and there is sea
enough beneath the glistening earth
to bear me toward the future
which is not so dark I see.

I was unsure whether those words were from Pollock himself, or were they from O'Hara who was well known for his own poems? So, I reread the words, but I was still confused. My guess after the reread was that it was O'Hara's poem, with Pollock in mind. It was strange and different, and I guess that was what Pollock was all about—strange and different.

The sun was close to setting and I had attached one more extension cord to a large standing lamp in the living room and my HiFi and played some Coltrane to drown out the noise of the generator. Coltrane was one of the fathers of jazz. And jazz was the thing that seemed to get my mind off of all my troubles, and relax my spirit. I opened up a bottle of Heineken, finished the beer, and turned off the stereo to extinguish the light. Normally, pure quiet out in the Hamptons, but tonight there was the additional roar of Mr. G.

After the beer, it was time to collapse. I walked to my bedroom, flashlight in hand and went over to my bed. I turned off the light and then reached underneath the bed. This was kind of a ritual out in the Hamptons. I felt for it. It was always there. A reminder.

Chapter 30

It was my bat! As I collapsed in bed, I drifted back to 1972.

My alarm went off. I looked up at the clock--eight a.m.

Within seconds, Mom and Dad and Sis arrived at my bed and sang "Happy Birthday." I had fantasized about receiving a surprise from my parents for turning thirteen, namely, Yankee playoff tickets. But they did not make the playoffs.

We lived in a modest Victorian house in a little North Shore town known as Sea Cliff. My mom told me it reminded her of San Francisco. Both locales had steep rolling hills with beautiful bay views. I went down for breakfast, and there was my favorite spread. Bagels and lox with all the trimmings. The trimmings included whitefish salad, tuna salad, and pickled herring.

"Nice trimmings for a gentile," I said to my dad.

"We have acclimated well to their foods," he joked. "Eat up quickly."

Dad was a modest jeweler who for many years had a small store, in Great Neck, called The Great Neck Jewelers. He worked there six days a week, and I helped him during the summers. This Saturday would be his sixth day of work. He had taken the day off, a rarity for my workaholic father. The Great Neck Jewelers was closed for my birthday, and he had a surprise in mind.

"Eat up," he said, "then get ready. We're going to the city."

Within an hour all four of us hopped into a black 1969 Cadillac Seville, a statement of mild success, and headed into "the City." The City to me was not just New York City with its five large boroughs -- it was that one majestic borough known as Manhattan. We parked at the Park and Lock, on Forty-Second Street, and took a taxi up to Fifty-Third off of Fifth Avenue, to an art museum. The MoMA.

"Not my Momma?" I joked to my family.

"Nope, MoMA"— my mother responded by emphasizing the long "O"—"MoMA. The Museum of Modern Art!" she said emphatically.

Art was an important element of our Sea Cliff home. Every wall contained a well-framed poster from some famous museum. The posters were very realistic and included a Rembrandt self-portrait entitled "Portrait of the Artist at his Easel," from the Louvre: a Renoir, "Two Young Girls at the Piano," from the Met: and an Ansel Adams photograph, "Clearing Winter Storm, Yosemite National Park". Mom, liked to paint and copied two Picassos: "The Seated Harlequin" and a-somber reproduction of Picasso's almost sickly looking "The Guitarist" from his Blue Period. The more cheerful "harlequin" sat on our mantel, whereas the starving guitarist was hung on a sidewall in our kitchen. The latter was perhaps strategically placed to encourage us (meaning me and my sister) to eat. Today, MoMA was featuring a temporary exhibit entitled "Contemporary Masters of the 20th Century."

We walked in and got our tickets. Inside we headed over to a very long horizontal painting that didn't look like art at all. It looked like someone just dripped paint all around the painting. It was nine feet high by eighteen feet wide oil and enamel on canvas. But, as my father explained, this canvas was not painted in the usual fashion.

"This is one of the great geniuses of our times, an artist by the name of Jackson Pollock. He didn't paint with a brush. He would throw, splash, splatter, and drip paint of all colors on canvas. And his canvas was not up on a wall or an easel, but on his floor in his studio at the East End of Long Island. He would even piss and throw cigarette butts right on the canvas." Dad enjoyed abstract art.

The painting was entitled, One: Number 31, from 1950. Jackson Pollock.

We walked through the rest of the exhibit. There was not a single Ansel Adams, but there were two Picassos. Each more bizarre than my mom's reproductions. "Les Demoiselles d'Avignon" from 1907. The eyes were twisted, noses exaggerated and disfigured, and everything disproportionate-seeming. Another was from his Cubist period and was called "Girl Before a Mirror," painted in 1932. The painting consisted of bright colors, with a geo-metric background and oval lines creating the girl's face, breast, and belly. One large oval formed the mirror, and similar curved lines formed the mirrored image, but col-ored differently.

After MoMA, my family took me to the Carnegie Deli on Seventh Avenue near Fifty-fifth Street to celebrate. We ordered corned beef and pastrami on rye with coleslaw and Russian dressing. Washed it down with Dr. Brown's Cel-Ray soda. Then Dad pulled out a box from the duffle bag. I tore off the silver wrapping paper and opened the box. Inside was the most fabulous present I could have ever imagined. A Thurman Munson–signed Louisville Slugger bat.

I awoke from the dream, felt under my bed and pulled out the bat. It was heavy—thirty-five inches long and weighed thirty-two ounces. Surprisingly, it had not browned despite the nearly forty years of time that had passed. It had the traditional Louisville branding. A brown oval, and inside it said: "Louisville Slugger 125, Hillerich and Bradsby Co., Made in U.S.A., Louisville, KY." Across the bat it said, "Powerized," with two lightning bolts. Sandy! I thought. Then I looked at the signature, in black—not a smudge, but clearly written in cursive, "Thurmon Munson No. 15."

Munson was not just any catcher—he was the team's beloved captain who led the Yankees to three consecutive World Series appearances. And he was my hero. One who met an untimely death. Right after he received his pilot's license, he crashed a small plane, a Cessna Citation, and perished! What a loss.

As I thought back, Munson's death was accidental. Pollock, on the other hand, also died in a crash. Not so accidental! Pollock was drunk, disturbed, and twisted. His mind was quite different than the more even keeled Munson's. I put the bat back under the bed and started thinking about the Pollock I had seen, nearly forty years ago, at the MoMA. I could visualize the large horizontal painting that was more than double the size of the one I saw today. There were no bright colors. At least, how I remembered it; only blacks and whites swirling on raw canvas. Was it just a faded memory? Could I only remember in black and white? Or was there something much deeper and more somber in Pollock? The one I saw today seemed more somber still than the one I saw at the MoMA. Today's Pollock was deeper in its intent, and also had more of a depth with respect to the buildup of the paint itself. Something was disturbing the artist. Yes, something was irking him. Was it his wife? Or his work? Or his own inner demons? His friends and inner circle? His art critics? The "art business"? The drinking and its effect on his brain? Or all of the above.

"He did kill himself," I said to myself. Yes, but he also killed someone else and his mistress, Ruth Kligman, was in the car! Pollock's career was going down the tubes. Sound familiar? Pollock had lost his ability to paint. That's a real killer! Was he suicidal? It was 1956 and Pollock was on the outs with his wife, who was away in Paris. He was carousing with two much younger women. Drinking and driving in East Hampton! Not a good combination, to say the least. He was heading around a curve on Spring-Fireplace Road, in his blue Oldsmobile convertible with the two hotties, arguing over a party, and accelerated off the road, hit a tree, and decapitated himself, also killing one of the gals. His mistress survived and wrote a book about their torrid affair, which I read between college graduation and medical school. *Love Affair: A Memoir of Jackson Pollock*, by Ruth Kligman. It was a great summer read, but now it hit too close to home. You know what I mean, with my marriage being fucked up and all. And the alcohol was just the least of it.

One theory regarding another great artist, Vincent Van Gogh, involved the possibility that he ingested a local flower called foxglove, which contained the cardiac drug digitalis, to treat his epilepsy. This drug, in too high quantities, could disturb the mind and make everything look yellow like the many Van Gogh sunflower paintings. And foxglove was out in the Hamptons. Could Pollock have ingested foxglove? It was just a thought, and a very improbable one at that. It was more likely that he ingested other substances. Alcohol was his demon! He had abused alcohol most of his life and struggled with depression. Did the alcohol have a twisting effect on Pollock's brain? It had to! Or was it sheer mental illness? He had received intensive psychotherapy. But how good is therapy, anyway? Everybody knew of his struggles with depression, but maybe he had more of the combo deal found in bipolar disorder, like so many other creative individuals. Was this mania or depression?

There seemed to be black and brown and grey drizzled paint that swirled around and built a base in my neighbor's Pollock. A base that looked more like a nest than anything else. On top of it there were thinly drizzled whites and yellows. The complete painting's milieu was a cacophony of Pollock's emotional physicality, plus his disturbed mental state. The end result—a Jackson Pollock masterpiece!

"Why would anyone buy this painting and put it over their fireplace?" I asked myself. It was not pleasant. There was no serenity. It was just plain disturbing. Plus, the fact that it was not only over a fireplace, but rather a waterfront fireplace. Plus, it faced his wife's masterpiece. A wife that he became estranged from, and was supposedly going to divorce! "Who on earth would subject these priceless paintings to the elements, and put them in harm's way? Any monster storm, such as Sandy, could easily turn those paintings into a worthless pile of debris.

"Perhaps the Weisbergs were so rich that the priceless Pollock was a mere pittance to them. I guess they could be multibillionaires? If the painting was even worth $300 million, that would be just a drop in the bucket for a multibillionaire." But what about its importance as *art*—to the art world as a whole, or a bona fide collector of prized "Postwar and Contemporary Art" as categorized by Sotheby's or Christie's auction houses? Or at least as a status symbol? Don't most art collectors care about the art, and also their own reputations as caretakers of art? How about the Weisbergs? Did they care, like I would have cared?

Chapter 31

The next day I returned next door in order to move everything back into the Weisbergs' compound. I opened the door and looked up above the fireplace towards the piece that attracted all my attention. My jaw dropped. Where there once was a priceless Jackson Pollock, now there was nothing but an empty wall with only two large picture frame hook fasteners.

Maybe I had moved the painting? I thought for a split second. Absolutely not.

I wouldn't have even conceived of touching the piece that seemed so secure to the wall. Unfazed by Sandy, a survivor! I had thought yesterday, but now it was gone. I glanced around the room, just to see what else was missing. The rest of the pieces were still there. The Krasner painting still stood above the breakfront, and the broken Calder mobile still rested on the kitchen counter. But those were worth only a tiny fraction of the Pollock.

My heart shook! I was spellbound. Everything else seemed right in its place. That was until I glanced to the right! On the other side of the kitchen counter, I could see extending from the counter's base long blond hair on the floor. Long platinum blond hair! My heart started pounding, and I began sweating profusely. As I made my way around the island, the blond hair was sitting in a pool of blood, attached to an ashen-grey lifeless body, a body that I easily recognized. No, it couldn't be!

I just stood there and stared. Then I bent down and felt for pulse, as if there were a glimmer of hope, as if I were treating another cardiac arrest victim in the hospital. But I knew from her pallor and the blood pool that there was no hope. The body felt ice cold, without signs of life. My breathing became even deeper and faster. My fingertips and mouth began tingling, and then I started to feel faint. I can't remember ever being in a panic like this. Not when I was fired, and not even when I caught my wife in the act! No! All time stood still and I just shivered.

"Dawson," I said to myself. "Get a grip."

I had enough of my faculties to realize I was hyperventilating. I knew the pattern and realized the medical sequence of events that was gripping my body. In my dizzying state I drifted back to the words of Dr. Lightfield, my pulmonary attending at Hopkins.

"If you're ever in a panic and start to hyperventilate, just breathe into a paper bag," he said.

I quickly glanced back to a shelf in the kitchen. Wedged between two books on the shelf, *The Joy of Cooking* and *The Barefoot Contessa*, was a folded brown paper bag. I grabbed the bag and began to breathe into it. Within a few minutes, I could feel my breathing pattern start to reverse, and slow down to a more normal pattern. The same thing happened with my pounding heart. It also slowed back to a more normal pattern. As the dizziness resolved, things became clearer.

"Thank you, Dr. Lightfield," I thought. Just like he taught us, breathing into the bag helped raise the carbon dioxide in the blood stream and reverse the effects of the hyperventilation.

I walked back to the body and looked down.

Chapter 32

Lying face down was a blond-haired woman, wearing black pumps with red soles, a grey woolen skirt, and a white short-sleeved shirt. I went to turn her over and saw what remained of Mrs. Charley Weisberg. That is, or shall I say was, Angela Weisberg.

Angela was a distant relative of a wealthy and historic family. Could have been the Astors or the Vanderbilts, for all I know. When Angela and Charley got married, their ceremony was featured in *Town and Country* magazine as the wedding of the decade. Lavish pictures from the Plaza Hotel flooded the magazine. Photos of Charley, in white tails, and Angela, in her elegant white gown, leaving by a horse-drawn carriage near Central Park and walking up the red carpet into the Plaza. It reminded me of the wedding of Prince Charles and Princess Diana, and we all know how that one turned out.

But now Angela was more than not breathing. She was dead. A death that was clearly was not accidental. Her muscles were partially contracted and her joints frozen in rigor mortis. But the body was almost at full stiffness, which typically starts about twelve hours post death. This would put the timing back to last evening after I left the compound.

Her neck had a sharp cut from what looked like stran-gulation. And bruises all the way around. Asphyxiation! But with what?

And then I glanced towards the doorway. A long, wrapped metal wire lay to the right of the entryway, nearly five feet in length. The same type used to hang paintings.

"Must have been the wire used to hang the Pollock," I thought.

Why did "they" leave the evidence?

Chapter 33

I dialed 631-288-0911, and Officer John McElroy answered, "Westhampton Police Department. How could I be of service?" The officer expected another downed tree or a local fire perhaps. He was inundated with calls from those battered by Hurricane Sandy. Dune Road was flooded, impassable, and trees blocked many of the side roads. Nobody had power. That is, nobody without a generator, which was 90 percent of the village. Our road was lucky.

"Perhaps the pull from heavy hitters such as Mr. Weisberg?" I thought. "The privilege of wealth and fame."

But all the wealth and fame could not bring Mrs. Weisberg back to life. She was dead. I felt so helpless. She was gone. Long gone. Yesterday's victim! Murder no less!

"Officer, you need to come quick, Weisberg residence, on Homans Avenue. Mrs. Weisberg's been murdered. Please send help!" I said with a shaky voice. It was hard for me to get the words out. I still couldn't believe what had happened. It was like a drooping clock in a Salvador Dali painting—surreal.

"Name, sir?" the officer questioned.

"Dawson, Matthew Dawson, Officer."

"Can you repeat the address, Mr. Dawson?" he said.

"Weisberg's place. Homans Ave."

"We're on our way!"

As I stood there in shock, I realized I forgot to mention something.

Chapter 34

THE PAINTING! I forgot to mention THE PAINT-
ING!"

I paced and paced and paced! Starting to slide back
into a *panic* again! Angela Weisberg—DEAD! Pollock—
gone! I grabbed the brown bag and started to breathe into
it prophylactically. After a few breaths, I proceeded to take
a more careful survey of the inside of their property.

By the time the officer arrived, I detected three more
pieces of evidence. First, I noticed footprints of mud that
came from the area where the Pollock stood and led out the
front door. Clearly, that was the path of egress of the painting. I took a sheet of paper from a leftover folded-up *New
York Times* crossword puzzle page in the back pocket of
my jeans. I took the newspaper and pressed the clearest
muddy footprint on the back of the puzzle page and created
an imprint of the footprint. Second, a MedicAlert Bracelet
was adjacent to the fireplace grill. I picked up the silver
bracelet and read it: "MDT Protecta and Cypher!" This
bracelet did not belong to Mrs. Weisberg! MDT was the
abbreviation for Medtronic, a pacemaker company. And
Protecta was their most recent brand of implantable defibrillator, a pager-sized box implanted in the chest to detect
and treat lethal heart-rhythm problems like the one that

befell Mr. Vicks. "Cypher" was the name of a stent manu-
factured by Cordis, part of Johnson and Johnson. There
was no way this belonged to Mrs. Weisberg. I looked over
Mrs. Weisberg's body very carefully, and even felt below
the left and right collarbone for the mass effect that would
have been created by a defibrillator implant. There was
none. No evidence of such an implant in her *whatsoever*.
Could it have been Mr. Weisberg's? Not a chance. I remember seeing him without his famous Yale T shirt, bare-
chested, when I helped him fix a backup from his cesspool.
There was no such scar. Only a blue tattoo that read "Eli!"
And the tattoo had no relationship to my cabbie from Miami Beach. I hooked the bracelet on my wrist for conven-
ience so I could continue scouring the place for clues.
Third, there, adjacent to the side moulding that abutted the
entryway, was a three-by-four-inch brown sticker, much
like a nametag that you would wear at a mixer. But this
was no mixer sticker. I picked up the tag, and turned it
over. The tag was aged and had lost its adhesive. On the
front I could easily read:

> *Sotheby's*
> *Artist: Jackson Pollock*
> *Title: "No. 5, 1948"*
> *Year: 1948*
> *Oil on Fiberboard*
> *8 feet by 4 feet*
> *POR*

"POR" stood for "price on request." Most people who
would have requested the price of this priceless painting
would have done so more out of curiosity than serious interest in a purchase. But someone did purchase the

painting? And it had to eventually make it to the Weis-bergs' private collection. I took the aged sticker and folded it up with the footprint-containing newspaper page—so that from the outside it showed only the crossword puz-zle—and stuck it in my back pocket. Lastly, when I looked carefully at the driveway, I saw only one set of car tire prints. Those tire prints had entered the Weisbergs' drive-way and led directly to my place next door. As I looked a little more closely, I felt certain I knew their source. They were the prints from my car's high-performance Pirelli tires. There was not another set of tire prints in sight. Any vehicle large enough to carry an eight-foot painting, even a minivan, would have made an imprint on the muddy driveway.

Four police cars hit the Weisbergs' driveway. Officer McElroy was the first to enter. I knew it was McElroy by the name on his uniform, but I also recognized him from town. He was a slender, well-kept policeman, who must have been in his mid-thirties. The Westhampton Beach po-lice officers all took turns patrolling the town's only real commercial thoroughfare, Main Street, and McElroy had his share of walking the rather mundane beat. The other officers followed. Seven in total: six men and one woman. Officer McElroy came directly to me, while two others in-spected the body and the rest searched the house.

Chapter 35

Mr. Dawson? What happened?"
Like many of the Westhampton regulars, McElroy was a typical blue-collar Irishman. Westhampton had two primary ethnicities. Many locals were of Irish decent. In fact, St. Patrick's Day is a national holiday on which the road-surface lines of Main Street are painted green and the locals are greeted with a festive St. Patty's Day Parade. The second ethnicity was the Orthodox Jews. On a typical Saturday morning in summer, one could see the Jews, from Dune Road and elsewhere, walking in suits and dresses to Hampton Synagogue. The temple, with a devout following, is a beacon for Hampton Jewry.

"Officer, their Pollock painting was stolen! And it must be worth millions—probably over a hundred million dollars! And Mrs. Weisberg is dead!" I nervously stated.

"Mr. Dawson, what are you doing here?" he abruptly asked. The officer looked at me, his puzzled face filled with distrust.

"Mr. Weisberg asked for my help. He said he was in Asia and needed me to check out the place. It was washed out by the storm. I tried to dry out all his stuff—and then the painting! Over there!" I pointed to the empty space, and the two lonely hooks hanging over the fireplace.

The rest of the officers were taking pictures of the body, grabbing evidence samples, including pieces of clothing. The whole entire area was treated as a crime scene. McElroy walked me over towards the other officers, who were inspecting the body. The female officer had donned some thin latex gloves to prevent her fingerprints from being confused with that of any suspect or the victim herself. "Why couldn't I have been that smart and worn gloves?" I said to myself. I had a box from the hospital just sitting next door at my place. I had no idea the Weisberg residence would turn into a crime scene.

"My prints are all over this place, including on Mrs. Weisberg's body," I anxiously reflected.

Dusting and collecting fingerprints. Hair samples, footprints, and bodily fluids! This was the blood and guts of an investigation, literally. Remnants of damage caused by either the perpetrator or the storm. It was hard to tell which was more devastating, Sandy or the murderer. The storm was bad enough, and now a grand theft of the highest order and a major murder, all next door to my "shed."

"Dawson, can I see some ID?" asked the officer.

"Sorry, Officer, I forgot my wallet," I replied.

"You what?" he snapped.

"Forgot my wallet. I left it back at my other house."

"How do I know you are who you say you are?" the officer questioned.

"I've seen you in town, and I know you know my face. You can ask anybody who is around. They all know me. Terry from Hampton's Coffee, Simon from the Beach Bakery, Fred Levy from True Value, and Hadley Ferguson from Prudential. If you need my beach pass ID, it's sitting on the windowsill in my kitchen next door. Do you want me to run next door and get it?" I asked.

"No, Dawson. Your beach pass will do you no good this time of year." He chuckled. He was not going to let me leave the premises anyway.

"And when was the last time you saw Mrs. Weisberg?" the officer asked.

"I had not seen her for a while. That is, I only met her a couple of times when we first moved to the neighborhood, and when I dropped off a package at their house a little over a year ago."

"Did you see her when you first arrived at their house the other night?" the officer asked again.

"No, Officer. I only saw her in her present state. Dead. Just plain dead."

"Were you having an affair with Mrs. Weisberg?" McElroy blurted out.

"Are you kidding me? I only met her a few times in the past. And that was not recently. It was about two years ago. When we first moved to the neighborhood. Don't know her from Adam. But I do know of her. But I respected the Weisbergs' privacy."

"Mr. Dawson, please come with me down to the station!" the officer insisted.

"I guess I was wrong," I said to myself. With his eerie stare into my eyes, I knew I had no choice.

Chapter 36

I rode with the officer back to the station. Went up the grand stairway that led into the modern large brick edifice, of a police building, that I always passed on the way to my place.

The officer led me to a back room and said, "Wait here," as he locked the door.

I waited—no, paced—for almost two hours, until the door was open.

Officer McElroy entered with another officer, who was much more intimidating.

"So, you are a doctor, I see," said McElroy. "Where do you practice?"

"Mount Sinai," I said. Then I thought, "*Did* practice at Mount Sinai."

"What do you mean, *did* practice?" asked the officer.

"I was just let go," I said in a softer tone.

"What do you mean let go?" he badgered me.

"Fired, sir." There, I said it. I'm sure this won't help matters. Being the first at a crime scene, and now a motive? Although I'm not exactly sure what that motive would be. But the way the officer was talking, I was certain they would find one. Or at least try to concoct some cockamamie story.

"When did this happen?" he asked.

"Two days ago," I said.

"And where is your family, Dr. Dawson?"

"My family? They're back in Port Washington."

"And Mrs. Dawson?" he asked.

"She's back there too. But don't call her. She . . . She . . . She . . . She . . . She just, I mean I just caught her screwing some guy half my age. No use calling her." All trust was gone! She did not have my back any longer. And since when? A year? Two? Five? Who knows? With deceit there is no trust. I just could not trust her. Calling Shari would not help my cause. But telling the officer not to call my wife? What was I thinking? Will he think that I was having an affair with Mrs. Weisberg as a reaction to my wife's affair? I was digging my own grave. Maybe I should have kept my big mouth shut like they do in the movies and just have called my attorney.

"Her name, Dawson?" he asked.

"Ah, shit. Do I have to?"

"Yes, Dawson. Now, give it to me and her number."

"Her name is Shari. You see, I got fired from Mount Sinai, drove home, and caught my wife fucking some guy. She's not going to be helpful, sir." I said.

"Dr. Dawson, please give me her number, I will have to call her." He said.

"Do I really have to?" I responded.

"Yes, Dawson. If you don't give it to me, I will get it some other way." He was continuing to raise his voice. Beads of sweat started to flow down the sides of his face. It was sheer, unmitigated anger, and all I wanted to do was get out of this mess. But just like McElroy, I was sweating as well. Slightly shaking.

"Now, give me the number!" he yelled. "Give it to me!"

"Okay, here it is, 516-767-2324. Just don't expect her to be on my side. That is not likely after I caught her in the act!" I explained. I think I was just aimlessly babbling at this point. Not helping my cause at all. They were going to call Shari one way or another. And whatever she would say would be out of my control.

"How did you know the painting was worth millions?" asked the officer.

"I saw it last night, a Jackson Pollock. Could be the one that sold for a hundred forty million a few years back."

"And how do you know that?" asked the officer inquisitively.

"Art, sir—it's my hobby. I collect art, and help out with the Art and Exhibition Committee at the Parrish Art Museum," I said. The Parrish was completing its move from the Southampton Village, to a rural location on Montauk Highway in the town of Water Mill. The new place, just east of Duck Walk Vineyards, consisted of two ultra-long ultra-high open barns to show off their art. The new Parrish was not yet opened, yet the building was nearing completion. Good timing. Had it been completed, the art on display there could have been destroyed!

"You saw the painting last night and now it's gone?" said the officer sarcastically. "And how about Mrs. Weisberg, did you see her last night and now she's gone? Have you heard from Mr. Weisberg?"

"Only when he called me to help him out with his house. He called me to ask for my help." I pulled out my mobile phone and showed him what I thought was an overseas number. "Officer, if you don't mind, I am going to try to call back Mr. Weisberg." I didn't wait for his permission. I just redialed the number, right in front of the officer. Surprisingly, I had not tried to call Weisberg before all this. Just shows how overwhelmed I was, in a state of panic. The dialing was complete and I heard: ". . . Your number did not go through. Please check the number and try your call later."

I hit redial and hoped for a different result, but:

". . . Your number did not go through. Please check the number and try your call later." It was to no avail. The number was not a New York number or even a United States cell phone number. It did not have any recognizable area code, and when I tried a third time, I got the same recording. I had no way to get in touch with Charlie, period. And who even knows whether he was still in Asia!

"And how long have you known Mrs. Weisberg?" he asked.

"I thought I answered this question," I responded, trying not to snap. Now he was starting to really irritate me. Each time he asked this question, he appeared to be approaching it from a different angle, a different vantage point. Did he feel I was going to crack and confess? The officer was beginning to remind me of the evil, Jew-killing Nazi Dr. Szell (played by Laurence Olivier) from the movie *Marathon Man.* Dr. Szell used a dental drill bit to torture the Jewish marathoner grad student Tom Levy (played by Dustin Hoffman). Levy, like myself, got innocently caught up in a twisted mess. In one horrific scene, he is kidnapped and then tortured by Szell, who repeatedly asks the restrained Levy "Is it SAFE?" Each time the same question is posed, Szell changes the intonation, i.e., "IS it safe?" And each time Levy fails to provide an answer, the crazy Nazi dentist drills into his healthy teeth, resulting in the ultimate torture.

I knew the answer to the "Is it safe?" question, I thought to myself. It wasn't safe then, and it is not safe now. I could hear the chilling screams coming from Levy as his teeth were being destroyed!

"No wonder I don't like going to the dentist," I thought to myself. I also thought that this McElroy guy was not just pulling my leg, he was pulling *my* teeth. This was my torture now. It was either cry or smile at the situation, and I chose the latter.

"What are you smiling about?" asked the angry McElroy.

"Just a stupid thought," I said.

"This is serious business Dr. Dawson, and no laughing matter."

Over the next fifteen minutes, Officer McElroy was clearly reenacting Olivier's award-winning role, by asking the same question over and over again. Each time with a different tone, in a slightly different way. Would I crack or slip up? Was he trying to break me down? Whatever it was, he was just plain annoying me!

"So, did you talk with Mrs. Weisberg at all before she collapsed?" he asked.

"What do you mean? I just found her dead. Right now. Right before I called you. I only met her a few times, just in passing. Neighborly stuff," I said.

"Did Mrs. Weisberg spend the night with you?" he asked.

"I told you no, Officer, I didn't even know she was in town." At that precise moment I knew my talking was not helping the matter. I was more than digging my own grave—I was burying myself!

"We're done with the questioning," the officer said as he abruptly got up, came around the table to my chair, and grabbed my wrist. He quickly cuffed my right hand and then my left, and escorted me to a cell in the back! "No more talking, Dawson," he retorted.

This was no laughing matter. I could see by the officer's expression. I was more than a suspect!

Chapter 37

Fingerprinted, mug shot taken, and strip-searched! I handed the officer my cherished Barenaked Ladies concert T-shirt that I had purchased from a Westhampton Beach Performing Art Center concert a few years ago.

How ironic, I thought.

I also tossed my jeans to the officer. I turned over my phone and bracelet, and emptied the rest of my pockets. There were just some spare bills I had taken from my sock drawer and the folded-up crossword-puzzle paper. No wallet!

"Nothing else, Dr. Dawson?" asked the booking officer.

"No, sir," I replied.

He went through each of my pockets a second time and found nothing else. All the contents were put in a large manila envelope labeled MATTHEW DAWSON, with my date of birth. I then got to take a world-class Westhampton Beach Police Department shower and was given a beautiful pair of matching Westhampton Beach Police Department jail attire. Oh, how stylish!

"You can put it on now, Dawson," said the officer.

I slipped on the attire and was led to my cell. It was made of cinder blocks covered with the usual jail-cell steel bars. There, I paced and paced and paced. Back and forth, forth and back, in my own little cell. All by my lonesome. Westhampton Beach was never a heavily trafficked area for hardened criminals. Yes, there was the usual vandalism or theft, but nothing on the scale of the crime occurred at the Weisbergs'.

And now I, "Dr. Goody Two Shoes" was being accused of the murder and the art heist of the century. Me, MD, the one who wouldn't even write off a cup of coffee on my income tax return for fear the IRS would negate it in an audit.

After moments of silence, a guard came back to my cell with a peanut butter sandwich and water. "Oh, how thoughtful," I said inside my head.

"I only thought they give you bread and water," I said to the guard. There was no response.

I wolfed down the sandwich and swallowed the water in what seemed like one large gulp.

"Guard," I called. "Don't I get one phone call?"

"Yup." He opened up the cell and grabbed me by my shoulder and took me to a phone down the hall from the cell.

"One phone call, Doctor, that's all you get," as the guard stood ten feet back from the phone.

"One call," I said to myself. After they had confiscated my cell phone, that was all I got. Just one phone call.

And whom did I call? My attorney? No! My wife? Not on your life! My mother? Are you kidding me? No! I called Shaw.

Shaw always told me, "You don't need an attorney, you don't need a tax accountant, and you don't need a financial advisor. All you need is me!"

"I don't know why I didn't just call my damn attorney—Mr. Seth Eisenberg, Esquire. Certainly, a decent guy. A real gentleman! He would have known what to do."

No, "Shaw" thing! I called Shaw!

Chapter 38

One hour later Officer McElroy came to my cell. "You have a visitor."

It was Dr. Alexiev Shaw.

"A fine mess you got yourself into this time, Ollie!" Alex joked.

It was no time for joking! "Alex what's going on? How long am I going to have to be in here?"

"Do you want me to tell you? One, you, my friend, are the leading suspect in the murder of Mrs. Angela Weisberg. Two, you are the leading suspect in the theft of the Jackson Pollock. They have a search warrant for your Hamptons home and are preparing to search your premises. Three, they called your lovely and delightful wife, who was absolutely useless in attesting to your character. You could imagine what *nice* things she said. No help AT ALL! What did you do to her?"

"Don't get me started, Alex!" I said. "What do we do now?"

"Tomorrow we have a hearing in Riverhead. You will plead not guilty. Hopefully, you will be released on your own recognizance for a one-million-dollar bail bond. And then I'll need your help."

"Alex, I know you are good with everything, but this is murder. Grand larceny. And a Pollock, no less! I need some serious legal help."

"Yes, you are right. I know my limitations. And there aren't many. I called an old friend of mine, who will meet you at the courthouse," Alex ended.

"An old friend?" I thought Alex was my *old friend*?

Chapter 39

I was brought by minivan to the courthouse in River-head. Cuffed all the way, and the ride was painful. En route, the driver hit two potholes and my head hit the top of the van. Just the beginning of another fun day out in the Hamptons, I said to myself. Riverhead was the capital of Suffolk County and had none of the grace or beauty of the Hamptons. It stood between North and South Forks of Long Island at the *head of a river*.

The courthouse was located in a desolate industrial area, not too far from the largest outlet this side of the Mississippi, Tanger, and way too close to the Riverhead Penitentiary.

Officer McElroy opened the van door, grabbed my throbbing hands, and walked me onto the stairs leading up to the Suffolk County Riverhead Criminal Courts building. It was a relatively modern concoction of concrete and glass and had none of the old-world grandeur of more popular courthouses such as the one in Baltimore from the movie *And Justice for All*, featuring Al Pacino. No, this was a relic that could use a facelift. But who am I to criticize? I was in the hands of the legal system, and let's hope there is "justice for all." As I reached the main courthouse entrance, there was Alex with his "old friend." Old friend, my ass, I thought. There stood what looked like a five-foot-eight-inch, striking thirty-eight-year-old defense attorney who closely resembled at first glance Cameron Diaz. And she was dressed to the kill.

Chapter 40

As I studied her more closely, I realized that *Cameron Diaz* was not Cameron Diaz at all. She was Amy Winter. The same Amy Winter I shared my first slow dance with in seventh grade, and my first kiss! I did not and could not forget that magical day in 1972.

September 30, 1972

After the religious service we all piled into a limo and ended up at Leonard's Palazzo—colloquially known as Leonard's—on Northern Boulevard in Great Neck. It looked like a large White Castle. But please, do not confuse this glitzy, gaudy catering hall with the hamburger joint. The castle structure had a massive parking lot in front, almost the size of a football field. It was more like a Sands Point estate, and if it were in D.C., it would be compared to the White House. As we entered, a stately doorman escorted us downstairs to the wine cellar for the "cocktail hour." The bartender was feeling benevolent and gave me a glass of some sweet, fruity drink with a splash of alcohol. After only a couple sips and some pigs in the blanket, we were escorted back upstairs to a large "ballroom" for the main event, featuring a seven-piece live band, "a Hank Lane Special." The band played pop music, and four sexy dancers decked out in black and white, wearing bell-bottom pants, grooved on the dance floor, hoping to get everybody "grooving." Yes, grooving.

I was very shy and had not yet had my first dance, date, or even a kiss. But if I were to do any or all of the above, it would be with the girl on the other side of the room. She was in almost all my seventh-grade classes but hardly even knew I existed. She was my secret heartthrob, and only one other person knew that information, my mother!

My mind wasn't hearing the band at this precise moment but was hearing something else. I had faded back to last week's conversation with my mom. The one where I told her about the prettiest girl I'd ever seen. And then she started singing that classic Frank Sinatra song "Once in Love with Amy."

Tear up the list, it's Amy. Mom's rendition seemed to evoke a silky-smooth young version of Sinatra. She had quite a good voice and actually acted as if she were singing on Broadway. At least in her mind. She was always belting out tunes from South Pacific, Oklahoma, and other classics, but this one only appeared after my maternal confession.

"You know, Matthew," she said, "I was your age when I first heard that song."

"I looked it up, Mom. Sinatra first sang that song in 1948. You were fourteen," I responded.

"Well, that's close enough," she said as she continued to sing.

"But once in love with Amy . . ."

By Amy she meant Amy Winter. Yes, Amy Winter. As I heard my mom singing in my head, even though the band was playing something else, I walked nervously across the parquet floor to this five-foot-tall girl with light ocean-blue *eyes and long blond hair, wearing a silky white dress and shiny white patent-leather dress shoes. There she was, all alone, just waiting to be plucked like a petal from a flower.*

Now was my chance, I thought to myself.

The band struck up another tune, and this time my obsessive focus on the song about Amy shifted to the Gilbert O'Sullivan slow dance they were playing, "Alone Again (Naturally)."

Perfect, I thought.

But its somber lyrics only made me more nervous . . . as I meandered closer to her.

"Do you want to dance?" I asked as my heart pounded in my chest.

"Sure," she replied as we listened to . . .

"I remembered I cried when my father died
Never wishing to hide the tears"

"Oh, could you give me a break?" I said sarcastically to myself.

As we walked toward the dance floor, I wrapped my shaking hands around her back. Moving close, she wrapped her hands around my waist. She put her head on my shoulder, and we danced slowly. At that instant, everything fell into place. My hands stopped shaking, and my pounding heart started to settle down. Although the room was filled, I felt as if it were just the two of us. How does our song go? Yes. "Once in love with Amy."

By the time the song finished, the beat switched to the more upbeat Sammy Davis Jr. hit "The Candy Man" and back to another slow number, "Summer Breeze," by Seals and Croft. Imagine two slow dances with Amy. This must be my lucky night!

We went to the sidelines and chatted after that. The whole evening was very, very special. Not just because it was Marty Scheinberg's Bar Mitzvah. It was special be-cause of Amy. And that evening, before my parents picked me up, I kissed her, right on the lips.

"Those delicious lips," I muttered inside my dizzying brain. The kiss must have lasted only five seconds, but it seemed to last forever.

Chapter 41

October 2012 Riverhead Courthouse

Amy had grown up to be very different than I remembered and radically unlike, in appearance, my soon-to-be ex-wife. Where Shari was small, Amy was tall. Where Shari had short legs, Amy had killer long legs. Where Shari had brown eyes, Amy's were a light ocean blue, just like I remembered. And oh, did she smell great, some fragrant perfume—I think it was Vera Wang!

"Dr. Dawson, I am Amy Winter. Alex filled me in on your predicament. You have to do exactly what I tell you. Nothing more, AND nothing less. You are going to plead not guilty. I am going to demonstrate that you are not a flight risk. And I am going to ask that you be released on your own free will. You are going to agree to post the requested bail. Do you hear me?"

"Yes, I do!" I replied. I think she had no clue who I was and how we were connected. She did not seem to recognize me or show any sign of prior knowledge of me. But my memories were as clear as day: the fireworks created by our first encounter. Here my life was in jeopardy, I was facing a future behind bars, and my heart was racing like a bat out of hell! I didn't have time to explain or even tell her where and when we'd met. Or even under what circumstances. It would only have confused the matters at hand.

The judge and county prosecutor were conferring and then separated.

"All rise for the honorable Judge Nielson."

Judge Nielson had straight greyish-black hair, at least what was left of it. It seemed just like in *Night Court*, but this appearance was during the day and for real.

The judge asked, "How do you plead?"

"Not guilty, your honor!"

"The prosecution has made a motion that you are a flight risk. They say you lost your job, your wife, and your money. They say you are an art expert and had the expertise and the motive to steal the Jackson Pollock painting. They also say that your fingerprints were all over the Weisberg residence, including Mrs. Weisberg's body, and that all evidence points to you having an affair with Mrs. Weisberg. What is your response?"

"Not true, your honor. Yes, I lost money, like many people did in the—" I was interrupted by Ms. Winter, who motioned me to be quiet.

"Your honor, Dr. Dawson is a well-respected physician. Yes, it is true that he was recently released from Mount Sinai Medical Center. And yes, it is true that he is an avid art aficionado. And yes, Dr. Dawson recently left his wife after he caught her philandering. But no, he was not having an affair with Mrs. Weisberg. In fact, he only met her on a few occasions and just in passing. He had no knowledge that she was even out in the Hamptons. Dr. Dawson is a decent man. A pillar of society! He is not a flight risk, your honor. I ask that you release him on one million dollars bail." Ms. Winter was cool, calm, and collected as she presented her argument, and evidently surmised it would be sufficient.

"One million dollars bail?" shouted the prosecutor with a raspy voice. "Dr. Dawson is a cold-blooded murderer, and a big-league art thief!"

The judge hit the gavel. "Silence. I am feeling kind today. Please release Dr. Dawson on one million dollars bail."

"Where the hell am I going to come up with one million dollars? And how the hell am I going to get out of this mess?" As Oliver Hardy put it: "well, here's another nice mess you've gotten me into!" Laurel and Hardy humor did not help. Not this time. I squared my slumped shoulders and tried to show some dignity as I was paraded out like the prisoner I was.

The bailiff unlocked my cuffs. But Westhampton Beach's Police Department had all my stuff. My iPhone, my clothes, and the bracelet, all contained within an envelope marked as my possessions. But I had to retrieve them just to get my life back.

Amy walked with me out of the courthouse.

"One million dollars bail?" I was still in shock over the amount.

"You are lucky they didn't make it three million. With your house as collateral, the million will not be a problem." I looked at her and then she looked at me. Our eyes met again. And then she realized.

"I've met you before," she said.

"Yes," I replied. "A long time ago."

"It was in seventh grade. Wasn't it?" she questioned.

"Marty Scheinberg's Bar Mitzvah," I said. Leonard's, the dance floor, you and me? It was my first slow dance. Do you remember?"

"'Alone again (naturally),'" she said.

"You remember," I said.

"How could I forget?" she replied. "It was my first kiss."

"Mine too."

At that moment I saw a twinkle in her eyes. It was as if time had stood still. She had remembered almost all the details, even the song. But still she did not know how I'd obsessed over "Once in Love with Amy" at that time, it almost drove me crazy. It was amazing that we both had never forgotten each other's names, together with the impact of what happened back in 1972. I could have seen almost anybody else from that year, and I would have never recognized a single one of them on the street. But who could forget their first love? Maybe if they were inevitably scorned, they would move on and forget. But a first dance, a first kiss, a first love, and then a presto change-o disappearing act? Those kinds of memories stick forever. And my Mom singing that stupid song embedded *Amy* in my brain forever.

"Oh my God, my car isn't here? I just remembered it's at the Westhampton Police Department."

"Can I offer you a lift?" she said to me.

"Sure," I replied.

We hopped in her red Miata sports car. Amy was kind enough to drive me back to the Westhampton Beach Police Department, where I signed for my personal items. I was happy to get my clothes back, especially my Barenaked Ladies concert T, and even happier to give up the WBPD jail attire. The manila envelope was untouched. I opened it up and found that my iPhone was nearly dead, and fortunately no one suspected the rest of my things were "evidence." It was all there—the bracelet, my cash, the folded piece of newspaper, even the sticker. Whew, I thought.

"I'd like to take you out to lunch, but I really need a shower. I don't live far from here. Do you mind, following me to my place, so I can freshen up, and then we'll go?"

"Okay," she said.

We then headed back to my place. I opened my side door and we entered. Still no power! I went out back and restarted the generator. I opened a bottle of the Bedell Cellars 2007 Musee with a daguerreotype label created by Chuck Close. This red wine blend was possibly the greatest Long Island wine byproduct, and Chuck Close was probably Long Island's greatest living contemporary artist, and, coincidentally, the guy who made the label.

"A toast," I said. "To old friends."

"Old friends? I've known you for forty years," she replied.

"Not really," I responded. "I lost track of you after seventh grade. What happened?"

"I moved," she responded. "Parents bought a place in Kings Point. I wound up graduating from Great Neck North. Sorry."

"Life goes on and then you die." I laughed.

"How about you? Did you stay in Sea Cliff?" she asked.

"Yes, all the way! I graduated North Hills High and eventually went to Baltimore, San Francisco, and then back east. What about you?"

"I stayed in Manhattan, Columbia all the way. 'Go, Lions!' Then went into practice at a small boutique firm, Eagleton and Siegel, Attorneys at Law. Eventually, I got the opportunity to run their Long Island branch. I've been out in Hampton Bays ever since. Inherited my parents' vacation home, just south of the highway."

"Did you ever get married?" I asked.

"No, my practice has always gotten in the way. I was engaged once back in 1985, but I chickened out on the way to the altar. My fiancé was a little too needy. My practice has always taken a front-row seat to my life, but I am getting older, and my biological clock is ticking. Tick-tock. Tick-tock." She just smiled and chuckled.

"Biological clock? Maybe we should go to work?" I joked. Amy was my age. But she did not look a day older than thirty-five. She was extremely fit, and I could barely see any wrinkles at all on her gorgeous face. I couldn't understand it. If I were meeting her for the first time, I would have thought we were from a different generation. I am most definitely a product of the 1970s and 1980s, at least insofar as my maturing years, and Amy would appear to be a product of the 1990s and 2000s. At least that was what I would have thought. My hair was greying. Amy's was as blonde as blonde could be.

I turned on Thelonius Monk and we each downed our Musee. I started to feel a little buzzed and very horny, but I knew I had to take a shower. I had not showered since that first night of cleanup at the Weisbergs'. The first time I saw the Pollock. And that included the day I discovered the Pollock missing and one dead Angela Weisberg—my stint at the Westhampton Beach Police Department—and my trek and adventure to and from the Riverhead Courthouse. "I'll be back in ten minutes," I left the room to freshen up. I was disgusting. I went into the bathroom, turned on the shower faucet, and turned up the water temperature. I took off my clothes and waited for the water temperature to get nice and hot and then hopped in the shower. The hot water felt so good, no great, as did the heavy water pressure. After about five minutes of just soaking under the hot water my muscles started to relax and melt. As I went to grab the shampoo, I thought I heard the door creak. I stopped for a second and tried to listen through the sound of the pouring water. Then the shower curtain opened.

Chapter 42

It was Amy, with the most amazing body I had ever seen. There was no way she was my age. Did she work out incessantly? I said to myself. Was this the same Amy that was with me in my seventh-grade class? She went to grab for the bar of soap, and I went to grab her. I placed my hands around her waist, and she put her arms around my shoulders and we kissed. This one was different than forty years ago, but it still made me quiver. The combination of hot water and soap, together with her voluptuous body, reminded me of *The Kiss* by Brancusi. No, that was wrong, way wrong. That sculpture was too modern, sterile. No, it reminded me of *The Kiss* by Rodin. More sensual and romantic!

Speaking of kiss, we began with our lips gently touching, and her tongue lightly sliding inside my mouth. Within sixty seconds, our tongues were deep inside each other's mouth, our bodies firmly pressed against one another. Then she started to slide the Irish Spring around my body and down between my legs. Then she took her long, red nail-polished fingers and grabbed me below with her left hand while she moved the bar of soap up and down my hard "obelisk" to the same beat as Monk's jazz, syncopating distantly in the other room. I wanted to cum, but I held back. I grabbed the bar of soap and began to stroke her down between her legs and saw her neck crank back. She gave a deep moan. As I went back and forth, I felt her harden and her moan turned into a much louder groan. She was groaning, louder and louder. At that particular moment I pushed her up against the tiled wall and went inside. Her body up against the tiled wall, and mine firmly pressed against hers. The warm water poured over my shoulders. As I pushed up and down, she started to groan louder and louder. I too began to scream as she dug her nails into my butt. "Yes! Yes! Yes!" she yelled as she started to harden with one of her legs tightly wrapped around mine.

The warm steam, together with my aroused autonomic nervous system, created a tingling aura and threw me into a dizzy spell. We held each other tight, soaped each other off, and then dried one another. Then we both collapsed on my bed.

I heard the song one more time, but this one was in my head, and it was not the music of Thelonious Monk!

Chapter 43

The next morning, I awoke at sunrise. I rolled over but Amy was not there. I went out to the living room and smelled something coming from the kitchen. It was pancakes and fresh coffee. The stovetop oven ran on a small tank of propane that worked only that one appliance, something I had forgotten with all the confusion during the storm. Amy found some matches in the utensil drawer and had started the stove, which provided an easy source to cook the pancakes even with a power outage. She had freshly brewed the coffee, using my French press. It was my favorite aromatic morning smell of Peet's coffee, which always reminded me of their café on Chestnut Street in San Francisco. My favorite of all was Major Dickason's Blend—Deep Roast, a rich dark java brew. Loved it even black. The table was set out in the sunroom, which faced out to the wetlands that backed up on to Quantuck Bay. Amy was sitting there, wearing a bathrobe that she found in my wife's closet. All she was wearing was the robe and a pair of black pumps. The latter must have been for the *effect*.

We both ate a stack of Jacks with fresh maple syrup that we found in the garage. I downed my Peet's. Delicious! "Now for the desert," said Amy. She pulled off her robe, with nothing underneath. Just her plump breasts, each the size of a ripe Florida grapefruit, with nipples that were stiff and firm. I touched them gently with my hands and began licking the tip of her nipples. Then she proceeded to pull down my boxers and began to go down on me. We moved quickly over to the couch in the living room and she began licking me up and down while I did the same to her. My tongue went deeper into her as she swallowed me up and down. She was on top and I was on the bottom. "Position 69, my favorite," she said as she dug her spiked heel into me. We were moving in unison, each of our mouths and tongues tasting each other's juices.

"Eureka," she screamed as we groaned together and shared the culmination. Nothing, and I mean nothing, has ever felt this good.

Chapter 44

How good was Amy? As a lover, there was no one who could hold a candle to her. But as an attorney? The best, at least, that's what I was told. Thank God, because my dear friend and fellow scientist, Alexiev was suggesting an insanity plea. I needed good legal representation. And I was lucky to have Amy. She got the Montauk Murderer off and was successful in other newsworthy cases. She represented a very famous East Hampton celebrity against her cheating Wall Street husband. Amy stuck it to that Wall Street scum! But was I confused? I'd done nothing wrong.

"Only a victim of circumstance," I said convincingly to myself. And my brilliant friend wanted to use the insanity plea to get me off? I was as sane as the day is long! Just a bit of misfortune. I was in the wrong place at the wrong time. Kind of like Sandy! You know, three events coming together: one, a full moon giving rise to a high tide; two, a Nor'easter from the west; and three, a hurricane heading in from the East. All three at the same time and place. And my predicament was not unlike that of superstorm Sandy. I too had three inopportune events: one, losing my job; two, catching my wife having an affair; and three, being at the scene of a high-profile murder and one of the world's greatest art heists of all time. All this I incredulously but silently recounted.

And, by chance, things have turned from bad to worse. That is, of course, not counting my newfound lust and love!

"Bang, bang, bang," came a noise from the front door.

It was Alex. Here "for Shaw," I joked in my head. He had stayed overnight locally, doing his own homework. "Nice of you to visit," I said. I escorted Alex inside and instinctively poured him a cup of the Peet's. It was no longer piping hot, but still warm and drinkable. And under the circumstance, warm black coffee would have to do, even for Alex.

"Alex, my only chance is to find the killer, and if we find the killer, I am certain we'll have our art thief!'"

"MD, are you Mentally Disturbed?" Alex always used to joke that that's what my initials meant. The confluence of circumstances points directly to you! Think about it— your job, your wife, the *hurricane*, and now THIS! Your fingerprints are all over the Weisbergs' place. Temporary insanity is your only way out: severe mental distress led to a mental breakdown! Yes, "Mentally Disturbed."

"Your friend, Matt, might be a heck of a scientist, but he makes a terrible attorney," Amy chuckled. "An insanity plea would be my last resort in your case. My strategy is simple. Our good doctor is an outstanding citizen and the truth will set him free. We will examine all the evidence as well as the timeline and put them all under a microscope. Any evidence, including DNA evidence, I assure you is only circumstantial. But because of the high-profile nature of this case, I will be bringing in a secret weapon.

"We have to catch the thief!" I proclaimed. Perhaps I watched too many Perry Mason reruns when I was growing up. Perry Mason was an LA criminal defense attorney, played by Raymond Burr. Perry Mason, according to IMDb specialized in "defending seemingly indefensible cases." He would gather the evidence and put it together like pieces to a puzzle. And in the end, Mason would always solve the puzzle. Speaking of puzzle pieces, I pulled out the MedicAlert bracelet from the manila envelope I'd been able to conceal from the police and showed it to both Alex and Amy.

"MDT Protecta and Cypher." He read it out loud, and then said, "What the hell does that mean?"

"It is a clue," I said. "I found it at the scene, and it does not belong to either of the Weisbergs. It is a piece of medical evidence that only a cardiologist would understand. And there's this. I pulled out a piece of folded-up *New York Times* newspaper that I had in my back pocket; it contained the Price on Request sticker from the painting and had an imprint of a shoe on the back. Unfolding the paper, I revealed the print. No, it did not show Bruno Magli shoes like in the OJ case, but it did say, "Cole Haan." There was a Cole Haan store at the Tanger Outlet in Riverhead, and we could see if we could identify the type of shoe and its size. The unfolded paper released the sticker, which I showed to my team.

"Sotheby's?" questioned Amy.

"Yes. This is a sticker from the painting I found at the scene, which proves some of the history, or shall I say more specifically the provenance, of the stolen artwork. It is a critical piece of evidence! I can't believe that they missed this one. Just got lucky, I guess."

"Did you give any of this evidence to the Westhampton police?" Alex asked.

"I gave it all to the police department when I was strip-searched, but they must have missed it. Quite an oversight.

Right? It was in my envelope marked personal possessions that they returned to me after I was released by the bailiff. If they don't want to play ball with me, I don't want to play ball with them. Besides, they weren't going to help me find the thief and murderer! And finding the thief and murderer should definitely exonerate me!"

Chapter 45

Wrongfully accused—now I am witnessing it firsthand. I had been following a New York City attorney by the name of Gale Schwartz, who grabbed national attention by taking on pro bono cases with his charity called the Exoneration Project, or *EP*. Every couple of months, Mr. Schwartz would appear on the front page of the *New York Times*, with a wrongfully accused pathetic soul typically trapped in jail for anywhere between five and twenty-five years and accused of some ridiculous crime. The sorry fact is that even when he found the real perpetrator, it still took him years to get his client out. I felt sorry for his clients, and every couple of months I'd send the EP a check for two hundred and fifty bucks.

Imagine my surprise when Mr. Schwartz arrived at my place shortly after Alex. Mr. Schwartz was of short stature and moderate build. Balding on top but a true tiger in the courtroom. He would perform nothing less than magic to get his criminally accused clients off. But how did Mr. Schwartz wind up at the vacation home of the former Director of Mount Sinai's Cath Lab? Ridiculous, I thought.

"Mr. Schwartz, you can't be here for me? I don't fit the profile of any of your cases?" He told me about the time he got his client off after being accused of an icepick murder based on forensic evidence and expert testimony provided to him by a cardiologist. And that cardiologist was *ME*! What I didn't know is that Mr. Schwartz had a thriving criminal-defense private practice separate from EP, and he knew exactly how to skin a cat.

"Perhaps I can repay the favor," he said. "You helped me out of a tight bind! And now you need all the help you can get."

"This was the secret weapon I was referring to!" Amy smiled.

Chapter 46

Now I had Alex's brainpower, Amy Winter (oh God, I'm glad I had her!), and Gale Schwartz's legal team. All examining the evidence! Gale and Amy went upstairs and spent the next hour reviewing the facts of the case. The two emerged and we met at my dining room table.

"This is an A-1 Felony murder as well as a robbery in the first or second degree with over fifty thousand dollars stollen. Ms. Winters will research whether this is a B or C Felony, but from your standpoint it is irrelevant. My strategy is the exclamation mark on Ms. Winters' assessment. Dr. Dawson is NOT a fucking murderer and he is not a fucking thief! He is an outstanding member of society. A renowned heart doctor. Our defense is the TRUTH. The truth is a fucking awesome weapon. It will explain your DNA at the scene. We will examine the timeline, and learn that it is NOT iron clad. The only evidence against our client is soft stuff. There is NO HARD EVIDENCE. And most importantly, Dr. Dawson, had NO MOTIVE.

"As for the evidence, we will research and determine whether there is any relationship between the specific implantable defibrillator, cardiac stent, and the pair of Cole Haan shoes that Dr. Dawson was able to secure as evidence." Amy's specialty was research. "We will need to determine if those artifacts fit anyone's profile."

"But it must," I said. "Let's research major art thieves or forgers, query the Medtronic defibrillator database, and crossmatch it with that of the Cypher stent's manufacturer, Cordis/Johnson and Johnson. Let's see how many Protecta and Cypher combinations we can find?"

"You're forgetting about a little thing called the Health Information Portability and Accountability Act, or HIPAA," said Schwartz. "It used to be much easier to access this information, but, now, with HIPAA, it is very hard for us to gain access to that kind of medical information, even if it is legally justifiable."

I knew his dilemma all too well.

"We'll have to get a search warrant to gain access, but this will likely take some fucking time," Schwartz said.

"What are you talking about," I vehemently protested. "We don't have time. Every day that goes by is one more day for the art thief and murderer to disappear. Time is of the essence!"

"What makes you think there is only one art thief and murderer? And do you really think they are one and the same? Certainly that is a possibility, but there could be multiple people involved. Isn't that so, Gale?" said Alex.

"Yes, that *is* a possibility, but unlikely based on Dawson's assessment of the shoe prints found at the Weisberg estate. If there were many people, I would expect a variety of prints recovered by the good doctor. Any luck with the shoe analysis, Amy?" asked Mr. Schwartz.

"Yes, the shoes," she retorted. "My friends over at Tanger identified the shoe as a size thirteen Cole Haan, of the general Nike Air type. Can we crossmatch that with the medical information?"

"This will all take some fucking time," Schwartz reiterated.

"I think I can get my friends from Medtronic and Johnson and Johnson to do this right away on the QT," I said.

For many years I had implanted the Medtronic AVE stent as well as the Cordis/JNJ Cypher stent. I called on my buddy Jason McCann, a local legend in stent sales. Yearly trips to Hawaii to celebrate his President's Club award and to meet the company's founder, Earl Bakken. He always came back with a Dole pineapple just to thank me. As I thought about the pineapple, I went over to my powerless fridge. I opened the door and pulled out his latest pineapple gift and grabbed a large serrated knife and proceeded to cut up the fruit in pieces and serve it to my team. Alex was on one side of my dining table with Amy, and Gale and myself were on the other side, enjoying the Hawaiian delicacy.

As we finished off the pineapple, I made an offer.

"Guys, we have a lot of work to do, and the roads are not great. Why don't you all hang out over here?"

"It would be my absolute pleasure," said Alex. He never did turn down a good offer.

"You could take the upstairs guestroom," I said.

Schwartz and Amy declined. "Let's meet back here in two days. I'll run the reports. MD, you get me the medical data any way you can. Amy, see if you can nail down the shoe information, and let's all reconvene here in two days to see *if the shoe fits*," said the New York lawyer as he exited through the front door.

"Sounds good," said Amy to the team as she headed out as well. "I'll be in Hampton Bays if you need me. That's only a hop, skip, and a jump away. Don't hesitate to call if you need me."

"I won't," I said. My head was still spinning from the Amy twist to my life! I regretted watching her leave, but I was too worried to think straight!

Chapter 47

Two days. Two full days of *Steven Seagal*. We talked about Sandy. We talked about politics. Oh, how he loved politics. France versus the US. US versus Russia. France's Sarkozy versus Obama. Obama versus Putin. Even though Sarkozy was no longer in office, Shaw was a socialist at heart. To Alex it was always socialism versus democracy, and communism was somewhere in the middle. He knew everything, and it wasn't arrogance. It was fact.

Then we talked about medicine. Changing trends in medicine. The US was becoming France with the Affordable Care Act and the goal of universal health care. This was the end of private practice, and the beginning of socialized medicine. Our health care would eventually transition to a governmental health care plan for all, much like that of our French friends. At least, that was our conclusion. Then we talked about Shari. What a fuckhead. I wouldn't have so much as looked at another woman, even with her alcohol troubles. The thought never even entered into my mind. Well, maybe a little fantasy now and then. But I would never have ever thought about cheating on her. I had endured years of no semblance of a physical or romantic relationship. No real connection, but still tried to stick it out. And then, "wham, bam, thank you ma'am." Screwing in our own bed. And I am certain that was not the first time.

"How long has Shari been cheating on me?" I asked Alex.

"Definitely, it was going on for a while. You just happened to catch her by surprise. How often do you just pop in during the middle of the week? Like never! MD, you are a workaholic. If you finished up early with your patients, you would stay late and work on your research. And if you were finished with your research, you would be helping the museum. And if you were not working with the museum, you were over at my place, working on our next startup company. MD, I know this might be painful for you to hear, but you were part of the problem. A bit of a disconnect with Shari's needs."

"Shari's needs, my ass. She never would call and say, 'MD, could you just come home early, or MD, could we have a romantic night out, or even MD, let's get away for the weekend,'" I snapped.

"She shouldn't have to. Love is a two-way street. And it takes two to tango," he said.

"And then the drinking started. I had no way to help this. Rehab did little good for her. It was no way to live," I said with somber frustration.

"I know, MD, but she *is* your wife. You have to face the music that you were part of the reason she started drinking."

"I'm not perfect, I guess, but I just trusted her too much. I thought that if she needed something, or wanted something, or wasn't getting something, she would have told me."

"MD, this is not like that asshole of a financial guy that you trusted with your money. This is your wife. What do you expect if you go days and days and days without giving her the attention that a spouse needs?"

"Alex, if you can't trust your wife, whom can you trust?"

"MD, you just don't get it. Shari is not a bad person. But she does have a problem. And I know that she fucked that cocksucker, but she is also a human being. If you had invested the same amount of time that you had invested in your medical practice and your inventions this might not have happened."

"But, Alex, there were no signs!" At that moment Alex just cut me off.

"MD, there are always signs. And it is your job to *always have your pulse* on the situation. No pun intended. Take your bigwig investor guy whose year after year performance is just too good, too perfect. Always getting double-digit returns no matter what. If it is too good to be true, it probably is. And Shari, she gave the signs. I never saw her exhibit warmth, the way we do in France, but I never saw you do it either. When was the last time you made wild passionate love?" he pressed.

At that moment Alex pulled out a folded piece of newspaper from his pocket, just like the one I had been keeping in mine. He had always made a habit of carrying a piece of the *New York Times*. Always the latest crossword puzzle. "Where do you think I got my habit from?" I muttered to myself. Alex was an expert with the puzzle. Monday took him literally less than five minutes to complete. As we went further into the week, the puzzle itself would get progressively harder, but not for Alex. He was legendary with the Sunday crossword. By the time I figured out a half dozen clues, he would have the entire puzzle completed.

But as he unfolded the newspaper, I realized it was not a crossword puzzle at all. My face just dropped, and my stomach sank as I looked at the paper.

"I didn't want to show you this, but I have to show you it, because you're going to find out sooner or later."

Chapter 48

It was the front page of the *New York Times*; it read: *POLLOCK PAINTING STOLEN, HEIRESS MURDERED, DOCTOR ACCUSED.*

Since Sandy, I have been out of touch with the news. I had not been able to watch any TV or even get a newspaper. But Alex had the latest *Times*, which I read in pure horror:

> *Dr. Matthew Dawson of Port Washington, Long Island, has been accused of stealing a priceless Jackson Pollock painting and murdering the wife of Mr. Charles Weisberg of Goldman Sachs. Dr. Dawson was recently fired from his position at the Mount Sinai Medical Center. He was arraigned at the Riverhead Courthouse and released on one million dollars bail. The* Times *has been unable to contact Dr. Dawson for a response at this time.*

"Oh shit," I thought. "Now everybody knows all of my business: My wife, my kids, my former employer. Everybody. How embarrassing! How could they publish this?"

And then I thought about it. If the *New York Times* would publish a story about a psychiatrist accused of having an affair with their patient, why wouldn't they publish a story about a cardiologist accused of murder and stealing a painting? Especially, the murder of a wealthy socialite and a priceless Pollock painting, no less. Of course, they would. "I just happened to be the victim of circumstances," I kept telling myself.

I still felt shaky and uneasy. Depressed, no less. I just wanted to crawl into a shell and never come out. Maybe even leave the country, if I could.

"Alex, I'm in trouble, aren't I? How the hell am I going to get out of this mess?"

Chapter 49

MD, you are not alone. I am here for you, and your legal team is all over this." On a dime, Alex changed gear. "And how about your kids? How are they doing? Just because they are teenagers or young adults, does that mean you are not their dad? You will always be their dad."

"Right, Alex. I guess I have been a little removed, distant perhaps, preoccupied. I only texted Jason once. That's it. I haven't even tried to call any of them. Just give me a few minutes, please, and let me give them a call."

I assumed Shari was taking care of our kids through the storm. Jason had returned to Port before the storm and never went back to school, and Bridgette was home as well. All without power. I was just so angry. But I knew if there was a real problem that at least Jason would text me or give a call. The fact that I had not received either led me to believe that for now, neither one of my kids read or heard my NEWS STORY. "Thank the lord," I said to myself.

I picked up my cell phone and dialed.

"Hello, who is this?" said Jason.

"It's Dad. How are you? Are you okay? I asked.

"Dad, Mom showed us the paper. It says that you killed someone and stole a painting. Is that true? I know that can't be true. Right, Dad?"

"Jason, something bad has happened, but it is not my fault, and I didn't do any of those things. It will all work out. How is it there?" I tried to console, and then knew the best strategy was to change gears.

"We are all worried about you, and you want to know how it is *here*? It is terrible here. No power at all. We are huddled in front of the gas fireplace in our living room. Barely keeping warm. Mom put sheets up with thumbtacks all around the living-room vestibules to hold in the warmth. Bridgette is here too. Do you want to talk to her?"

"Sure. Love you," I said.

"Love you too," he replied.

Within seconds I heard her voice. "Hi, Dad," exclaimed Bridgette.

Bridgette was going through her senior year of high school madness. She had applied early decision to my Alma Mater and felt an intense pressure coming on—uncertain as to whether she would be accepted, and if not, she would have to rapidly file all of her college applications and apply within a few days just to get everything submitted in time. December 15 was the date that she would find out whether she was accepted. Would she be a Blue Jay and go to Hopkins? I asked myself. It was out of our control, I replied inside my weary brain.

"Bridgette, how is it there at home?" I asked.

"Dad, we all saw the paper? Did you kill Mrs. Weisberg?"

"Of course not, Bridge!"

"But, Dad, the paper says that you stole the neighbor's priceless painting and then killed Mrs. Weisberg. Mom told us that you were fired from Mount Sinai. Did you just lose it and go off the deep end?"

"No, Bridge. That's not what happened. It was just a fluke that I was even out east when that all happened. I was just trying to help out our neighbor, and I was just in the wrong place at the wrong time. This will all work its way out. Please don't worry."

"When are we going to see you again, Dad?"

"I don't know, Bridge, it could be days." If not longer, I thought to myself. "Is everybody there? When do you think you'll get power back?"

"Yes, Dad. Mom, Jason, and I are all here. The house is okay, and there is still no power. We are eating leftover bagels that we're frying on our gas stovetop. And the water is fine. We are very fortunate we have hot water. Our school has been turned into a shelter for those in the flood zone. There's been no school the entire week and I don't even know whether there will be any next week."

"Like a snow day," I said. "I miss you. Just stay warm. I love you."

"Dad, I'm worried about you. Please come home soon? Love you Dad!" she said.

I loved my kids with all my heart. And then I heard the voice, and it was not pleasant. It was abrupt and screaming.

Chapter 50

It sounded like the phone was pulled right away from Bridgette. And then I heard silence for about thirty seconds, and then . . .

"MD, did you kill Mrs. Weisberg? What happened to you? What the hell happened to you? Were you having an affair?"

"Me? You were the one doing 'Leave it to Beaver.' How long has that been going on?" I asked.

"Let me walk somewhere in private. Wait a second." A five-second pause ensued while Shari wandered out of the living room to a quiet corner of the house. "MD, you haven't been exactly the perfect husband. You missed our twenty-fifth wedding anniversary, and we haven't had any spark for the most of that."

"Thanks for telling me that now," I said sarcastically. "I guess the tide has turned since I saw you last."

"You didn't even give me a chance to explain. I've been lonely and have felt very empty. There was nothing else for me to do. I had to do something," whined Shari.

I didn't buy that for a second. She could have tried talking. Okay, I guess I wasn't the great talker either. I was just doing my thing. But come on, she was screwing the local kid next door. At least, that's what it looked like. The whole thing was totally ridiculous. And the drinking, what was that about? Was Alex right that my own self-absorbed life drove her to drink and provoked the entire thing? Who knows? Not me.

"You could have tried talking," I snapped.

"I did. At least, I thought I did. Remember last Valentine's Day? I wanted to go out to dinner and made a special reservation at La Piccolla Liguria. And you just had to finish your presentation. You never would make time for me. Never! And now this? A murder and the stolen painting? I guess I just don't know who you really are!" She began to weep—then the phone call abruptly ended. A deafening silence.

I had no chance to respond. No chance to clear the air. But in reality, there was no chance in hell for any salvage of our relationship. A relationship that I thought was originally built on trust.

"Alex, Shari grabbed the phone from Bridgette and gave me an earful. She seemed to feel it was my fault. Then she hung up on me! But at least Jason and Bridgette are safe. Still no power in Port."

"MD, what did you think? Did you think she was going to take all the responsibility for your marital woes? Are you crazy? Of course, she was going to blame you. Just like you are blaming her! And yes, my wife confirmed that there is still no power. One of the LIPA workers told her it could be until Thanksgiving by the time we get our power back."

Alex then proceeded to make some phone calls. I did too, and eventually we got our answers. At least to the questions we were asking now. We were trying to hit the "trifecta" and find the individual with a particular brand of stent, defibrillator, and pair of shoes. Like pieces to the

puzzle. We were starting to find the pieces and put them
all together.

Chapter 51

The doorbell rang. Like clockwork, Mr. Schwartz was back and so was Amy. We gathered around the living room couch as Alex passed out the French press this time. Black Peet's, no milk. I did my part.

"I have a list of names. My buddy identified sixty-eight people nationwide with both a Medtronic Protecta defibrillator implant and a Cypher stent. Forty-eight of those individuals were male, and twenty female. In all likelihood, the true killer and thief was a male!" I said. The latter comment may have seemed somewhat chauvinistic, but it was also a scientific fact. "Just playing the numbers, the male-to-female ratio of those with defibrillators and stents as specified on the MedicAlert bracelet was greater than two-to-one. And there was also the size factor. Mrs. Weisberg seemed to be strangled without a struggle. And the shoe size was large as well."

"Unless Mrs. Weisberg was the thief, and someone else was the killer," said Amy. That theory I seriously doubted.

"I took the shoe print MD had provided over to one of our forensic experts," Amy continued. "They created what they call a forensic print map, a copy of which I have here. You could see that this print copy has quite a bit of detail regarding the sole of the shoe, more than just the name."

Amy pointed with her index finger, with its perfectly pol-
ished red nail, to the top of the shoe. "Proceeding from the
toe to the heel, in order, you can see a very precise pattern.
There is a half-moon figure with a line cut right through it
at the toe, followed by three rows of dots, each about the
size of a pea. Four in the first row and then five in the next
two rows." As she moved her finger down she said, "After
that come two rows of three dashes, followed by two rows
of six dots, and then three dashes again, then a row of five
dots and then three dots, and then two dashes."

"Get to the point," Alex said. "It sounds like SOS! This
is not Morse Code."

"But indeed, it is a very precise code, Dr. Shaw. I just
described the toe and not even in complete detail. Special
stitching visible in the print surrounds each row. And I am
just talking about the toe. The heel has a different but
unique pattern, and in between the two you could even see
a curved leather pattern in which the word *Cole Haan* is
imprinted, with some type of figure between the two
names. To me it looked like the image of stirrups, from
riding horseback, which separated the two names. But after checking the website and examining the Cole Haan
logo, it became clear that the logo was the name with a
vertical needle and thread between the *Cole* and the *Haan*
name.

"When my associate took it to the local Cole Haan manager, she told him that this pattern is only specific to one
shoe. The Cole Haan 'Men's Air Grant Penny Loafer.'
And the size was specific to a large-width number thirteen.
The shoe is quite popular, according to the manager, but in
a number-thirteen width, only one hundred twelve pairs
had been sold from the northeast region. The manager was
kind enough to provide us with the complete names and

dates of each purchaser, as well as the store in which the purchase occurred. Incidentally, of the one hundred twelve pairs sold essentially in the last two years, only thirty-eight were from a New York Cole Haan retail store, and only five were from the Riverhead outlet."

"Good work Amy," I said.

"Better than OJ's shoes or gloves. These Cole Haan, with their detail, are like a fingerprint biometric. And speaking of fingerprints, our forensics even looked for those on your muddy newspaper print. None were found."

"Too bad," I sighed.

"Not really," Amy said. On a flash drive she had compiled a computer file that contained the names of everyone in the northeast who had purchased Cole Haan shoes of the precise type and size that matched the shoe print on the paper. "You see, the size thirteen, 'Men's Air Grant Penny Loafer' names, together with Dawson's medical-implant names, are so unique they will almost certainly provide a match."

I placed all of this into an Excel spread sheet on my MacBook Air and looked. This took a few minutes. Only three names turned up that matched the defibrillator, stent, and shoe type and size in the entire country.

"Our matches are a Maxwell Foster from Milwaukee, Wisconsin; Fredrick Fox from Duluth Minnesota; and Seymour Vicks of East Hampton," I said.

"Only one is local! Seymour Vicks. And not only local, but also a family name from across the street no less. Coincidence?" I said.

"I doubt it," Amy asserted with a grin that said, "Of course, stupid, it's him."

A relative of the Vicks? I toyed with the idea. The Vicks had to be involved somehow. How could that be possible?

Mr. Vicks was still in the hospital, and his kids were attending to the old man's medical woes.

"I guess we'll have to figure out who Seymour Vicks really is," said Mr. Schwartz. Schwartz continued: "Perhaps a visit to East Hampton is in order. I have nothing better to do right now. I'm going to take a drive and head out that way."

"I think I'll head into town and pick up something for us to snack on. I'm sure you're all tired of Dr. Dawson's stale snacks," Amy rejoined.

I proceeded to walk Amy and Gale to the door. We had made considerable progress, but there was still work to be done if we had any hope of catching the assailants. I had not lost an ounce of interest in Amy, in fact, quite the contrary. I just hoped I was not overdoing it with my formality when she was around the other folks who were working on my behalf.

"Goodbye, Gale and Amy," I said. "Great work." I escorted both of them out to their cars and could not help giving one last Dawson pun.

"I guess we'll be "Seeing More" of you guys and hopefully "Seeing More" of Mr. Vicks! I smiled, knowing full well that my life might depend on it.

Chapter 52

The place had no electricity. It was pitch black before the storm and pitch black after the storm. It had been there for over a century. It was never repaired or updated. At least, that was how it appeared from the outside. It was a large clapboard structure, much like a reinforced barn, that to the outside observer was associated with peace and serenity. The only apparent thing that may have been repaired at some time was the roof. It was impervious to rain, sleet, and any other wrath that came from Mother Nature. Sandy had no effect on this ancient remnant that withstood all the big storms that any living soul could remember. Its owner remembered all of them, every single one of them, including that bastard of a storm from the late 1930s. But this time he wasn't there. His underlings would have to sit in and do the legwork to get it done.

There were two large barn doors at the back that were invisible from the road. Each door was made of thick, solid oak and weighed at least one hundred pounds. The two door panels were split down the middle vertically and rotated on a strong black hinge in order to open up. A large, mangy, dark-haired man pulled the handle on the door to the left and swung one side of the barn door open, revealing the interior. Another large-framed man with a mustache followed him.

The inside of the structure looked nothing like the outside. The outside was "old school" farm barn. The inside was neon-light bright, state-of-the art high-tech, and none of the sparkle and glimmer made it outside. In fact, at night, the barnlike structure was as dark as night. No light penetrated. Every window was boarded up, and all the neighbors thought that it was just deserted—another refuge for someone's junk. That someone would have been Mr. Vicks. But no, junk was not what was inside.

Inside, a man stood behind a camera on a tripod directed to an easel against the backdrop of white drapes. The cameraman was using the latest Olympus SLR camera with a superhigh-resolution lens with state-of-the-art digital capabilities. In stage one, he would first photograph the easel-supported painting front and back before the piece made it to stage two. But this painting was much too large and heavy to sit on an easel. No, this one had to rest against the clapboard wall, and the cameraman used three large photography spotlights, all rotated towards the piece, in order to reveal each and every detail of the painting. On the side stood a number of already-crated pieces.

"It's here," came a voice from inside the structure. The voice was not talking to the two gentlemen that were standing at the doorway. It was directed at a flip-top cell phone held to his ear. Harry Massino was a chubby, balding, squat Mafioso type who barely made five and a half feet. Though short in stature, Massino was *huge* as a master art forger. Harry was not only a master forger—he was a master forger of Pollocks. A trove of Pollocks recently came out of the woodwork and hit the art market. Even without any provenance he had the experts baffled. Seven Pollocks in all, and not even a record of the pieces' prior existence, and the authorities could not distinguish the type of canvas, medium, age of the materials, quality, and type of images from a truly bonified Pollock painting. This included the Pollock authorities from the MoMA and the Pollock catalogue raisonnée authentification team.

Yes, Harry was good, very good.

But nobody knew who Harry was. He was always too obscure and elusive and one step ahead of the authorities.

"Harry, are you done with this one?" said Mustache Man.

"Yes, got the front and back. Now let's move it to stage two. Stage two was a technique of forging not yet known to any other art forger in the whole wide universe. Unlike any other forger who used a skilled artist's eyes and steady hand to replicate a masterpiece, Harry used high tech 3-D scanning and printing. In this second area, the large painting was hoisted onto a conveyor belt, and multiple precise laser beams scanned the entire painting surface front to back. Samples were taken to duplicate the materials, and the precise color and type of canvas was chemically analyzed by a mass spectrometer. The 3-D scanner would not only capture the precise colors and swirls of the Pollock in two dimensions, but also its entire surface structure. The red laser light went back and forth along the entire surface of the painting, which spanned 8 feet by 4 feet. Each pass was slow and methodical, and each additional pass was elevated by a fraction of a millimeter in order to replicate the surface's complete topography. In essence, the 3-D scanner created a 3-D image of the surface that included the exact color, surface texture, brush stroke, depth, and thickness of the paint. Even a stray hair, bristle, or fingerprint in the paint was precisely reproduced. The information was all captured and stored on a state-of-the-art computer that stood across the room. After scanning and recording each and every aspect of the Pollock, the job was nearly complete.

"You guys can pick it up and pack it in that large crate on the other side," said Harry.

Across the room was a seventy-inch computer screen, which recorded the high-definition-image photograph and the 3-D scanned image. On the full screen appeared an image, of the yellow, white, and red swirled painting. The image was labeled front. Alongside that was another more mundane image: the back—with its raw, aged canvas; some writing including the name of the piece; and a number of stickers. The image fell into this sophisticated database, which catalogued the name of each piece, the images, the dimensions, medium, date, signature, provenance, and then the ZIP file. The final row of the database was entitled "ZIP," which stood for the computerized, compressed scanned 3-D image file and included the chemical composition of each of the paints used in the picture.

Harry checked the computer and double-checked the name and all the rest of the details. He looked at the computer and saw "Pollock No. 5," with its HD front and back images and the not-yet-compressed surface analysis. Harry then pressed "compress and encrypt." The custom-made program did just that, and all the information fell into the ZIP file and column. When all was complete, every detail of the canvas, including the period writing and stickers, were all reflected in the files and would assure the authentication of the piece's *provenance*. Provenance for each piece was critically important! Any painting can be copied, but without the aging, the medium, and the provenance, it would be very hard to sell even the best of reproductions. Harry's process was not just good, no, it was perfect.

Damn perfect! He had been running the operation for years and had never been caught.

"A okay!" Harry hit the send button, and the information went electronically via a secure, scrambled service over the World Wide Web to a secure cloud storage service. That service could be securely accessed and used by the rest of the team in order to re-create an identical copy of whatever object was catalogued. And the object at hand was Jackson Pollock *No. 5*!

Harry's partner was also there. He sat at a desk alongside the fine-art cataloguing computer, with an old cell phone at hand. But even seated, he appeared much taller and more slender than the rest of the men in the clapboard barn. Lanky, like Ichabod Crane from "The Legend of Sleepy Hollow"—with a prominent jaw or *jowls*, a result of his unusual facial features and absent adipose tissue. If anything, his face looked like a *fish*. He spoke into the phone. "It's here. Now what?"

"Good," said the *big* voice on the other end. "Have them take it, and then give them the envelope."

After a few minutes of lifting, packaging, and crating, the two men, one with a mustache and another by his side, grabbed the large wooden crate, which was almost nine feet tall by five feet wide. The two picked up the heavy crate and placed it in the back of a concealed truck. The truck had entered the property from an obscure entrance not visible from the road. The jowled, fishlike man holding the cell phone handed them the envelope. And the larger, clean-shaven man opened it and counted the Benjamins. But they were not Benjamins. They were *Grover Clevelands*. The two large-framed couriers were not familiar with Grover Cleveland, and they may not have even been familiar with President Obama, for that matter. But they were familiar with the number on the bill, and it had one more zero than the more familiar Benjamins, namely one thousand dollars. The man counted each and every bill. There were one hundred in total. "There's only one hundred thousand here," he said angrily to his compadre. "We were promised two hundred thousand."

"Not until it's safely delivered will you get the rest," stated the jowled man. The full name of this gentleman was a mystery to almost everyone. He was called, as one would guess, almost jokingly, "Fish." In reality, the jowled man was Jimmy "the Fish" Facone. Jimmy or "The Fish," or just plain "Fish," as he preferred to be called, got the name from not only his fishlike looks, but the recurring fact that his deceitful clients wound up swimming in the East River, and they never got out!

The man with the mustache approached the seated, jowled, fishy man. He grabbed the seated man and threw him into a headlock. "Where is the rest of the money?" Mustache Man asked. Fish could not speak. He began to choke and then gag. If the headlock were held for thirty more seconds, he would not only lose consciousness but would likely meet an untimely demise. But before that could even occur, a large shadow of a man came out from under another desk, having been lying underneath it, on the floor.

He was dressed entirely in black and wearing a black, hooded sweatshirt, which covered his head, revealing only a shadow of a face. The Shadow resembled Darth Sidious, the scheming Sith Lord from *Star Wars*. Cloaked in black, none of his features showing. He must have been sleeping on an old couch cushion beneath the desk. There invisibly with The Shadow was what appeared to be a gun, and not just any gun, but a PO8 Luger no less. It must have been hidden under The Shadow's cloak. The Shadow pointed the pistol right at the man with the mustache. "You have sixty seconds to let him go or you will die."

As The Shadow waved the gun near his face, Mustache Man immediately eased up on the jowled man, who gasped for air. The Shadow now redirected his Luger to the clean-shaven man's head. "Like your mustachioed friend had, you have sixty seconds to give the money back, or else." He pulled out a pocket watch and clicked the start button. The clean-shaven man was no dope. He had seen this *timed killer* in action before. Always a stopwatch, always sixty seconds. And if he didn't get his result, a pulled trigger followed by a brain-dead victim, or a quick blow to the heart with the equivalent result. Within ten seconds, the clean-shaven man released the money, and The Shadow withdrew the pistol. He then counted half of it, put it in his own pocket, and then gave back the other half. "You get only fifty thousand dollars, asshole! You'll get the rest once *it* is safely delivered and *it* reaches its final destination."

The pistol was directed loosely towards the man with the mustache as they made their way back to the truck. These two larger gentlemen, if you could call them that, closed up the back of the truck and left. With only a quarter of what they thought they would get. "Fuck you," said the pissed-off Mustache Man.

The cell phone was still connected and The Fish continued. "The delivery is on its way."

"I heard what happened," said the voice on the other end. "We have a *big* problem. Those two are troublemakers. But more importantly, those two troublemakers can lead the Feds to us. Only one local person met these bozos, and that's our friendly neighborhood Dr. Dawson. Our *intel* tells us he could be a problem. I want you to dispose of him."

"But, sir?" objected The Fish.

"Don't 'but, sir' me. Get rid of him. No, better yet. Bring him to me, and I will see to it that he is properly disposed of."

Chapter 53

There was too much talking. My head was spinning. I had to go for a walk, get some fresh air. Alex and I walked energetically down Homans and around the peninsula, past the waterfront mansions, each one with its own character. Most were cedar shingled, painted light grey, yellow, or an occasional white, some with gabbled roofs, others with a widow's watch, but all with the grandeur of the Hamptons. Every house was still in place, but who knew what internal damage the storm's tidal surge caused. Debris was still on the street, and many of the downed trees had already been carted off to the side of the narrow road. The sea had receded, but a fair amount of saltwater debris was left behind. Some houses had major damage to their bulkheads. Waterfront pools were badly damaged, and docks were almost universally destroyed.

As we walked, we saw almost no signs of life. The Vicks' place was unfazed in the middle of the neighborhood, well off the water. I paid particular attention to that one, given the matching last name from our research. The Tudor-style house and its historic barnlike structure still stood in complete silence, and there was no sign of a light or Mr. Vicks' sons. The rest of the residences also showed no life, except at the very end of the road where a roofer was repairing a roof and securing a large blue tarp across its corner.

There were no cars on the road, and no sounds other than a stray egret, or some local Canada geese. When we headed back around the circle, I caught a glimpse of a truck pulling out between two houses on Shepard, a side road off Homans that ran perpendicular to Quantuck Bay. Was I seeing something? As we approached the truck's egress, I examined the driveway. It was not a driveway at all but a loosely graveled path between some trees and brush between two of the smaller neighborhood houses, each however considerably larger than "my shed." I walked up the path to get a glimpse of where it headed.

It was the same house that stood catty corner to the Weisbergs' estate. The one that was central to the neighborhood and belonged to the Vicks family. As I looked in again from this vantage point, I still saw no signs of life and proceeded back to the road with Alex.

"I have no clue what that was," I said.

"Maybe a contractor checking on their house?" he responded.

Within five minutes we were back at my place, but this time there was no coffee to be had. "Shaw would not be Shaw without coffee," I thought. I heated up some water and gave him a mixture of that and a stale, opened-up Lipton Tea bag that was sitting on the shelf in my closet.

"Tea? For a Frenchman?" Alex complained.

"Alex, the tea should be the least of my worries. Here are some biscottis to keep you going."

The doorbell rang, and I opened it with barely concealed anticipation. It was Amy back with a caramel walnut apple pie from Holy Moses Bakery. She had picked that one up from Cor-J's, the local seafood store. They just reopened, and even though fresh fish was their specialty, they also carried an array of freshly baked breads and cakes. "Holy Moses is legendary out here," I said. "Perhaps we needed a taste of religion to solve this crime."

Amy smirked at that one. Perhaps my puns were getting to her. When I am nervous and tense, I would always use humor as a release. But with Amy, I now had a better release.

"How the hell, did Holy Moses get the power to bake pies?" I asked.

"He must have had some divine help," replied Amy.

"Touché," I said.

"Two could play at the game," she rebutted.

I was lucky I didn't pig out on the biscotti. Although Alex already had two, he took a big hunk of pie and washed it down with black tea. I savored each bite, as did Amy.

My cell phone rang and it was Gale. Checking into Mr. Seymour Vicks of East Hampton, he had gone first to City Hall in Riverhead and then over to the Village Hall in East Hampton. No luck. He was trying to see if he could get the address of Vicks, as recorded at the time of the Cole Haan purchase. After two hours of work, Alex decided to bid me a fine adieu and head back west.

I was all alone with Amy, and I had our one and only sexual escapade on my mind. Naturally. Constantly. But that would only get us so far, and eventually we would have to convincingly find Mrs. Weisberg's killer and recover the Pollock. It was nice that I had a pleasant walk with Alex, but I was curious as to what might be open in Westhampton Beach.

"Amy, do you recall what was open in town?" I asked. By town I was referring to the little thoroughfare called Main Street that went through the Village of Westhampton

Beach. Quiogue had no downtown. It was just a quaint, little historic hamlet slightly off the beaten path at the beginning of the South Fork on the East End of Long Island. And Quiogue didn't even have its own post office. In fact, Quiogue and Westhampton Beach shared the same zip code: 11978. All our deliveries and packages said "Westhampton Beach" and went to the Westhampton Beach Post Office. Despite this fact, those who resided in Quiogue did not share the same privileges as the Westhampton Beachers. Quioguers had to pay for a beach pass and would only get one car pass to Westhampton Beach's Rogers Beach or Lashley Beach. Guests of the Quioguers were ten dollars per day. The Westhampton Beach Villagers had their passes covered by a modest village tax and received two, not one, car passes, plus free endless guest passes.

"I went the back route down Mill Road and saw Hampton's Coffee and Cor-J's open," she said. "Then I looped around back through Main Street. Not a sign of life. That is, of course, except Simon's Beach Bakery.

The Beach Bakery was a local legend. With its old Victorian façade and showcase windows with their signature yellow-and-white awning, locals and tourists all flocked there for their baked goods, coffees, and sweets. In Westhampton Beach there was no better place to sit and have a coffee, other than the beach or bay, of course, than in front of Simon's place.

Prior to the storm, everything was boarded up. And immediately after Sandy hit, when I passed through Main Street, I saw everything—and I mean everything—still boarded up. The most memorable was the plywood-boarded window on the front of the Shock clothing store on Main St. On the sign it read in black magic marker:

SANDY SHOCK YOU! Nothing was open then, but that was days ago.

"Would you like to go back to town and get some coffee from the Beach Bakery?" I asked.

"Maybe," she responded. "Looked like a happening place!"

Of course, it was a happening place. It was a happening place when everything in town was open. But now it was even more of a happening place, when almost everything else was closed. Simon, the Beach Bakery's owner, had a captive audience much like Terry's much smaller and more out-of-the-way Hamptons Coffee. The latter would have been another half mile and was a less-spacious hangout in comparison. The thing I liked about the Beach Bakery was that place essentially never ever closed! "The Bakery That Never Sleeps," I thought. Kind of like Manhattan, you know, "The City That Never Sleeps."

But there was a difference between never closing on New Year's Eve and never closing from a hurricane. Power is Power. And you need power to run a bakery, and at least some kind of power to brew coffee.

"Let's check it out," I said. I grabbed her hand and proceeded out towards my car by the side of the driveway. As I opened the passenger side door of the Honda Pilot for Amy: "BAM!" I didn't know what hit me. All I could remember was being struck in the head by heavy object.

Chapter 54

Harry Massino, The Fish, and The Shadow all walked unobtrusively into town and got picked up by a black Mercedes and dropped off at the Francis S. Gabreski Airport just outside of Westhampton Beach. Within seconds they were on a NetJets plane headed westward.

"Massino, I hope you have this one done," said the shadow of a man.

"No problem! Just another roll in the hay. This one should be a big payday." Massino chuckled.

"Just do your thing," said The Fish. "Hey, any news on Sam?"

"Yes, The Shadow responded. He is recovering in the hospital. Jared told me he would be released Tuesday. It's hard to do his job."

"Hey, somebody has to play tough guy," said Massino.

"What about that troublemaker Dawson?"

"Our two guys have him and his girlfriend covered. In fact, as we speak, they are sitting in a warehouse, waiting to be interrogated by Maxwell. Well, more than interrogated. Shall I say, interrogated and then disposed of properly."

At that instance a stunning cocktail-waitress-dressed airplane stewardess walked by.

"Cigars, cigarettes?" she joked. She was wearing an old-fashioned miniskirt with her boobs hanging out up top. She was not there for the usual flight safety or security, but for pleasure. "Who goes first?" asked The Fish.

"Hey, Massino, you've had a full day of work. How about you get the first quickie," leered The Shadow.

"Nah," not in the mood. "Take it Tiki." Tiki was The Shadow's first name, and his only name. He had earned it by his well-timed killer instincts. In fact, Tiki stood for just that: Timed Killer. His targeted victims only got sixty seconds to squeal. If they failed, they would die, by either a shot to the head or a knife to the heart.

"Well, okay." Tiki got up and headed with the hooker acting like an old-time "cock"-tail waitress to the back of the plane, where he pushed a folding door open that lead to a makeshift playboy pen, toys and all. When they were both inside, Tiki closed the door.

After four hours of fun and frolic, the plane was ready to land. The jet plane hit the Tarmac, and Massino, The Fish, and The Shadow, aka Tiki, left through the Chico Municipal Airport's terminal.

Chapter 55

When I woke up, I was on the floor in the back of either a van or truck of some sort, gagged with what felt like duct tape. My eyes, arms, and legs were immobilized. My arms were pulled around my back, and I felt the pain. Lots of pain, mostly coming from my head. In medical school they talked about the worst headache of your life, referring to an intracranial hemorrhage, or bleed within the head. Such a bleed could be caused by an aneurysm, in which a weakened blood vessel spontaneously burst. Or by trauma, such as a fall, car accident, or some motherfucker hitting you in the head with a blunt object. The latter was clearly what happened. But still my head was ringing and hurt like hell. Certainly, the worst headache of *my* life. I could not feel for a bump on my head, due to the physical restraint, but I knew at least one was there. And pain is pain—I was seeing double. This sensation had only happened once before.

It was in 1979, when I went with the Johns Hopkins sailing team down to Annapolis to compete in a sailing regatta. My partner was almost as much a novice as I was. We were sailing a traditional NAVY 420 dinghy, on a leeward tack, and there was an abrupt change of wind. The boom swung around and hit me squarely in my head, knocking me overboard. Within seconds, a seaman in a tall naval ship threw me a life preserver, to which I hung on for dear life, until I was pulled to safety. After the entire mess, I saw double for two days.

And now I had the same kind of headache. "Annapolis Bay all over again. That was merely a concussion and eventually went away. But this time it could be different," I thought.

I couldn't see, speak, or move.

But I could hear and smell.

And I smelled the fragrant smell of the Vera Wang that Amy had been wearing. And heard her breathing as well! Thank God.

She too could not see, speak, or move!

And I could also feel the movement of the vehicle we were trapped in. It was driving on some sort of busy road, maybe even a highway, I could tell from the background noise of moving traffic, a honking horn, and even an occasional police siren in the distance. If only I could get some message to that officer, I thought.

Chapter 56

But I also heard one more thing.

It was Mustache Man talking to Sidekick from the front of the truck. The voices were unforgettable. I listened very carefully and was able to make out the following:

"Do we dump the bodies in the river?" Sidekick asked.

"No, that's not what Mr. Big wants," replied Mustache Man.

"They are just trouble—that's all they are," snickered Sidekick.

"Trouble, but trouble that the Big himself wants to deal with personally before we do what we were paid to do," said Mustache Man.

I started shaking in my boots, even though I wasn't even wearing boots. Our destiny was being determined by two assholes. And the ending was not looking like it was going to be pleasant. Not unless we were able to do something and escape. But at least I realized something. Someway, somehow, Mustache Man and his sidekick were certainly involved. Not at the highest level, but as muscle, *thugs*, and *scum*. The latter two terms, Alex had used time and time again. Mostly referring to corrupt politicians. But the terms were still relevant to these two assholes, nonetheless.

"Thugs and scum," I said to myself. They were thugs and scum, and the kind of thugs and scum that would give me a headache for a long, long time.

My mind was spinning. Question after question followed. And each of these questions was spoken inside my aching head!

"This Mr. Big, who the hell is he? Is he the head of the entire operation? And what precisely is the operation? Stealing priceless paintings? And what about Angela Weisberg's murder? What could she have done to justify her death? All this to meet Mr. Big? What the hell did he want from me? And what did I ever do to him?"

Chapter 57

I could not see a thing. Just pure darkness, and my eyes were starting to hurt from the pressure of the duct tape. That pressure combined with the pain from my headache was making me nauseous. But I believe we had pulled up into an area where there were other trucks. I heard a loud honking sound coming from what was probably an 18-wheeler or some other large transport vehicle. I heard the noise of different engines, mostly loud noises, with a variety of bass and vibrato. More like the sounds at Port Authority. A bus or dump truck perhaps. Or both? I also heard the sound of sea gulls, and some type of foghorn. How much time had passed by? Was it an hour? Maybe half a day?

Then the door opened, and I was crated out by the two of the thugs, one grabbing my feet, the other my shoulders. I was being tossed around like a sack of potatoes. But where to? Will this be my final resting place? Was I—God forbid—going to be tortured? And—not only me—Amy too? I tried to push aside the pictures that began to crowd into my brain.

A large, heavy metal-sliding door screeched open. I based this deduction almost entirely on my hearing sense, although I knew my feeling sense also detected the motion and vibration. The sound and pitch of metal sliding on metal, as well as the duration, all helped me come to that conclusion. At least, that's what it sounded like to me a large heavy, metal garage door that led to a storage facility of some sort. And then both my beautiful Amy and I were brought inside and tossed in the back. But the toss was just another PAIN as I hit what felt like a metal floor. No soft landing, just some more pain. But this one was on my right side, my right gluteus maximus—or buttocks, for those nonmedical readers. The same one that had been giving me pain from my sciatica: a long-standing condition from wearing the heavy lead vest and skirt protection required by my profession. I heard a second thud echo from within the chamber and knew it was Amy. Then they departed and slammed the door shut with a repeat of the screeching sound, followed by another loud thud, as the garage-type door hit the ground with its heavy mass. Besides our breathing, there was only one other sound, the *sound of silence*. A typical oxymoron, I thought. No, the true sound of silence, and I'm not talking about Simon and Garfunkel.

Chapter 58

Silence, that was, until I heard the door open up, with the now all-too-familiar screech, though slightly more distant. It was not coming from our door, but another one nearby—close enough that I could hear everything the man said. His voice was much less gruff than that of those other two *scum and thugs*, working for Mr. Big. And whoever gave him that name was certainly not trying to hide his role in this mess. No matter what, this Mr. Big had to be the mastermind of the murder and the art heist. Or more precisely, he was the mastermind at least of the art heist! My headache started pounding, and again I heard inside my head a rash of questions that came along with it! "Was the murder a consequence of Mrs. Weisberg's seeing something she shouldn't have seen? Maybe she caught the thieves in the act? The same way I caught my wife in the act? And what would the Pollock thieves do, just take the painting and say goodbye? Did they have any choice? Couldn't they have just knocked her unconscious on her head like they did mine and let her recover? Not if she saw too much or knew too much and could easily identify the thief or thieves. Was that our problem too?" But more immediately, Mr. Big appeared to be pulling the strings to whatever was to become of Amy and myself. Our final resting place.

"RIP," I thought again as my head continued to pound.

He spoke like a high-powered salesman. "Yes, I am the Schlepper! That is what they call me. Ship My Bike, Ship My Art—all the same biz. Three months ago, Mr. Trump wanted me to ship his Harley to him. Gave him the best price in all the US. Saw the guy at the US Open in Flushing Meadows, but he wouldn't even give me the time of day. Not even a pass to the Open. Cheap bastard!"

"Well, if I could do all this for 'the Donald,'" I'm sure I can help you. *Ship My Bike, Ship My Art*. Been in business nearly twenty-five years, and let me tell you, it ain't pretty. But you want a deal, I'll give you a deal. Crated and shipped to wherever you want. Think of me like "the Transporter". And I don't ask questions. Ship My Art, Ship My Bike!"

The voice continued. But I was sure this was not MR. BIG at all.

"Contract—ah, yes, contract! Have I got a contract for you! I am an attorney, you know. An attorney and a shipper. A shipper and an attorney. Almost as unique as what I ship, just *Bikes and Art. Art and Bikes*. Nothing more, nothing less."

This guy was as talkative as Crazy Eddie, that weird techno-commercial guy who used to come on TV, trying to sell you a TV or stereo, with his famous ending: "Crazy Eddie, Our Prices are INSANE!!!!" But where is Crazy Eddie now? Not sitting pretty on some remote island in the Caribbean, for that I was certain. Crazy Eddie was Eddie Antar of Brooklyn fame. Crazy Eddie was also the name of a chain of popular electronics stores that started in Brooklyn around the same time I first met that little cute girl named Amy. The same Amy who was trying to help get me out of this mess, and the exact same Amy I could still smell, though we were both bound and gagged. How ironic!

The Crazy Eddie commercials were memorable. Even spoofed on *Saturday Night Live*. Crazy Eddie grew to forty-three stores in all and grossed more than $300 million. But eventually he was accused of fraud. The company went under, and Eddie fled the US for Israel. He returned to the US for trial in 1993 and was found guilty. Prison! That was where he went. Not a resort in the Caribbean at all, at least initially. Was I headed for the same place? Sing Sing? "Only if I am lucky enough to survive this," I surmised to myself. He was sentenced to eight years in prison but served much less and was released in 1999. Would I be so lucky? "Hey, wait a minute, I never did anything wrong, whatsoever!" I said to myself.

Chapter 59

Before the new, Mr. Crazy Eddie-sounding guy left, I did hear that the shipper was shipping the package to "Fort Mason." I heard it as clear as day. "Fort Mason." The only Fort Mason I knew of was in San Francisco. Every year, the San Francisco Museum of Modern Art, or SFMOMA, had their Artist's Warehouse sale there. Two years ago, Shari and I were vacationing in Frisco and went to Fort Mason and bought six paintings for our Hamptons house at their Annual Warehouse sale. We got all those great pieces for a song and a dance, and they now filled our place on Homans Avenue. The warehouse sale was always in May, and it was now November.

Fort Mason was an old army barrack with yellowed concrete buildings, casement windows, and green-tiled roofs, all touching the San Francisco Bay, facing out towards Alcatraz. Oh, how ironic!

"Too many ironies," I thought. First, the new Crazy Eddie and now Alcatraz. Maybe I was getting a little paranoid. The artists I like all committed *suicide*. The people around me right now are *thugs and scum*. And me, little old me? I'm being accused of *murder and grand art theft*; and now this? My mind must be playing tricks on me or perhaps it is the concussion. Am I delusional?

"We've got to get out of here and get to San Francisco," I thought. But was I sure of *the plan*? Was the new-fangled Crazy Eddie really talking about shipping the painting or something else? Or was it just a coincidence?

Chapter 60

I had no alternative. I knew where this was heading, and there would be no happy ending! I had to do something, get myself free, release Amy as well, and escape!

Myth busters demonstrated the ability and strength of duct tape, time and time again on their popular TV program. Duct tape could hold a broken-apart car together and survive the stress of driving at sixty miles per hour. It could create a suspension bridge strong enough to allow a group of large adults to cross over a ravine. But even with that strength, there was something that was even stronger.

The human jaw!

The amount of force applied by the human jaw is many times stronger than the strength of both a human's legs and a human's arms combined. It is the masseter muscle, or jaw muscle, that gave me hope—the hope of cutting through the tape.

I wiggled and moved my mouth for about five minutes until I was able to get my tongue out. I used the moisture from my tongue to loosen the tape, and its contact with my face together with my jaw's movement. In another five minutes, I was able to get my teeth on the tape and began gnawing. When I got through it, I was then able to work on my legs and ankles. I tried to reach towards my feet with my mouth, but they were just too far way. Maybe if I was double jointed and had the flexibility of a circus contortion expert, I could have reached with my teeth and grabbed the tape that was restraining my ankles. But I wasn't even close. I wiggled my body towards the side of the storage container and started to work on my hands instead.

There was a razor-sharp edge by the metal container door, and I was able to swing myself around and work the tape off of my hands, which were numb from being pulled around my back. I got the tape off my hands, then off my ankles. I then ripped off the tape that was covering my eyes. Then I saw her!

My precious Amy had a large bloody bump on her head. The blood was dried and crusted over her left ear and ran down the left side of her face. She was lying on the floor, completely bound by duct tape, just like I had been. I carefully, as gently as possible, pulled the tape off her eyes and mouth, and freed up her arms and legs. I could see that she was conscious, but barely. "Was she drugged?" I wondered. "Or was this the effect of the head trauma."

"We have to be quiet," I whispered to her.

"Thanks, but we have to get out of here," she whispered back.

"So great to see you," I said affectionately. "I reached over to her and gave her a big warm hug. I felt tingles all over! But did she?"

"I didn't know what happened to you. I thought you were dead," she said.

"I don't know exactly who we're dealing with," I whispered. I motioned with my finger over my lips, the universal sign for *quiet*, and then we just listened. But we did not hear much.

Chapter 61

With my ear to the door, I listened again. "Only the quiet of an abandoned or remote outdoor spot!" I thought. We had to take a chance. I wanted to try to open up the large storage-container door. But I had feared Mustache Man and Sidekick would be waiting for us outside. We had to be careful. I listened again and again and again. I didn't hear a thing. I listened for about another twenty minutes and still heard nothing. If they were going to try to dispose of us, we would at least have to risk trying to escape. I looked at the large metal container door, which must have weighed eighty pounds. In my mind, there was no way this door would open. Besides its weight, it had to be bolted shut.

But I gave it a shot. I heaved the large, sliding storage-container door upward, and it barely budged. By its movement, however, I knew it was not bolted shut. Then I gave it another full "heave ho" with all my might, and it opened about halfway, providing us just enough space to escape. We both made our way out of the container, and then I pulled the door back down.

Sunlight greeted our eyes, and lots of it! It was an enormous shipping yard, and this end contained twenty oversized storage units, with one large wooden sign overhead which read: SHIP MY BIKE, SHIP MY ART. Mustache Man and Sidekick, as well as the Crazy Eddie guy, were nowhere to be seen. And the storage bin next door was wide open and completely empty. I looked out, away from the shipping yard and across a body of water. The water was polluted with floating bottles, cans, a dead fish, and a full page of the *New York Daily News*. "No place for a swim." I grinned. The body of water was more like a small man-made river, inlet, or canal. There was bulkhead on both sides, reminding me of the channel that led between Dune Road and the main part of Westhampton Beach, but much wider and dirtier. Across from the so-called canal were a number of brick high-rise apartments. Queens or the Bronx? But it could also have been someplace in Staten Island. Or Jersey, for that matter. I had no way of knowing. The area looked nothing like any I'd ever seen before.

A tugboat anchored on the other side of the bulkhead said, HELEN MCALISTER. Was Helen McAllister the owner? Or was McAllister some other dead-end. "Perhaps an Irish relative of McElroy?" I speculated to myself. The boat showed no indication of life—just anchored on the other side of the body of water.

It would have helped if I knew how long we were knocked unconscious. A few hours or even a day? I looked at the sun—dead straight overhead, it appeared to be after-noon, though I couldn't be sure. I had no sense of direction. How far were we from Riverhead? Could we be in Con-necticut? I doubt it. It looked like some of the more built-up areas near the City—New York City, that is.

Amy and I made our way around the side of the com-plex that faced towards the water. I was holding my breath while anxiously looking for the perpetrators. A number of trucks were parked there, and there were still no signs of movement, or any sign of human life, for that matter. I gave out a big sigh while gasping for breath. Just seagulls, lots of them. I looked to the right of the shipping yard and saw what looked like a towering pile of landfill encircled by seagulls. The air smelled of this refuse. "Oh, how pleasant," I said to Amy. "We need to get the hell out of here."

Chapter 62

W e made a mad dash for it. Racing out of the parking lot, I instinctively grabbed Amy's hand. Near the exit out of the parking lot there was a large shipping truck parked next to an evergreen Jeep Active Drive 4 x 4. A relatively short guy got out of the Jeep and walked to the much larger shipping truck, and opened up its back door. Then went to the front of the truck. I glanced at the truck's side and saw the now very recognizable insignia we had just observed outside where we were imprisoned.

On one side was what looked like a historic emblem with a picture of a Harley-Davidson motorcycle.

SHIP MY BIKE, said the draped upper emblem.

As we carefully circled to the other side, there was another historic emblem, with a picture of the *Mona Lisa*.

SHIP MY ART, read the draped emblem above it.

The back was open, someone was coming. I caught one quick glance of him. That was it. The real Crazy Eddie was a six-foot-plus beast of a man with a roaring voice. My made-up Crazy Eddie was a five-foot-four middle-aged Jewish grey-haired guy of medium build. The back of the truck gave it all away, and the new Crazy Eddie was coming toward us. Amy and I before he even noticed hid around the back near the truck's doors. There was a full artist's rendering on the back of the truck door that looked quite familiar and historic.

It was a classic picture of Uncle Sam, and above it read: UNCLE DANIEL WANTS YOU." Below, it had the address:

Ship My Bike, Ship My Art
Principal: Mr. Daniel Kleinman, Esquire
355 East Rockaway, New York
www.shipyourbikes.com

This guy must be a comedian.

There was no way we were going to run out of the shipping yard without being seen. And there was no way I was going to let Mr. Kleinman escape with what may be the world's most valuable piece of art.

I jumped inside the truck, then grabbed Amy's hand and pulled her up as well. Inside there appeared to be twenty to twenty-five boxes, even crates, and fifteen motorcycles, all bubble wrapped. One of the crates was quite oversized, large enough to house the Pollock. We wedged ourselves together in a corner between a "Bike" and a "Box."

"Oh, this is cozy," I whispered to Amy. The box shielded us from anyone glancing inward through the back door. Thirty seconds later the back door was slammed shut, and we were trapped in the dark again.

"One last pickup and we're off," said the Crazy Eddie-type voice. "We're going to Ghost!"

"Could it be? Could we be going to where I think we're going?" I whispered to Amy.

Chapter 63

Ghost Motorcycle was another one of those legends, but this one was not in the Hamptons.

"They can't be heading there," I said to Amy incredulously.

"Why's that?" she replied.

"Because Ghost is located in Port Washington, my hometown. The town where I raised my kids!"

"Sorry," she said sympathetically.

Ghost Motorcycle had been located in an off-white, dilapidated, concrete building on Main Street many years, in what was an overbuilt Long Island Sound sea town. In the past, the large sign GHOST hovered above the store's edifice. For many years it was stocked with an array of used and rebuilt Harley Davidsons. And a seedy-looking crowd of bikers. The male bikers were either bald or had long grey hair, often accompanied by unruly facial hair. They reminded me of the rock band ZZ Top, with their black leather vests and matching biker boots, and their unsightly tattoos! The Biker Babes were equally tattooed and stuffed into similar black-leather garb, always too tight, and definitely unseemly. This group seemed harmless to the mostly white-collar workers that inhabited Port Washington. The GHOST sign had long since been removed. And

Ghost was really a ghost. I had no inkling that there was even any life left in Ghost. No pun intended.

Port Washington was on the water, and Main Street led from the Manhasset Bay water park, up past the shops, past the modern Port Washington Library, past the stately Landmark Senior Center, past even more shops, and then up to Ghost. The meandering, wooded village streets of the affluent village of Sands Point and the eclectic little Port Washington neighborhoods and villages all wound up on the "Main Street" of Port Washington. A number of the elite Wall Streeters, New York professional athletes, including New York Ranger greats and Mets veterans, as well as some well-known TV personalities all came from the storied village of Sands Point. Hey, even the sportscaster/NBA broadcaster Marv Albert and the National Hockey League legend and Hall of Famer Wayne Gretzky once lived here. And many of the neighboring doctors, lawyers, and other businessman all hailed from that area, as well as the less affluent but still gentrified Port Washington. This included the New England-style neighborhoods, such as Baxter Estates, Beacon Hill, and Port Washington North.

If you went a little further up Main Street, you hit the Long Island Railroad, or LIRR—a unique feature of the town. Since Port Washington was the end of the Port Washington Line of the LIRR, you could always get a seat to Penn Station in downtown Manhattan.

Everyone knew that Ghost had had tax problems and essentially disappeared. At least, that was the story.

"Ghost essentially became a ghost." I whispered into Amy's ear. "I thought they were in foreclosure."

The truck came to a halt, and Amy and I immediately hid behind the large crate in the back. I did, however, get enough of a glance out the back to realize we were on Main Street in Port Washington. After a few minutes of apparent serenity, I slid out from the crate toward the back door of the truck and quickly caught a glimpse of the vacant, sign-less Ghost building. I then returned back to Amy, where we both hid, in the back corner behind the crate.

Chapter 64

Amy," I whispered. "We are so close to my old place. If I could only run to my house, and get some things, it could be helpful to us."

"I don't think you have enough time," Amy replied.

"But all I need is an hour, tops. That's all I need. I really have to get some things, especially if we are going to head across country. We'll need water and nourishment at the least, just to stay alive."

"Don't risk it," she said.

"Amy, I hope you'll understand. But I have to risk it. We will get to the bottom of this mess. And we will figure out who is behind the art theft. Sixty minutes, tops. That's all I need." I was hopeful that she would understand.

But she didn't. "MD, don't even think about it. What if they leave in the next few minutes? I would be trapped on board in the back of a truck, potentially driven by the murderer and thief. On a trip to who knows where. Plus, you would not be with me."

I thought about what she said. She was right!

I resisted the urge to run out the back and up Main Street. It was too risky, heading to my house in Beacon Hill, literally a twenty-minute walk from Ghost. I had no clue how long the truck would be there. If it were only ten minutes, Amy would be up the creek without a paddle. But weren't we up that creek anyway? Was this our opportunity?

After what Shari did to me, I did not even want to see my old place again. But I needed my wallet, and other essentials. And what if I ran into Shari. What would she do? Call the police? In my mind, our relationship had ended. Finito! And it ended with a bang, not a whimper. I was literally and figuratively *screwed*! The *literally screwed* part was the blond buck Shari was doing in our bedroom.

Rather than run, I reached into my pocket and found something that I had forgotten I had.

Chapter 65

My iPhone. It had been turned off to conserve energy, and I flipped it back on and switched the phone to "silence." When it rebooted, I saw ten text messages.

Six were from Alex, all wondering where I was: two from Mr. Schwartz, asking for me to give him a call, one was from my mother, wondering if I'd started dating, and one was from Mr. Edward Ginsberg, Esquire, Shari's new attorney, stating that divorce papers had been filed, that we were legally separated, and that the papers were in the mail.

I quickly called Alex but only got his usual message, "Hello, this is Alex," followed by a bunch of French pleasantries, and then back to English: "Leave your name and number at the sound of the beep. *Merci et passez une journée agréable*." I spoke quickly and concisely into the phone.

"Alex, where the hell are you? Amy and I've been kidnapped and have escaped, but now we are in Port Washington, hiding inside the back of a large shipping truck. We need your help. We are on Main Street in front of the old Ghost Motorcycle building. We are inside the large white truck with a SHIP MY ART/SHIP MY BIKE emblem painted on it. I believe the truck is headed to San Francisco. Amy and I plan to go with them. I know it sounds strange, but I think it will all come together where *I Left My Heart*.

Alex knew this song well. It was my wedding song, but now it might be my swan song.

"I don't want to let this painting out of my sight, Alex. Please keep your phone at hand, I will need your help in Frisco. They are loading the bikes on board and will be off to the West Coast shortly."

The message ended abruptly and I knew I had to act fast.

I snuck out of the truck for an instant and listened from the right side of the Ghost building. Peeking my head around the corner, I saw Mr. Kleinman—who appeared harmless enough in the distance—giving his best Crazy Eddie sales pitch as his team started to wrap up five more motorcycles. When I heard him tell their customer that it would take an hour and a half, including a detour down to the Harbor Deli for snacks, I knew I had time to make one more trip.

Chapter 66

I snuck Amy out of the truck, and brought her catty-corner across the street into Finn MacCool's, an Irish tavern and restaurant, frequented by the New York Mets. Amy would be safe in their foyer, and would have full view of the truck from their front door. I texted Alex and let him know what I was doing. Each time I used my phone, I turned it off to conserve energy. There was no place for me to charge it. The text was as follows: "Alex, making a dash for my old place. Need to stock up for trip to survive. Keep u posted in case I need help." I pressed send. Within an instant, I looked at my screen and saw, "K. Got message. Will be nearby in case." I then turned off the phone again.

I ran up Main Street and saw an old banged-up Schwin bike leaning against "BALTIMORE," the design studio of Keith Baltimore, on the north side of the road. I grabbed the bike and peddled quickly past the center-hall colonials in Monfort Hills, up Orchard Farm Road, and around Ridge. I turned up Crescent Road in Beacon Hill, built on top of a large bluff overlooking the old sand mines that were essential to building the skyscrapers that make up Manhattan. Some of the Beacon Hill homes had views of the Arnold Palmer Harbor Links Golf Course down below. Mine was one of them.

My home, or shall I call it my soon-to-be ex-wife's home, was a large brick center-hall colonial with a three-car garage in this all-too-quiet suburban neighborhood. It wasn't quiet the day I caught Shari humping that motherfucker! I thought. Hopefully, this time I would have more luck than my last visit, I said to myself.

I jumped off the bike and ran up to the house. There were no suspicious- looking cars out front or in the garage. Not a peep. I was fearful of being seen by a neighbor or an old acquaintance, ever since my story appeared in the newspaper. That would not be good for me, and not good for my chance of recovering the Pollock or finding the murderer.

What luck, I said to myself. Shari's car was gone, but Maggie was still home. She was a beautiful Soft Coated Wheaten Terrier that saw me from the front door and started jumping and wagging her tail.

"At least, someone missed me," I said.

Were the locks changed? I nervously reached underneath the planter to the right of the door and pulled out a key, unlocking the door.

It was great to see Maggie. She gave me the usual lick and promptly returned to her crate.

I first went through the mudroom into the kitchen and opened up the drawer that was built into the kitchen island. My wallet was still there. It had my license, credit cards, and a few hundred dollars in cash. I took the wallet and put it in my pocket and then quickly went upstairs to grab my MacBook Air and charger from my office. I ran into the bedroom, past that disgusting scene where my wife fucked up our life, so to speak, and through to our large walk-in closet. I went straight across to the far wall, where I kept all my clothes. To the right of the built-in shelves were my dress socks, all neatly folded. Underneath the socks was a small letter envelope. I grabbed the envelope, stuffed it in the dollar-bill section of my wallet, and left down the hall.

Then I glanced up at the wall. There it stood, in its wooden frame, surrounded by a linen mat. The letter!

Chapter 67

The letter was in the form of a card that I purchased from the Museum Shop at the MoMA. The front was a beautiful Rothko painting with slabs of magnificent glowing colors. It was entitled *No. 3/No. 13 Magenta, Black, Green on Orange*—oil on canvas, 85 3/8 by 65 inches. "Why two different numbers?" I wondered. "Perhaps a lucky three, our marriage?" I thought. "Followed by an unlucky thirteen, our separation?" No, it was ironically a reference to the date I popped the question. Our engagement date. March thirteenth. The Rothko was not that different in size from the Pollock. The first three colors floated on an orange background, and the painting itself belonged to the MoMA's permanent collection. I had placed the front of the card side by side in the frame next to the written text that originally appeared inside the four-panel card. Mark Rothko, like Jackson Pollock, was a first-generation Abstract Expressionist. Both had an alcohol problem. Pollock died, after getting drunk, from a car crash. Rothko committed suicide after overdosing on anti-depressants and slitting his wrists. And there was the text to the letter written by me,

Dear Shari,
I have been looking for you my entire life! But what do we need to be happy? What do we strive for? What do we need in life? What things do we as human beings yearn for? Success? Contentment? A Job? Art? Family? Love?
Well, now that I have found you, I have each and every one of those things! A Great Job, A Great Family, and most importantly, the Love of My Life!
And now I ask you? Will you marry me?
Love you Forever and Ever
MD

And signed right underneath:

I Will! Love you too Forever and Ever,
Shari

"Forever and Ever?" I thought. I starred at the Rothko and could not get my mind off of his painting and the two untimely deaths. Rothko at age sixty-six and Pollock at only age forty-four!

In the mudroom I found my MacBook Air laptop computer still hooked to a charger, as was my iPhone's extended-battery charging case. I threw the computer, my iPhone charging case, a dozen or so water bottles, and two boxes of Kashi Cherry Almond energy bars in a backpack, ran out the back, and grabbed bike. I peddled as fast as I could back to "BALTIMORE," and returned the bike where it had previously resided. Then I grabbed Amy from Toscanini.

The whole trip took twenty minutes. And I now had my wallet plus some other goodies. Mr. Kleinman's crew was about to bring the wrapped bikes out to the van. We quickly slid into the back of the truck, behind a "Box" and a "Bike."

Chapter 68

After making sure my phone and computer were both on silence, I slid the phone into the battery-charging case to give it some extra juice. I also made sure the phone stayed off when not in use, otherwise, the power would be depleted after about twenty-four hours. When we were on our way, I sat up in the back of the truck and briefly got web access on my iPhone, using a hotspot. The phone created enough ambient light that we were able to see the silhouettes of most of the boxes and crates and bikes being shipped. But I also saw the silhouette of a beautiful angel, one who had entered my life at the worst possible time. She was my only glimmer of hope. My salvation.

I used the flashlight app designed by a fifteen-year-old kid from our town by the name of Felix Mayer, who already had his own company, "App-ealing, LLC"; he had developed another twenty or so iPhone apps. "He's probably worth millions," I thought.

To my surprise, the largest crate, wedged up against the side of the truck container, was the one we were sitting next to. By my best approximation it was the only one large enough to contain the painting.

"Amy, this is the one!"

The crate was a solid wooden box, which appeared to be roughly nine feet by five feet by ten inches. It was stamped FRAGILE in red in multiple places. Smaller wooden crates were just visible as well, also marked FRAGILE in red.

"Are there other stolen paintings?" I whispered to Amy. "Perhaps Picassos, Cézannes, or even a Degas?"

"I wouldn't be surprised," she whispered back. "Evil is evil. And if they could steal a Pollock and kill an heiress, they could certainly steal other great paintings. Maybe art heists are their modus operandi?"

But the most *fragile* or shall I say *precious* thing of all was the woman wedged up against my side. Even with a bruised head and bloodied clothes, nothing, and I mean nothing, was as beautiful as Amy, or as important to me.

"I still can't believe it has been nearly forty years since we first met," I said.

"I can't either," she replied softly. "But I am so glad to be with you."

My right arm was draped over her shoulder, and she was resting her head on my shoulder. She turned her head towards mine, and I turned towards hers. And we kissed. As if nothing else mattered.

I shut off the flashlight app and went onto the Google website and searched for Jackson Pollock *No. 5*

Chapter 69

An image of the *No. 5* appeared on the screen. A classic Pollock! But not just any Pollock, the one I'd seen over the Weisbergs' fireplace! We both closely scrutinized the screen.

I went to my iPhotos folder on my iPhone and pulled up the painting from the Weisberg place. Again we both looked at that image very carefully.

"They are identical!" Amy whispered.

The Google image appeared to have the same brown-and-white drips in the same pattern. And there were greys and oranges, and even the same red splatters in identical places as the one on my iPhone from the Weisbergs' estate.

As I zoomed into both the web image and my image, every detail was the same. Apparently, this painting was shrouded in mystery. At least, we gathered as much from the web. Snuggling around the computer, we learned the following facts.

According to the *New York Times*, David Geffen sold the painting November 2, 2006, privately. With two other well-known celebrities—Steven Spielberg and Mark Katzenberg— Mr. Geffen was a cofounder of DreamWorks SKG. The article went on to say that one David Martinez, a "wealthy financier" from Mexico, purchased the painting for $140 million.

According to multiple articles, including one on Wikipedia, Mr. Martinez later denied he was the purchaser. The true owner was reportedly unknown.

"But how the hell did it get from Mr. Geffen to Mr. Weisberg and NOW next to me? If that is where it is?" I whispered.

Chapter 70

With an uncertain but long drive ahead, I had to conserve my computer and iPhone usage. Estimating I had only seven hours max in the MacBook, I turned it off and put it away.

I used my iPhone to text both Alex and Mr. Schwartz to let them know we were okay and apprise them of what was happening. I typed in the following text:

> Guys, in back of shipping truck with painting. Painting is what I believe to be the 1948 Jackson Pollock *No. 5*, which sold for $140 million. Going cross-country to San Francisco. Believe drop-off point is at Fort Mason. Please send help! Should be there in three days, though not sure how long it will take. Need to conserve cell and computer power for the trip. Will go dark for hours and keep you posted. Reply by text or email. Will check periodically.

I pressed send.

I turned to Amy and melted next to her. She did the same with me. We were both exhausted. I began to doze off into oblivion, rocked by the bounce of the truck. Within seconds Amy was snoozing. I started drifting, drifting into another world.

I was back in 1972, after "the Bar Mitzvah." I had received a folded Leonard's napkin stuffed into my pocket before I left the event. Written on it were the words: "Call me, 516-364-9212, Amy."

I called her that week after my algebra test.

"Amy, would you like to catch a movie and a bite?"

"Sure," she replied.

"How about The Heartbreak Kid?*" I asked.*

"Sure," she replied.

"My dad will pick you up at six and we can grab a bite and catch the movie."

I took her to Friendly's Ice Cream Parlor and grabbed a burger and a milkshake, while Amy had a tuna melt followed by a Swiss Chocolate Almond Fudge Sundae with Toasted Almond Fudge Ice Cream.

Then I held her hand as we walked up Northern Boulevard to the Manhasset Bay Cinema and bought two tickets to The Heartbreak Kid.

"What a screwed-up movie?" I said when we left the theater.

"Yeah," Amy said. "If I ever got married and then got a bad sunburn, I hope my husband would not go astray."

"If it were me, I would be there through thick and through thin," I replied.

The next few months I must have seen her at least a dozen times. And then in 1973, I will never forget the last time. Another trip to the Manhasset Bay Cinema—for the opening of Jeremy, *starring Robby Benson, a tearjerker of a love story. It was so romantic and so intense, at least for a thirteen-year-old. It was a love story between a cello student, Jeremy Jones, and a ballerina, Susan Rollins. Love at first sight! Just like Amy and me, or should I say me and Amy, to be less grammatical and piss off Mrs. Parker, my English teacher.*

I was in the theater, the next to last row, making out with Amy. I slid my hand underneath her blouse, inside her bra, and cupped what was a well-formed breast. I was blown away and had a hard-on throughout the entire film. At the end, Amy turned to me and said, "I have to go."

"What's wrong?"

"It's too intense," she said. "I'm just not ready."

I called and called and called but never got an answer.

That was the last time I saw Amy—that was, at least until we reconnected at the courthouse in Riverhead.

Chapter 71

The syndicate was a well-oiled machine, a worldwide network—Berlin, Mumbai, New York City, Dubai, Los Angeles, San Francisco, Shanghai, London, and Paris. Fine art objects would find their way to the super-rich buyers. The buyers were first identified and their money secured. Then the objets d'art would magically appear. But it was not magic, it was work. Hard work, led by none other than Mr. Big. The master organizer, or kingpin, from the very beginning was Mr. Big, as he was called. He was BIG in stature, and in so many other ways. He had built the empire, and in doing so made BIG connections, he made BIG decisions, and most importantly he made BIG money. He had a myriad of regional directors in each of the world's art hubs. The directors would find the buyers and sell them the works of art as they were secured.

Lucky for Mr. Big he had formed a solid—or should I say BIG—relationship with Harry Massino. You see, Harry, and his master forging team were a perfect complement to Mr. Big. Harry gave Mr. Big the opportunity to more than double his ROI, that is, his "return on investment." In other words, his profits! All of Mr. Big's clients were so secretive and anonymous—and from such diverse geographic area—that Massino's forgeries were often good for two, maybe even three, and sometimes even four sales of the same exact painting. And only Mr. Big got to keep the original. Oh, how thoughtful.

Mr. Big was still lying in bed, looking out the window onto a parking lot. As he looked out, he saw a few leafless trees, a mostly filled lot, and an ambulance pull up to the façade. He was alone for the moment. But that could change in a split second, with something as simple as his lunch tray. He picked up his antiquated flip cell phone and whispered with his scraggly voice, "The buyer has already paid the two hundred million dollars for *the piece*. It must arrive on time," he stated to Jimmy "The Fish" on the other end of the line.

"It is en route," replied The Fish. "Should be in San Francisco by the end of the week. I've arranged a boat for direct shipping and a land courier right to your client's destination in Shanghai. I'll need the first half of the wire transfer to my offshore account before the piece is loaded on the boat. That's twenty-five million dollars—signed, sealed, and delivered now. And another twenty-five million when the piece arrives at Fort Mason and is secured on the ship."

"And the others?" asked Big.

"The deal is going down exactly like you outlined. All works are in transit. Once in Fort Mason, your piece will go into short-term storage, then be delivered to your Carmel Estate."

"When?"

"One week later." I have that shipment all coordinated. And the money, Biggie?"

"Consider it done! Just make damn sure that '*the piece*' is on board the ship." This time when he said *the piece*, he used both hands to indicate the quotations marks and emphasize its importance. "Our client has paid dearly for it. I don't want any mistakes. If there are any screwups, you will be dealt with in an appropriate manner." Mr. Big always threatened his connections. It was his way of making sure everything fell into place. And yes, he had a *BIG* temper. You just didn't want him to take it out on you.

"And how about our loose ends?" asked Mr. Big.

"You mean Dawson and his lawyer? They were in custody, but . . . but . . . but . . . they somehow got away," stammered the embarrassed Fish, who knew he had to squirm his way out of this one.

"How did that happen? You should never have let them get away! If that was even a possibility, you should have taken care of them the old-fashioned way"—he paused—"the same way you took care of Mrs. Weisberg! What the hell are you doing about it?" demanded an angry Mr. Big.

"We are on the lookout for him. Remember, he is a wanted man. And how are you doing?" Fish tried to change gears.

"I'm fine. Just a shock to my system. I will be out in no time. My sons have the rest of the business covered. They are flying into San Francisco to make sure everything goes as planned. Where is Massino?"

"With me and Tiki in Chico. Everything is fine. Files are uploaded in the computer and we're waiting delivery of *your piece*. They should be here in less than twenty-four hours. You have nothing to worry about." The Fish was very reassuring. He had to be. If Mr. Big sensed an iota of a problem, he would have sent his own assassins to take care of business.

"I certainly hope not!" Mr. Big hung up his phone, then slowly got up from his mechanical bed and proceeded to open the top drawer at his bedside table and pull out a six-inch- long rubber replica of a grey rat. He grabbed the whiskered fake animal in his hand and started to squeeze it tighter and tighter. This was just a toy, but at home, he had a cage of real rodents and would do the same activity until the beast started to squeal. This was his way of letting out anger. When he had a veritable rodent, he would continue to squeeze until the rat stopped breathing altogether, and began to shake until it became motionless. He would then and only then drop the dead rodent into the garbage. In this sterile place, the toy would have to do. Mr. Big squeezed the fake rat like a stress ball, and after two minutes, imagining its demise, just put it back in the drawer. "Ah," he said as his muscle started to release, and he felt a warmth spread over him.

Chapter 72

We awoke to a large pothole, which jarred us both. No more Dreamsville. It was back to reality. Where were we? I wasn't sure. I was in a fog about everything, just a whirlwind tour of the US. One that made me feel apoplectic, partially from the cerebral contusion and partially from the pain of the past week. But Amy was my painkiller now. My touch of hope!

I opened up two bottles of water and two Kashi Cherry Almond Bars. I passed one of each to my soul mate. I was starting to get dehydrated. We had a limited supply of water, but enough to get us by for the next few days if we rationed ourselves to one bottle per day apiece. I easily could drink the entire bottle, but knew that was not in my best interest. I drank half now and wolfed the bar down! Amy did the same. Then she nuzzled her head back against my shoulder as I leaned against the crate. With the vibration of the truck, I drifted off to sleep again. And so did she.

The back of the truck opened and suddenly there was light!

"Pull out the Ghost Bikes," one voice shouted. "Take out the four in front."

We were well hidden behind a large crate box. The bikes were pulled out and the door slammed shut. Where are we? In OshKosh? Could I remember anything from the door opening to figure out where we were? The thought caught my mind, but I knew it was impossible from the angle of the back of the truck. But after they removed the bikes, I moved my head and for an instant I caught a glimpse of some other motorcycles in the parking lot.

"Hell's Angels, perhaps." I joked to Amy.

"No, Bike Babes," she laughed back.

Chapter 73

It was my inner humor that kept me sane. Little thoughts like that. Amy had the same instinctual humor. She seemed to read my mind. We talked, and talked and talked. Our entire lives shared an endless whisper in each other's ear.

Love and life. Love for life. My love for her life. How does that song go?

"Once in love with Amy . . ."

But this time, it was my humor that reminded me of the most simple of cell phone features. One that I had forgotten in all the hoopla; namely, my iPhone Maps app.

I'd made use of the app many times to locate exactly where I was, especially when lost. Last time was one month ago, when I was in Manhattan and got really lost. I knew I was in Chinatown but had no idea how to get to the Bowery. I was visiting the former artist studios of a husband-and-wife team of Abstract Expressionist painters. No, not Jackson Pollock and Lee Krasner, but Milton Resnick and Pat Passlof. Passlof, was the lesser known of the two, and previously resided at 80 Forsyth Street. The residence was an old synagogue, which at the time had been a massive art factory for the now-deceased artist. I needed to get from Forsyth Street to Bleecker, but had no idea amongst the confusing Chinatown hustle and bustle. So I pulled out my iPhone, tapped on the Google Maps app, and hit the corner arrow, which immediately pinpointed my exact location. Then it was simple to type in where I wanted to go on Bleecker and within seconds the app gave me the directions.

The ability to perform this function depended on cell phone access and service, which for me had never been an issue. That was, unless I was in jail, where luxuries, such as a cell phone, were frowned on by the local jurisdiction. Fortunately, my iPhone was sitting right next to me, resting on the floor of the truck's storage container. I could also have used the same feature with my computer tethered to the iPhone, but why use two batteries when one will do? "How could I have been so stupid?" I thought. "I could have done this back when I awoke in the storage warehouse." Did I have a concussion? Perhaps, but at least now I was thinking straight, so I opened the app, and hit the angled arrowhead in the lower-left-hand corner.

Within seconds it showed a blue ball in the center of a map, with a surrounding round circle. The ball showed that we were in the outskirts of Chicago in Villa Park, Illinois. A few clicks of my phone, and I soon realized we were just pulling out from a place called Wild Fire Harley-Davidson.

"Where else would we be?" I chuckled toward Amy.

All of this I forwarded to Alex.

Chapter 74

Two more days, and two more stops and all the bikes were gone. The last stop was in the big city and bright lights of Las Vegas. Again, I glimpsed out to see LAS VEGAS HARLEY-DAVIDSON, but this time some new crates were loaded in the back of the truck, the doors were slammed shut, and we were back driving in no time.

I crept forward with the flashlight app on my iPhone to look carefully at the new crates.

This was not car parts, and it was not "Art" nor "Bikes." This was something quite different.

The long wooden crates were labeled: AK-47.

The smaller crates were labeled: GRENADES.

"I don't think Alex or the Feds predicted this," I said to Amy.

"And we could be right in the middle of the line of fire," Amy retorted.

I texted Alex: "Heavily armed crew with AK-47s and grenades!"

One of the crates was half opened, probably checked out by the driver or passenger to confirm the load. So, I opened up the crate. It was a long, semiautomatic rifle, similar to the M16 used by the military.

I had fired this gun before, when I went hiking with one of my dear friends, who served as a physician in the Vietnam War, Dr. James Nicholas. James, or Jim as he was called by his friends, was a practicing general cardiologist, who liked to go fly-fishing and target shooting in upstate New York near Hamilton. He was kind enough to invite my son and me for an outdoor adventure approximately ten years back.

We hiked into the woods with my son Jason and threw axes into trees, shot arrows at targets. But most importantly, we were instructed in the way to load, handle, and shoot an AK-47.

Jim placed an Osama Bin Laden target against a tree and we stood back about forty yards, loaded, aimed, and fired.

Most of my shots at first missed the target, but with a steady arm and keen eye, I was quickly able to take out his disgusting beard and his smirking face.

I picked up my phone, flipped it on, and texted Alex: "Leaving Vegas. Be prepared."

Then pressed send and turned off the phone. Only twenty percent of the battery life remained. We cuddled up behind a large wooden box and quickly fell asleep. Amy was snuggled into my chest, and I had my arm around her shoulder.

When I awoke, I turned back on my iPhone to check our location, and we had entered California.

She looked at me. "I knew you didn't do this, from the start."

"Then why did you look at me incredulously when you first met me at the courthouse? I thought you were going to be as ridiculous as Alex and push the insanity plea non-sense."

"Any half way decent lawyer would never argue the insanity plea from the get-go. The insanity plea is notoriously either an obvious plea or one used in desperation. It's not even used in one percent of felonies, and is rarely even successful. Alex may be a hell of a scientist, but he would make an awful attorney. There were too many things pointing to you as a suspect. I knew they were all circumstantial, but as your buddy Schwartz would say, it is 'fucking' hard to refute the facts. My job, Alex, is to do everything I can to help my clients. And bringing Schwartz into your team was one of the best things I could do. He will dissect the timeline like a medical student dissects their cadaver. Then he will look not only at the evidence and its timeline, but he will also examine how and by whom the evidence is handled. Every detail will be examined with a fine-tooth comb."

"Nice to know that now," I exhaled with great relief.

"I knew something else," she continued.

"And what was that?" I quipped.

"I knew there was something about you, something very endearing, and very sincere. Something very special."

The light that emanated from my iPhone's screen shimmered like candlelight, and our little hideaway became very romantic. Even more romantic than a fancy night out at *Star's*. Star's was short for Star Boggs, the upscale eatery behind Main Street in Westhampton Beach.

I kissed her lips. There was no taste of lipstick! No smell of perfume! But we both shared a long, drawn-out French kiss one that I will never forget. I held her tighter, and she grabbed me. My heart was pounding, and I could feel her heart beating as well.

Then I slipped off her blouse and slid my hand beneath her soft silky bra, and cupped her breast. I have not felt these emotions for anyone, at least not in the last twenty years!

Chapter 75

W e're going to find the killer!" I professed.
"And we're going to live happily ever after?"
she asked, but in a manner as though she knew
the answer. Her facial expression was quite serious, as if
she were giving the closing arguments in a murder trial!
"But just not my murder trial," I chuckled to myself.

We were pulling over, and again I was clueless as to our
precise location. I only had a limited amount of juice left
on my iPhone, and that was even with the use of the extended-battery carrying case. I was trying to limit the usage
to just an occasional few minutes at a time, but I just had
to find out where we were.

"Amy," I said as I gently nudged her. "I think we're
coming to a stop. Let's be real quiet." We both hid behind
the crate and did not say a thing. Though I needed to find
out a little more information.

"Careful with the phone," she said. "If they open the
door and see the light, we'll be dead meat."

I knew she was right but I still had to find out.

Were we at Fort Mason? I didn't think so. Not enough
time had passed to make it all the way to the West Coast.
Where were we? The suspense was killing me.

The Maps app showed the location as Chico, California. I quickly opened Safari and typed in "Chico, California," to look on Wikipedia. I had heard of the college town before. One of my old classmates, Brian O'Hara from North Shore High, had gone to college there, Chico State, I believe. He was more of a burnout. You might call him a pothead. But Brian was also quite the artist. He won our school's art prize and got a full ride to Chico.

As I studied the screen, I learned that Chico was northeast of Sacramento in the northern Sacramento Valley and was home to Chico State. Yes, the school Brian went to. That place had a reputation as a big party school. Lots of stoners. According to Wikipedia, it was also apparently an education and cultural center for the region. "For potheads," I thought. But it also had a highly recognized art and art history program. Perhaps that's what made it quite the cultural center, though it was in the middle of nowhere.

"Another bike drop-off?" I first thought. "No, it couldn't be. There were no bikes left!"

Chapter 76

Amy and I continued to read from the cell phone's screen the description of Chico, California. We read that that Jackson Pollock had also lived in Chico when he was very young.

"Just another coincidence?" she asked.

"There are no coincidences," I replied confidently.

"Pollock moved here when he was a little boy," she said with an inquisitive eye.

The truck stopped near Orville, where Highway 70 intersected with Highway 99. The door opened only a crack, and I quickly turned my phone over. "Whew," I said to myself as my pulse started to race.

From the side of the crate, I could see out the back. Not a glimpse of the driver or his passenger. What I saw was a large black, yellow, and white sign that read:

PICK AND PULL, SELF-SERVICE AUTO & TRUCK DISMANTLERS

There was an old yellow car on top of the sign.

I looked around and realized what it was. One vehicle on top of the other. Junk! Compressed vehicles. It was a junkyard, a place to find used-car parts and to dispose of a totaled vehicle.

"What are we doing here?" I whispered to Amy.

She shrugged her shoulders and raised her eyebrows. This was a universal sign, which indicated that she was clueless.

This time, when the back opened up completely, I knew we were in trouble. Amy and I had hidden almost the entire trip behind the crated bikes, but we were at the end of the road as far as transported merchandise. If these last few crates were removed, there would be nothing left. How does that 1967 Herman's Hermits song go? You know, the one that was remade by the Carpenters in 1976: "There's a Kind of Hush (All over the World)." The line I was referring to went like this:

"Just the two of us and nobody else in sight . . ."

or maybe it was this line:

". . . you can hear the sounds of lovers in love."

No matter which one it was, we were dead meat. A team of oversized men in army fatigues started unpacking all the remaining crates, and as they came towards us, we made a dash out the back. A tall, lanky, heavily jowled man grabbed Amy and threw her to the ground. Another large, somewhat-hidden shadow of a football player tackled me as if I were going to score the winning touchdown.

"What were you two doing in the back of the truck?" said the man with the fishlike face.

"Hitchhiking," I said.

"And you?" asked the all-black-garbed, hooded tackler as he glanced toward Amy.

"With him, just trying to get home."

"Likely story," The Fish said.

"Ah, shit," I said to myself. "I left my phone in the truck. Now I really will be out of touch."

We were firmly escorted to a large multi-garage complex located right in the middle of the junkyard. Storage, at a car junkyard, is always used for something related to the selling of car parts, that is, of course, unless something else is being sold under the cover of *junk*. If one had to guess what that *something* was at a shithole of an out-of-the way place like this, it would have to be drugs. The door opened up, and there were no car parts, and no drugs.

Chapter 77

Inside the garage complex was a room that looked more like NASA's Mission Control than a junk warehouse. There was a series of centralized computerized workstations with a number of terminals with large flat-screen displays. On the wall was an oversized monitor with none other than a 3-D image of the Pollock painting rotating about its axis. The painting on the screen looked exactly like the one that was stolen from the Weisberg Estate, to a T. It was not a flat image, but rather a slowly rotating image, showing all the details front and back. The front had the colored swirls that by now were fixated in my mind. The side of the painting looked to be about two inches thick, and the back had several aged Sotheby stickers, including one browned-out space for a missing sticker. "The one that fell off," I thought. There was no wire attached to the back, only the two secure fasteners. "All consistent," I thought again.

Amy and I were then forcibly escorted into an even larger room. The room contained catalogued storage shelving for paintings. To the side of the room was a slave computer and monitor workstation with the same Pollock 3-D image as appeared on the previous NASA-styled Flight Control Room wall. In the center of the room was a twenty-foot-long conveyor belt. On the belt rested a painting, but not just any painting. It was "the Pollock." A large horizontal steel bridge was mounted in the middle of the belt, with hydraulic tubes hooked to a number of colored tubes in what looked like a triangle. The central array of rubber tubes included the primary colors of red, yellow, blue. Two of the outer tubes were black and white. I quickly counted the remaining tubes in a variety of rainbow colors, and there were fifty-nine other gradations. The tubes were actually not tubes, but hexagonal pipes in a geometric array and pattern that I had seen before. "Pascal's Triangle," I thought.

I had looked at the screen in the room and saw that they were using the latest CAD/CAM software to accomplish their task. This was the same program Dr. Shaw and I had used to create our MATAL system. The CAD/CAM computer program could take our concept and create a rapid three-dimensional prototype. Here, they were scanning a masterpiece painting and creating an exact 3-D replica. The original Pollock was already reproduced, using this same software. The painting I was looking at, on the conveyor belt, was an EXACT 3-D replica of the Pollock! Two guys in army fatigues picked it up and flipped it over; another applied the aged Sotheby replica stickers to the back, and a third attached a hanging wire. The black writing on the aged framed read in cursive: "Pollock No. 5."

If someone was going to copy the painting, I would have anticipated a skilled artisan standing and reproducing every little detail. I envisioned an artist in his or her forties, paintbrush in hand—like the forgers that were identified through the Knoedler Gallery in New York City. But our forger was not an artist, artisan, or even a human being. No, our forger was a computerized machine: a 3-D machine, no less.

The finished "Pollock" product was picked up and then put under a heat lamp to "bake." This team had the process down to a science. They used a finely refined "bake and fan" method to seal in the finished process and simulate the aging. The painting was then packaged in coffee beans to absorb and mask the smell of the paint.

Amy and I were forcibly brought over to the side by the shadow of a man and both handcuffed to a lally column, while the rest of the truck's crates were hauled inside. The large crate, nine feet by five feet, which accompanied our cross-country trip was placed on the floor alongside the conveyor belt. First, the wood crate was carefully opened up. The remaining Plexiglas cover was quickly unscrewed and removed. Then the veritable Weisberg "Pollock" was exposed. There was no perceptible difference between the two paintings; they were identical in every respect. Except for two things that were absent from the original: one, the missing Sotheby's sticker I had in my back pocket, and two, the missing hanging wire used to strangle Mrs. Weisberg.

The replica Pollock was carried over by the team's gorilla-type men, laid carefully back into the crate, covered with Plexiglas once again, and secured. Then the wooden crate cover was hammered shut. The crate was reloaded back on the truck, while the original Hampton's Pollock was repackaged in a different, less-secure container, which was more bubble wrap and cardboard than plywood and Plexi.

"Confusing," I thought.

The other "Pollock" was also loaded in the truck. I heard the back doors of the truck shut and then the noisy engine sound as wheels took off, then faded into the distance. The vehicle vanished.

Chapter 78

D r. Dawson, I presume," said a short, chubby, bald-headed man. The man spoke with a heavy Brooklyn accent. He wore a gold chain around his neck with a large cross in the middle. The cross intermingled with his greyish-black chest hair and almost touched the V made by his half-unbuttoned black silk dress shirt with a wide collar. My only thought was that this man was very *Guido*.

"Who are you?" I angrily replied.

"Let us say, I am not a big fan of yours," he taunted. He paused and then continued. "Call me Harry!"

"Let us go! You are not going to get away with this," I shouted back without getting an ounce of sympathy.

"Says who, Dr. Dawson? You don't even know who I am."

"No, *Harry*, but I did recognize the two guys out front. The man with the mustache and his oversized sidekick helped me with the mess from the storm. At least, I thought they helped me." Helped me my ass. Yeah, they hauled and cleaned and worked for their money, but what they really did was aided and abetted the art theft, and who knows what role they played in Angela Weisberg's murder.

"Anything else you want to say, Dawson. If so, say it now, before it's too late." Harry was not one to mince words.

"Yes. Who the hell are you, Harry? Come on, this is some operation you've got here. And that one over there is a great artist. A regular Leonardo da Vinci." I pointed to the large 3-D printing machine that had just re-created a duplicate masterpiece. What a joke. This was not art, but science, just like I do science.

Tiki and The Fish were orchestrating the loading of all the crates into the truck. Mustache man and Sidekick provided the muscle.

"Hey, Tiki, come here," shouted Harry from inside. Tiki brought Fish back inside the complex.

"Get a load of these guys," said Harry. "They are who you were looking for, aren't they?"

"That's them, bastards! How the hell did you guys escape?" The Fish was puzzled. He had orchestrated the kidnapping of the good doctor and his female attorney friend. And the word was out on the street. Kind of like an APB to the police—the Mafia equivalent. Yet there was no sign of either of them. Not until now.

"Let's take care of them the old-fashioned way!" shouted the shadowy Tiki.

Mustache man returned, interrupting the party.

"Hey, boss, do we take these crates and that sack as well?" He was pointing to the smaller elongated crates on the ground and a green army sack nearby.

"Yes," responded Tiki as he walked the guys out. "Just be careful."

Mustached Man and Sidekick hauled the ten elongated crates, along with a green army sack, into the back of the truck, along with the replica painting. The door quickly closed.

"We are in trouble," I whispered to Amy.

"I hope you have Plan B?" Amy asked.

"I don't," I quietly snapped.

"We are in trouble," Amy stated.

"Well, I might as well, tell you and your friend Dawson who I am. You will not live to tell anyone. So here goes. First, I am a master, just like you are. The best there is. You could take samples, analyze X-rays, even place the painting under an electron microscope, and you would be hard pressed to tell my paintings from their originals. Second, I am a *master scientist*, and yes, also an *artist*!" He paused and paced for a few seconds, then smiled back at us and continued.

"I am the supplier of the best forged paintings throughout the world. In fact, it is my belief that what I am doing is actually *cloning*. Because in the art marketplace, I can take a priceless painting such as the *Mona Lisa* and with 3-D computerized scanning and printing I can create two *Mona Lisa*s." If one painting was worth a billion dollars, now my two paintings, the real one and the clone, could yield two billion dollars. Simple math! Not just anybody can do this! Like you, Dawson, I have put my IVY LEAGUE education to good use!"

Right then and there he paused and looked me in the eyes. And then he turned to Fish and Tiki and said, "Guys, you have my permission to slit Dawson and his beautiful friend's throats. Do it now!" Massino quickly exited back into Mission Control. Tiki pulled out his Stiletto knife and started moving towards us, along with the Jimmy "The Fish."

"Give me one good reason why I shouldn't kill you, Dr. Dawson? You have sixty seconds," said Tiki as he pulled out his pocket stopwatch and pressed start!

Chapter 79

"CRASH, BAM, BANG!"

"SMASH!" came from the front Mission Control Room.

The rapid-fire sound shook me right to the bone, reminiscent of that semiautomatic AK 47 machine gun that I had fired with James Nicholas at Osama Ben Laden targets!

"What the hell is happening?" I whispered to Amy.

And then I saw him.

Olive-skinned, tall, and muscular, like Steven Seagal in *Born to Raise Hell*. He was wearing all black, including his classic black leather jacket, and was wielding his semiautomatic shotgun. And the best part of it all was that he was on our side.

It was Alex.

He quickly immobilized the tall, shadowy Tiki. One spin and a forward kick knocked the Stiletto to the floor. Another roundabout, and two forward thrusts and he removed Jimmy the Fish's sawed-off shotgun. The result was both victims were barely alive on the floor, reeling in pain.

"Krav Maga," I whispered to Amy.

"Quick Draw McGraw. Is that what you said?" she replied.

Both remarks were technically correct. He was a master martial artist for *Shaw*, quick at taking down his opponent's weapons and inflicting pain. The other folks—Massino, Mustache Man, and Sidekick—all exited stage right, whereupon Alex took out a special tool and *jimmied* open the locks, freeing us from our handcuffs.

"Alex, how the hell did you find us?"

"Been tracking you ever since you were in Port. I knew your phone was seldom on, but while it *was* on, I tracked it, found your whereabouts, and then followed you to this place. What the hell is going on in here? I was hoping you would make it all the way to San Francisco, but then I smelled something was wrong!"

Alex always had this sixth sense about him. Always knew the right time for everything.

He continued: "I was actively tracking your phone up until an hour ago and knew it was on. When you failed to reply to my text, I knew something was wrong—way wrong!"

Thank God for Alex's sixth sense.

Chapter 80

The three of us ran out from the back and into Mission Control. Not a soul. Then we exited the complex into the junkyard parking lot. Everybody was gone, and so was the truck.

"Ah, shit," I said. "We lost our chance."

Alex looked at me, and then back to his cell phone screen.

"No, you didn't, MD. Look here." He pointed to his Find My iPhone App, which showed a *moving* blue dot on a map. "Your phone is still on, and moving closer towards San Francisco. It is now on an interstate, Route 5, and heading towards 505 South. Follow me." He gave us the universal "come with me" arm swing, and we followed him back to his all-too-familiar Honda Pilot.

"Hop in," he said.

Alex quickly pulled out the Pilot, and Amy and I with it, out of Pick and Pull and raced to Route 5.

"You guys look like hell. What happened? How'd they catch you?" asked Alex.

"Just another joyride cross country. Let's just say we got a little banged up." Putting it mildly.

"Banged up is an understatement," laughed Amy.

"Anything to eat, Alex? We have been through hell, and I had no clue where it would end. Food was not our main concern, survival was. But now that you're here, Alex, I'll take anything. Just lucky to be alive!"

"There's a case of Muscle Milk in the back, MD, and plenty of Tiger Milk bars as well.

"Oh, yummy!" I said sarcastically.

"Got Milk?" joked Amy.

"Can you picture Shaw on a billboard, with his oversized physique in a business suit, doing a karate chop with a milk mustache, and the caption GOT MILK? Shaw, you missed your calling," I joked.

In fact, I didn't have to picture it. I once saw or dreamt of Steven Seagal on a "GOT MILK" billboard!

From the back seat, Amy reached way back into the Pilot, pulled out the Muscle Milks and Tiger Milk bars, and tossed a few to me.

"Want any, Alex?" she asked.

"No, thanks. I am well fueled," he replied.

Amy and I were like savage animals. Ripping the gold-and-silver wrappers off Tiger Milk bar, after Tiger Milk bar, and wolfing them down like they were nothing. Nearly simultaneously we both yanked the little plastic off the tiny juice box type straw attached to each Muscle Milk, then punctured each container with said straw, and sucked down the protein-filled concoction.

"Quite a combo of nutrients, Shaw. I guess you need your protein. Hey, Amy, just like when we were kids with our juice boxes, aye?" Humor was the salve for our dehydrated, beaten, wounded state, but the "Milk" bars and drinks didn't hurt.

"Yeah, just like when we met," said Amy almost tearfully.

Alex had the Pilot at full throttle, roaring straight down the highway. The occasional curve's centrifugal force threw us to the door.

"Look out, Alex. You're going ninety-five!" I shouted.

"No choice, MD. We've got to catch them," he replied.

"Not at the expense of our lives!" shouted a tremulous Amy.

"We'll be okay. Just hang on! They're twenty miles ahead of us," Alex said as he made the looped turn onto Route 5.

"Twenty miles and we're dead?" I shouted.

"No, twenty miles ahead," Alex shouted back.

Chapter 81

None of us felt good about this, and the speeding was the least of it. A passing sign said, SACRA-MENTO WILDLIFE REFUGE, but there was no glimpse yet of the shipping truck. Ten more miles and the DELEVAN NATIONAL WILDLIFE REFUGE sign loomed ahead. Then we spotted the truck.

"There it is," I shouted. "What's your plan?"

"My plan, for now?" answered Alex. "We're just going to follow from a distance, and stay out of trouble. Our low-tech tracking system works like a charm."

"You think you can do that all the way to San Francisco?" asked Amy.

"Think so, especially if it is just the shipping crew in the truck," replied Alex.

"Shaw, Harry something is in that truck. I don't know his full name, but he claims to be the artist behind the forgeries. What an arrogant asshole! The truck also has the operation's muscle. You know, the guys that helped me at the Weisbergs' Estate before this whole fiasco unraveled. They were involved from the get-go. How do you think we got so banged up? We're just clumsy? No, these were the goons who took us captive and almost got us killed. Plus,

I think they're armed with guns as well as knives that we've already seen."

As we pulled around the bend, we began to lose visual sight of the truck.

"I can't see them," I stated.

"No worries. They are still on the screen, a half a mile ahead. It's good to give them some distance. Remember, MD, the Honda Pilot was at the Weisbergs' when you first met your Mustachio friend and his sidekick!"

"You got a point there!" I was jarred by this fact, shaken to be more precise. Shaw always had a point. He was sharp as a needle, and never missed a beat, and he was *Shaw* good at what he does! Whatever that will be."

The plan worked great! South on Route 5, then South to Route 505, all the way down to Route 80. We even knew the destination—heard it as clear as day. Fort Mason! And then it happened.

Chapter 82

Just like a bad magic trick. Presto change-o. It happened. We were just getting on the long, expansive Oakland Bay Bridge into San Francisco. We were closer to the truck than we were on the interstate highway. It was much safer, now that other cars, trucks, and buses all were flooding the highway into the beautiful metropolis by the Bay, and I'm not referring to Oakland.

The view was magnificent—gorgeous bay water on both sides of the bridge, Treasure Island to our right, and San Francisco in the far distance. Treasure Island was a real treasure, with its 1939 World's Fair exhibition buildings. What remains is not only a historical relic, but also has the island's Administration Building which serves as a museum, while other hangars have been used for filmmaking. Parts of *The Matrix*, *Indiana Jones and the Last Crusade*, and even *Bicentennial Man* were filmed on-site. And even though this bridge did not have the glamour of the more familiar orange facade on the other side of the bay, i.e., the Golden Gate Bridge, it was still magnificent.

There they were on the phone screen. The moving blue dot was just ahead of us on the cell phone's map. Their truck, though on the bridge, was nowhere to be seen by our eyes. They were too mixed in with the crowded bridge traffic to be visually identified from all the other similar-looking vehicles. I looked back at the screen, and the blue dot appeared to be heading for the Freemont Exit. I knew this route all too well. That was the way to the Marina District, and the best way to get there. After about thirty seconds we were in the same position. As we pulled off the exit, I looked at the screen to identify the truck's San Francisco location.

"Alex, the blue dot is GONE! It just disappeared. What the hell happened?"

"MD, just try to reboot it. It should bring it back."

I did just that, but no luck!

"Not working, Shaw," I said anxiously. "What do you think happened?"

"MD, this is a no-brainer. No, I don't think they detected your phone and tossed it in the Bay. I think your phone died! How long did you think that thing could last, no matter what you did, and that includes your extended-charging case powering off your phone, etc.? It has been days. Your phone is DEAD! We'll just have to do this the old-fashioned way."

As we pulled off the bridge into San Francisco, Alex took his Pilot into hyper mode. He went left down the Embarcadero, and then left on Bay Street, and within a minute or so he was heading down Buchanan and crossed over Marina Boulevard, entering Fort Mason Center.

"Lucky we didn't get caught by the police," I proclaimed.

Chapter 83

Alex had notified the authorities of the fact that there was a major interstate transport of stolen goods in progress. The notification included the FBI, CIA, New York Police Department (NYPD), and the San Francisco Police Department (SFPD). Based on intel gathered from my text messages, Alex had arranged for the FBI's Special Weapons and Tactical (SWAT) team and SFPD's Special Operations and Security Unit's Tactical Operations Division, a division of Homeland Security, to stake out Fort Mason. How Homeland Security got involved was anybody's guess. But it was not really anybody's guess, it was Dr. Shaw's insightful decision. Shaw was seldom wrong! Both tactical units arrived at MacArthur and Pope Streets a full day before we even entered California.

According to the bronze plaque near the entrance, "Fort Mason was established November 6, 1850, on the site of Battery San José. Erected by the Spanish Government A.D. 1979."

FBI and SFPD saw nothing out of the ordinary. Fort Mason consisted of an upper and lower area. The upper area had an array of army barracks, and the lower area had a number of warehouse buildings and pavilions. From the upper area, one could see a magnificent view of the Golden Gate Bridge.

The Feds and police all caravanned down a lengthy road to a long, white building with a large blue sign that read: HOSTELLING INTERNATIONAL, SAN FRANCISCO—FISHER-MAN'S WHARF. This was a hostel, laid out as a large lodge with multiple rooms filled with bunk beds.

It was an inexpensive place to stay, but for the time being, it was where they would hide out. Six SFPD police vehicles and five unmarked FBI SWAT vehicles parked far to the left of the hostel, out of sight. They entered the hostel and set up camp—one plainclothes officer near the entrance and one near each barrack.

Chapter 84

We pulled into the quiet stately entrance to Fort Mason and followed the eucalyptus tree lined road around to the back of the upper state park-like area near the hostel. Nothing looked out of the ordinary. There was no sight of the delivery truck, any other criminal activity, or even a strolling policeman. At the hostel, the SWAT team's leader, Sergeant Peter O'Leary, greeted us. He flashed his badge towards us. "Another Irish cop," I thought.

"Park your car back here," instructed O'Leary. He was a somewhat oversized, six-foot-tall, middle-aged man. There was not too much hair on top, and his shirt was hanging out from an equally oversized belly. He seemed to be quite familiar with Alex.

"Good to see you again," said Alex.

"Top of the morning to you too, Dr. Shaw," replied the sergeant.

"Do you know where we can catch a thief?" asked Shaw.

"No sign yet. Come with us," he replied.

Alex pulled out an army-green sack from the back of his Honda Pilot and swung it over his shoulder. We followed him inside the hostel.

"They should be here any minute," I said.

"We know that, that's why we're here in the hostel," replied the sergeant.

We waited patiently in the hostel for the fireworks. Amy and I were crouched behind a window in a small room with two bunk beds. Holding hands! One minute went by, then two, then four, and then ten. Still no truck!

The truck had arrived at Fort Mason, but not at the upper old Military Barracks, or hostel, where the Feds were stationed, but at the lower warehouses and pavilions of Fort Mason. Lower Fort Mason consisted of the buildings that I recalled from the SF MoMA warehouse sale. There were three long piers or pavilions that jutted into San Francisco Bay, facing out to Alcatraz. The Herbst Pavilion 2, and then the Festival Pavilion 3 followed the most western Pier 1.

"Sarge, they're at the lower pavilion. The truck just pulled up," reported an out-of-breath junior SWAT team member, carrying a half-smoked cigarette. He had run over from the cliffside woods just to the left of the hostel, which overlooked the Lower Barracks. The officer now stood huffing and puffing right in front of the hostel, facing O'Leary.

"Guys, send Shaw and his crew around the front through the main gate. My crew and I will head through the woods down the cliff, and trap them from the other side." O'Leary was ready for action. But now he had to reconfigure and redeploy his troops.

The first-pier pavilion, part of the Lower Barracks, was the one I remembered the most, since it included the SFMOMA warehouse. It also included the ever-popular and long-standing San Francisco vegetarian restaurant known as "Greens." I had eaten there once before, nothing but fruits and vegetables, and definitely no steak.

The Lower Barrack buildings were labeled by letters A through E and consisted of long, concrete yellow structures, tilting casement windows, red fire escape-type stairwells front and back, and large storage facilities. Each building had such storage, and at least one of them must have had something to do with the stolen art.

"Guys, you six take the back trail. The other half come with me around the front."

O'Leary seemed to know what he was doing. Alex grabbed his army-green sack, reached in, and pulled out two shoulder-strap bags—each concealing a weapon. He unzipped a bag, which revealed an Uzi, an Israeli open-block submachine gun, and then zipped the bag back up, handing one bag to Amy and the other one to me—motioning for us to follow behind him.

"Just aim and fire, Dawson. Amy, you may have to do the same." Shaw just stared into our eyes.

I just nodded and swung the concealed weapon over my shoulders. Amy did the same.

This was not my plan. Amy and I had talked about a plan if we made it all the way to San Francisco in the truck by ourselves. Our plan was to run for cover and let the Feds do everything else. But Alex needed us, and we were not going to stay out of harm's way. It was *all hands on deck*! I looked at Amy and whispered, "Without capturing these guys and the painting, my life is over."

"Mine too," she whispered back.

We followed Alex and the SWAT team through the lower Fort Mason gate. We quickly ran through the parking lot shielded by Pier 1. When we reached the yellow concrete façade of the building, Alex looked back and put his finger over his lips and glanced at all of us.

From our angle, we could see the very back of the white truck, and then I saw the rear doors swing open. Concealed by the western wall of Pier 1, Amy and I quickly glanced towards Building C. Two men walked out the main entrance and stood below a big green sign with yellow letters that read GOODY CAFÉ. They stood motionless on the grey outdoor steps. It was the Vicks brothers, Maxwell and Jared, enjoying some San Francisco brew and a goody, so to speak. Fortunately, they were looking eastward and didn't see either of us. We peeled back in order to remain hidden.

Maxwell yelled to the driver, "Not here, you idiot. The Herbst Pavilion, over there." Max pointed eastward to another building that—with large orange, oversized garage doors—looked more like a seaside funhouse than an old army barracks.

"Alex, the Vicks brothers are standing right in front of Goody Café. Everything is going to the Herbst Pavilion," I whispered as I pointed eastward.

Chapter 85

Something bad was going down, and we were not safe. The paintings were quickly unloaded, and rapidly placed in the Herbst Pavilion storage. We followed Alex around the back of Pier 1, completely out of the assailants' view. I heard a large sound overhead and saw two low-flying black Apache helicopters hover just over lower Fort Mason.

"I hope they are on our side," I whispered to Amy.

Alex silently intercepted and said, "They're SWAT. Stay alert."

I hoped and prayed that I would not have to use Alex's latest gift. But the Uzi was a necessity, not a choice. From the waterside edge of the building we could see that the back of the truck was now completely empty. Standing right in front of the landing were Max and Jared. They spotted us!

"It's Dawson," Jared said, "Get them!"

Jared pulled a handgun from his pocket and fired two shots.

Luckily, he missed. Amy and I ran around the building between Building B and C, under an overpass between the two structures.

Two additional shots shattered some of the building's outer concrete, not human flesh.

We could see the rough waters of the bay, with Alcatraz in the distance. Twenty yards from where we stood, there was a large freighter docked on the side that stretched between the two buildings. "Was that for the Pollock or Pollocks?" I thought.

Following Alex, we turned right and quickly ran up the red fire escape-like stairwell into an open door, which led to the second floor of Building C. Alex pointed for us to go one way, while he proceeded in the other direction. Amy and I ran down the stairwell onto a landing. We could hear footsteps getting closer. We came out by a grey second-floor landing that consisted of four doors: three separate bathroom doors and one regular door. I pulled Amy's hand, and we slipped into the bathroom to the right, hoping that no one saw this move.

"You two cover the entrances, and we will check out the bathrooms, and the stairwell," said a familiar voice. It was Sidekick.

I heard a few doors open, and then our door slammed opened. We were hidden behind the toilet stall. We had no choice. As the door opened up, I could see through the bottom of our stall door a pair of dirty black shoes approaching the stall, and then I heard heavy breathing. I smashed the stall door outward against the body with all my force and saw Sidekick go down! He had fallen to the floor but was shaking it off. I then kicked him in the jaw in order to silence him.

It worked!

Chapter 86

Amy and I fled out the door, around the corner, to the stairwell. When we got down to the first floor, I saw Max with a gun, staring at the entrance to the bookstore. There was an Italian American Art Show going on across from the bookstore, and we quickly slipped in. The artwork was of an artist from the Bay Area, Alberto Tonnini, something I would definitely have enjoyed if the circumstances were different, but not while we were running for our lives. I looked at the large-scale landscapes, all of the Bay Area, not too dissimilar from our current surroundings minus the army barracks and warehouses. Their calming affect had no impact on our heightened adrenaline levels. It was "fight or flight," "them or us," or as Charles Darwin put it "survival of the fittest."

We slipped around the corner into the deepest end of the art show and leaned back against the wall that abutted a canvas entitled *The Marin Foothills*. Then I glanced back out of the entrance.

The coast looked clear.

We re-entered the bookstore, which sold a large selection of used San Francisco books.

"Who knew?" I thought.

Amy and I made our way through the bookshelves, and around the display tables and meandered to the right into Goody Café. A long line of people stood waiting for their orders, and I could smell the fresh zucchini bread coming right out of the oven. I looked towards the door that led out. There was Jared standing with a gun on his side. We quickly jumped in line with the rest of the customers and tried to blend in.

As we got to the counter a young lady asked, "Can I help you?"

"Yes, we'll take two slices of your zucchini bread and two mocha lattes," I replied as we covered our faces by looking down—away from any entryway or exit point. Always facing away from the door, trying to mix in . . . Our order eventually came. We each sipped our mocha lattes and gobbled down the zucchinis! This was the calm before the storm.

Chapter 87

Mustache Man was coming out of the bookstore's entrance into the Goody Café. His gun was evident to the crowded café customers. Once the customers saw the weapon, they panicked. Most of them ran right past Jared, who stood on the other side of the café, manning the entrance.

Amy and I were now out in the open. The short, flat shape of our over-the-shoulder harnessed weapon was easy to conceal. I had the meaty part of the "package" strapped across my back like a backpack. Amy's was on her front side. The case was not long and flat like a shotgun or rifle, and it was not short and squat like a pistol either. It was shaped more like a musical instrument, such as a trombone or French horn, than a semiautomatic submachine gun. And the both of us looked more like members of an orchestra, perhaps the SF Philharmonic, than members of a SWAT team.

Mustache Man ran towards the both of us as we tried to head back out towards the bookstore. To no avail. He grabbed Amy by her shoulder-strapped package and threw his left hand around her neck in a tight headlock. As she screamed from pain, I could see her struggling to breathe! I was out of sight, back out in the hall just behind the rear entryway to the café. I slipped off my shoulder-harness package, unzipped the Uzi, and proceeded back inside.

"Let her go!" I screamed, pointing the Israeli submachine gun towards Mustache Man's head.

"Drop it, Dawson," said Jared, the younger of the two Vicks brothers, who seemed to appear out of nowhere with a pistol now pointing directly against my cerebral cortex. I did not know what to do. I knew if I lost the weapon, we would be finished. But if I kept it up towards Mustache Man, I would probably be totally finished. My grey and white matter would be splattered all over the place. No *matter* what happened! I decided to hold my position.

"Dawson, you're making a big mistake!"

A crash came through the front door. As Jared and Mustache man turned their attention away from the both of us, I closed my eyes and pressed the button on the Uzi.

The loud rapid fire took down Mustache Man.

A similar barrage came from the front towards Jared, followed by the sight of another Uzi charging through the front door. Glass shattered from a pastry-display case. A framed poster of Golden Gate Park crashed down, and its glass shattered.

"The SFPD," I guessed to myself, "or the Feds." I expected a storm of troopers would follow, but there was no such storm.

Chapter 88

A tall, olive-skinned man walked slowly through the door. The man was wearing all black, including a black leather jacket with matching work boots, and he was wielding an Uzi submachine gun. His black hair was slicked back, held by an elastic band in an all too familiar ponytail. When I looked closer at the face, it was even more familiar than the back of my hand.

It was Dr. Alexiev Shaw.

"Drop your weapon," Shaw said, pointing the Uzi directly at Jared.

"No, Shaw. You drop yours!" Jared hardened his stance. But he was no dope, he knew his Luger was no match for Shaw's Uzi. He tossed the pistol towards Shaw. And Shaw put the Uzi down and started to walk towards the younger member of the Vicks clan.

I gave a sigh of relief. I held Amy in my arms and felt like this mess was over.

"Not so fast," said a similar-appearing but slightly older Vicks member. Maxwell had now entered the café. He too was holding a Luger pointed directly at Shaw.

Instantly, Jared grabbed the Uzi away from Shaw. Max came even closer, with the Luger pointed right at Shaw's heart! Shaw grabbed Jared's left arm and twisted under and then back till he held Jared in front of his body, his arm in a painful hammerlock hold.

"Your brother is my shield. Go ahead and shoot!" Max threw down the gun and, pulling out a knife, came at Shaw with a downward thrust. Shaw cracked Jared's arm, and split the bone right out of its socket and threw him down to the ground.

In a split second, Shaw missed the knife's blow, then grabbed Maxwell's arm with both wrists and kneed his wrists with one big blow, freeing up the knife. Jared managed to stand up with only one functional arm, his right. He picked up the Luger and pointed it back at Shaw. Max was again in front, and Jared was now at his side.

Two quick thrusts forward into Max's chest, and one on the side of his neck, followed by a roundabout and a sidekick to Jared's chest and head, and both Vicks were reeling in pain, just like those goons in Harlem.

"MD, are you okay?" asked Shaw.

"Shaw, feeling better now," I joked. But this was not over. The elder Vicks brother got up again, and so did his junior sibling, who was pointing a pistol right at Alex. Alex had his back turned and didn't see what was coming. I grabbed my Uzi and did what I had to do. I pulled the trigger.

Blood spattered everywhere! Down went both brothers. And this time for good."

Seconds later Sergeant O'Leary and the rest of the SWAT team came busting through the door into the bloodied café.

"What the hell happened here?" asked the sarge.

"You missed it, sir. Amy and I were held hostage by the Vicks brothers. Dr. Shaw saved us but almost died in trying to do so. I pulled the trigger, sir. There was no alternative. I had to kill the brothers to save Shaw."

"I don't know how to thank you enough, MD! It was always my turn to save your ass. But today, you returned the favor." I looked at Shaw and he looked back at me and we both started to cry. Amy just held me tighter, and then I let go. There was something I had to do.

"Sarge, I know this is a crime scene, but I have to check the bodies very quickly." I wasn't looking for permission. I was looking for the facts in the case.

I went over to inspect both of their bodies. First, I looked at Max and pulled off his shirt. Nothing out of the usual, a few old scars, one that looked like an incision from a cholecystectomy and another from what could have been an umbilical hernia repair. There was nothing other of interest. And the soles of his black shoes read, "Johnston & Murphy."

I now turned my attention to what remained of Jared, who was face down, and ripped off his shirt. A bulge was evident from below his left collarbone; a three-inch horizontal scar approximately one inch below that bone. It was a piece of metal, an implant that had saved thousands and thousands of lives. But it would do no good for Mr. Jared Vicks now. It was a defibrillator in the shape and configuration of the Medtronic Protecta, as indicated on the MedicAlert bracelet I'd found at the Weisbergs' waterfront compound. I looked at his shoes. They were Cole Haans, with a pattern identical to those at the Weisbergs' place. I pulled off the shoes and read the label: *Cole Haan Men's Air Grant Penny Loafer, size 13.* I pulled the newspaper out of my back pocket and placed it against his right shoe. "An exact match," I said as I showed the matching evidence to both Amy and Shaw!

"I bet he had a Cypher stent," I said to Amy.

Looking at his hands, I found what appeared to be wire burn marks from the fight that must have ensued before Mrs. Weisberg bit the bucket. The burns were from the painting's metal wire used initially to hang the Pollock but later to strangle Mrs. Weisberg. They were present on the front and back of both of his hands and were now in the healing phase. The scars were linear and scabbed over. They were there as a reminder.

"It's all there, Amy—the hand marks from the murder, the implantable defibrillator from the MedicAlert bracelet, and the shoe imprints—a complete match!" I said.

I threw my weapon down and went to comfort Amy. She was both shivering and crying and crumbled into my arms.

"Its over!" I said.

Chapter 89

Amy and I walked out of the Goody Café and saw Alex smiling at us in the parking lot.

"They are all dead," Alex said. "Jared and Maxwell Vicks, and his accomplices!"

"What about Sidekick, his accomplice upstairs?" I asked.

"He is the only one that made it," Alex said. "He is handcuffed in the back of that SFPD car."

"And what about Harry? You know, the gentleman that I told you about, that claimed to be the master art forger? The guy we were following from Chico to San Francisco? Where the hell was he during this mess!" He had to be somewhere. He was in the white truck and had to be nearby. I knew he hadn't gone far.

"Choppers found a bald-headed guy in a pontoon boat, motoring his way towards Alcatraz. He was a short, heavyset guy with a heavy New York accent. Wouldn't give us his name. But he's now in custody down at our San Francisco Police Headquarters. They will want you to ID him, MD."

That was the least I could do, I thought. And how about the paintings?

"The Feds are inspecting the crates as we speak," Alex caught me up. "The freighter was from an Asian cartel dealing in stolen art. The FBI was onto a worldwide high-end art-trafficking network. If we had been a few hours late, that boat would have been on its way back to China. The boat and its crew have been seized by the Feds, and their immediate team is in custody. The Feds agree that there must have been what you call a "Mr. Big," but they have no idea who or where he is. It's always the little guys who get caught and the Big guys continue to stay afloat."

We walked toward the shipping truck and saw the crates pulled out onto the parking lot. There were a number of crates, but only one large crate was lying right on the asphalt pavement. The crate itself was a work of art, and must of cost thousands of dollars. The Feds opened it up very carefully with a hammer and crow bar. Inside was a large Plexiglas cover. This cover was screwed into the wood itself. One of the authorities had a Black and Decker battery-powered drill with a Phillips screw bit. He unscrewed the Plexiglas and revealed a tight Styrofoam packing approximately an inch thick surrounding the back of a painting. The painting lay on its front, only the back was showing.

The wire to hang the painting was not missing. The fake, I thought. Around the painting we saw multiple Sotheby's stickers, similar to the browned one I had found at the Weisberg residence. There were no missing stickers on this one. Double proof of the forgery!

I couldn't see the sides of the painting, but the little bits of canvas that made it towards the back contained a brown, yellow, white, and black color similar to what I recalled from the night before the theft, as well as what I remembered from Chico. Two gentlemen wearing white gloves carefully lifted the painting from the crate and swung it around. "Easy," said a Fed who appeared to know something about art preservation. One would hope an expert knowledgeable about handling fine art would be involved in fine art recovery, and Cecile Donovan was their man. He was very instrumental in helping to recover a very valuable painting by a Norwegian artist by the name of Edvard Munch called *The Scream*. Mr. Donovan also recovered many of the paintings stolen by the Nazis in World War II. Those included many German Expressionist paintings, twelve Picassos, seven Miros, and five Matisses. But even those probably paled in value compared to the painting now resting on the Fort Mason parking lot.

The confusing thing about this painting was the identical-looking piece that was lying next to it on the right. That painting was not wrapped in plywood, Styrofoam, or Plexiglass. It was wrapped the way I received my prints back in New York, that is, in bubble wrap and cardboard. Both pieces were identical in every respect from the front.

Both had identical-colored splatter, with their twirls—the whites and yellows built upon the reds, and the swirling blacks. The back was the difference. The painting removed from the expensive wooden crate had all Sotheby's stickers in place and an intact hanging wire. The one packed in a cardboard box was missing a sticker and a hanging wire. I still had the folded *New York Times* pages in my back pocket. I pulled it out and unfolded it carefully. Out dropped the Sotheby's sticker that I found at the Weisbergs' Estate. I looked at it closely. There were areas of paper loss on the back of the sticker. Those areas of removed paper were evident on the back on the cheaply packaged painting. Those areas fit like a puzzle.

"A match," I stated firmly to Mr. Donovan. "This is the original! You can test them both, but I believe the hanging wire discovered at the Weisbergs' place and this sticker should help prove which is which." I was certain that this was confusing to the authorities. But at least they had the paintings.

"Jackson Pollock *No. 5*!" I said as I pointed to the one to the right.

Chapter 90

We spent a few hours down at the San Francisco Police Headquarters in the Property Crimes Bureau. Jared and Maxwell Vicks had been transporting stolen art for years. They were tied into a much larger underworld that was forging and selling art worldwide. Some of the names that were thrown at us I had heard along the way: Jimmy "The Fish," Tiki, also known as "The Shadow," Mustache Man, and Mr. Big, to name a few. The latter was the mastermind and was still at large. Apparently, the other crates contained a variety of paintings including, ironically, a Pablo Picasso, a Joan Miro, a Salvador Dali, and a Marc Chagall. All of substance, but none like Pollock *No. 5*.

I was brought into a room where we peered through one-way glass at a police lineup. Four men were lined up on the wall—a teenage thug with two tattoos; an African American man wearing a tank top; a middle-aged, short, bald guy who had taunted me, by the name of Harry; and a cross-dressing junky type that looked like he came from the Tenderloin district.

"That's him," I said as I pointed to Harry. "That was the guy that had us in Chico, and that was the guy who claimed to be the master forger!"

We answered some more questions and then were turned over to the Personal Crimes and Forensic Services Division. They had many questions about how and why I killed the Vicks brothers. After examining the evidence, and talking separately to Dr. Shaw and Ms. Winters, they came to the only logical conclusion. The Vicks brothers and their gang were the criminals, and I acted in self-defense. After two painful hours we were all released, free and clear to go.

Mr. Schwartz ran a detailed search on Seymour Vicks of East Hampton. Seymour's full name was Seymour Jared Vicks. Apparently, he couldn't stand the name "Seymour," although I didn't understand why. All his friends and family called him by his middle name, "Jared."

All the evidence about the painting theft was clearly related to "the operation." But there was still the case of Mrs. Weisberg's murder. Mr. Schwartz was able to do his fancy footwork, especially with evidentiary findings of the recent hand scars and cuts on Seymour Jared Vicks. Within a few hours, Schwartz had the DA convinced that all the evidence pointed to the Vicks brothers, and we were released.

"Amen," I said to Amy as we walked out of the SFPH.

Chapter 91

We had one night in Frisco. And it was a night to remember. I took Amy to my favorite little bistro located on Fillmore Street in Pacific Heights, the Jackson Fillmore. We dined like there was no tomorrow.

I had the bartender, or shall I say *sommelier*, select a boutique 2008 vintage Californian red wine from Napa Valley with an interesting name: "Forlorn Hope Sangiovese."

"Maybe he knows something we don't?" I said to Amy. We enjoyed our sangiovese wine. together with their spectacular sourdough bruschetta, compliments of the chef. We then shared a delicious California salad and their pasta special, and for dessert there was tiramisu and a classic California espresso (one to make the "Shaw–man" proud). But no evening would be complete without a cherry on top of the whipped cream.

That cherry was one night and only one night. For years and years and years whenever I went to Frisco, I would stay three blocks away from the Jackson Fillmore Trattoria at a century-old bed-and-breakfast brownstone called the Jackson Court on the corner of Jackson and Buchannan. The inn was only two blocks from Danielle Steel's mansion, and I was able to reserve the quaint Library Room on the second floor. That room was especially large and quiet. We walked to the Jackson Court, and I buzzed Evelyn, the manager, who let us in and escorted us up to our room.

"Evelyn, this is Amy, an old friend," I said.

Evelyn was smart enough not to ask questions, like any smart proprietor, and I did not have the energy or desire to tell her the whole entire story anyway. At least, not tonight. Every ounce of energy I had remaining was saved for only one thing.

I closed the door, and we both had to shower and purify ourselves from our imprisoned trip. We were too tired for an upright adventure like in Quiogue, but we were not too tired for a supine physical Fiesta Americana, California style.

After toweling off, it was just Amy and me. No props, nothing, just pure our physical attraction. But it was much more than that. It was deeper. Not lust or love, but our heart, body, and soul. And that, coming from a cardiologist. We had a connection, a sixth sense if you will, and an understanding. One that stood the test of time.

Forty years, to be precise!

Chapter 92

Evelyn had arranged an early wake-up call and a taxi. I got up early and walked three blocks back to Fillmore Street to grab two cups of Joe from Tullys, which happened to be catty corner from the Jackson Fillmore. I brought them back to the Jackson Court to surprise Amy. And she had a surprise for me. One block away from our B&B was a small beer boutique called Ales Unlimited, which had beers from every corner of the world, but in particular Belgium and Germany. She had an assortment of interesting bottles, which she was having shipped back to New York. Although I am not a big beer guy, the gesture was very thoughtful!

Within thirty minutes the Yellow Cab was out front. Unfortunately, there was no vacation left. No vacation in San Francisco, that is!

We took the next plane back to New York—a Delta flight out of San Francisco International to JFK. Amy treated me to first class. "Ah, the leg room, and even food!" I said as I turned to her.

"Louis, I think this is the beginning of a beautiful friendship," I said as I turned to her. She was a big fan of old movies.

"I love *Casablanca*," she said. "But I really want you to see *Vertigo*, with James Stewart and Kim Novak. That film treats the viewer to the beauty of San Francisco in the 1950s, with its hilly streets, trips to the Legion of Honor Museum, and a mysterious romance. We can watch it on Netflix back in New York and still enjoy San Francisco."

"Amy, we have so much in common: old movies, art, love, and time. And Lord knows I now have a lot of time. No more early-morning trips to Mount Sinai. I guess I could do what I always wanted to do. That is, to try to write a novel, go to museums, and maybe work on my next big invention with dear old Alex."

She kissed me on the lips and we opened a goody bag from the SF Police commish for all our help. It contained Ghirardelli chocolates in small, colored tinfoil wrappings. We chose the dark chocolates. There was a half bottle of PlumpJack cabernet, from a winery owned by San Francisco's former mayor, and then there was a small Boudin sourdough bread and a container of fresh Dungeness crab. The commish had arranged a heated New England clam chowder that the stewardess poured into a scooped-out sourdough bread bowl!

"Just like down at Fisherman's Wharf," I said to Amy.

"Delicious," she said as she licked the dripping clam chowder off my lips.

We feasted on this and toasted to our future.

Chapter 93

When we arrived at Kennedy, we walked out the door towards the cabbies. They were not the Yellow Cabs of San Francisco, but they were still nice and pleasant. The weather was not like in San Francisco either. It was after eleven p.m., cold and rainy. The temperature felt to me like it was in the low forties.

"Taxi, sir?" the attendant asked.

"Yes," I replied.

"Where to?"

"Westhampton."

Amy and I rode the cab all the way back to my place. We took the Belt Parkway and sat in some traffic until we hit the Southern State, which melted into the Sunrise Highway.

"All Roads lead to Rome," I said.

On the way, I finally spoke to Mr. Weisberg. AT LAST! Finally, the police did get in touch with him overseas. He apologized for his inaccessibility and confirmed that his report substantiated his request for my presence at his residence. You know what they say—better late than never. But I always prefer the statement: better never late! He was very appreciative of my help but still reeling in pain from the loss of his beautiful wife. He apparently took the next flight home from Asia, after he learned about her murder, and the funeral occurred while we were on the West Coast.

Mr. Weisberg said to me, "I knew it wasn't you, Dawson. I always knew it wasn't you."

When we hit exit 63 off the Sunrise, we headed south past Gabreski Airport, over the railroad tracks, across Old Montauk Highway, and then around the circle. Amy had fallen fast asleep in the passenger seat. This time I did not stop at Hamptons Coffee, but proceeded past the Westhampton Beach Police Headquarters, and eventually made it to Homans Avenue.

"The Shed," I thought to myself.

Chapter 94

The cabbie pulled up to my circular driveway and let us off. I nudged Amy and she awoke and got out in half a stupor. The cabbie deposited our bags on the sidewalk, and I paid his fare plus a generous tip. The neighborhood was pitch black. There was no life to be seen, even three weeks after Sandy. I looked out at the bay and heard an errant seagull in the distance, then went to the side door. There was a yellow-and-white DHL shipping envelope wedged between the screen door and the wooden one. From Morgan Capital Associates. I was too tired to deal with it then, but I had some idea what might be inside. I picked up the envelope, opened up the door, and then flicked the light switch. It went on. Power had been restored to our quaint little hamlet and our entire neighborhood. I tossed the envelope on my kitchen table, and then Amy and I brought our bags inside and didn't even bother to carry them up to the bedroom. We were so completely exhausted we didn't have the energy to do anything other than pull off our clothing, except our underwear, slide underneath the covers, and melt into bed.

"There's no place like home," I said to Amy.

"Yup," she said as she spooned into me.

"Goodnight, my love," and I meant it to the bone.

"Goodnight, darling," she replied as we cuddled each other to sleep.

At two a.m. I heard a door creek. The wind, I thought as I tossed to the other side of my pillow and thought nothing more of it. Then, as I started to doze back to sleep, my wooden floor creaked again, and then again. I looked up and saw a silhouette of a man. A man with a gun!

"Dawson, you are a dead man!" he yelled.

I reached under my bed, and there it was. Old reliable. Like the day my dad gave it to me. My Munson-signed Louisville Slugger. And with one large swing I whipped the bat around and hit the man on his ankles.

I made contact the way Munson used to, right in the meat of the bat.

And then—

"BANG." The gun fired.

Chapter 95

The sound echoed in my ears. I wasn't hit, but what about Amy? She was okay too. The bullet had hit the ceiling. "Close one," I thought as I grabbed the bat and quickly hit the man with all I've got in his chest. The gun was knocked loose. But the man was unconscious. At least. it seemed.

I went to pick up my cell phone to call the police, and then the man grabbed me with his rough, wrinkled hands, right around the neck. I could barely breathe. He then kneed me right in the solar plexus. I was doubled over with pain and still could not breathe. Any attempt to swing at him or kick him was futile. I was running out of steam and would surely fade away in unconscious oblivion unless something happened and quick.

Then I heard a smash. "BAM!" Amy shattered the vase on the nightstand over the figure's back. As he turned to look behind him, he released his grip and I was able to free myself and catch my breath. Then Amy flipped on the desk lamp and I could see his face. I checked for his pulse—it was still regular and he was still breathing. He was alive but unconscious. I could clearly see his face.

It was Samuel Vicks, the senior statesman from the neighborhood.

Again, I grabbed my cell phone and finished dialing police headquarters. But before I could even hear the voice on the other end, Mr. Vicks had risen and now was holding the gun to my head. I dropped the phone to the floor and just froze. "This guy had more lives than a cat," I thought to myself. I was helpless.

"Dawson, you didn't think you would get away with what you did. You killed both my sons and destroyed my entire network. You and your lovely friend are not going to get away with it. Say your last prayers, Dawson!"

Closing my eyes, I began to pray fervently for salvation. Then within a split second I heard it:

"BAM!" followed by a loud scream. I opened my eyes just in time to see Mr. Vicks, crash down to the floor with a big thud! This time he went down for good!

I looked at Amy. She was standing there, shaking, with the Louisville Slugger in her hand. She had picked up the bat and, using every ounce of energy, hit Mr. Vicks on the head. He was lying there, completely out. I went over to her and just hugged her.

"It's over," I said. Amy just shook in my arms.

I picked up my phone from the floor, and there was a familiar voice on the other line.

"Hello, hello, anybody there? Please pick up," said the voice. He had heard the smack of the bat over Mr. Vicks's head. It was Sergeant McElroy. "Address, please, I'm sending help!"

"It's Dawson, this time at my place, Mr. Vicks tried to kill us and we knocked him unconscious. Come for help!"

"Not you again, Dawson? I heard what happened in Frisco. Be right over."

I looked at Mr. Vicks, who was lying face down with blood running from the back of his head to the nape of his neck. He was lying motionless on the floor. I checked his pulse and breathing. His pulse was rapid and thready and his breathing shallow. I examined his pupils with my phone's flashlight app; they were fixed and dilated. Vicks was in a deep coma from the blow to his brain and the intracranial bleeding that ensued. Then he started to shake. He was having a seizure.

Three squad cars arrived. McElroy entered, to find Mr. Vicks unconscious, shaking on the floor. One of the officers was part of the Westhampton Beach EMT unit. I noticed his breathing had stopped and immediately checked his pulse and breathing. They were both gone. The EMT started CPR and for the next twenty minutes we both worked to revive the bastard. It was to no avail. The code was called. There would be no more lives for Mr. Vicks. His party was over.

I got up from the dead body and looked at McElroy.

"The Feds had alerted us to what happened to the Vicks brothers, and I always had a suspicion about Samuel Vicks's involvement. This time, I'll take the report right here. You won't have to come down to the station, Dawson," he kindly stated.

I looked at McElroy and then I cried.

Chapter 96

H onk, honk!"
I looked outside and saw that the Four Ones taxi-
cab had arrived. Amy and I packed a combined
small travel bag, and I grabbed the unopened yellow-and-
white envelope from the kitchen table and gave the bag to
the cabbie. We were on our way. We just had to get out of
New York! Enough was enough. The taxi dropped us off
at the Southwest Airlines terminal at the Long Island Mac-
Arthur Airport in Ronkonkoma. We were on our way to
Miami Beach!

"Amy, it was Samuel Vicks and his family all along.
Sam was the mastermind, the kingpin, the leader of the operation. I saved his life, and for what? We almost lost ours
because of him. Who would have even thought that the old
geezer was capable of doing what he did! And you, Ms.
Amy Winters, saved my life!" I just looked and smiled at
her.

"Well, MD, you resurrected mine!" Then we kissed.

Thanks to my dear friend Christian, we got a complimentary room at the W South Beach Hotel with all the
trimmings. The flight was seamless. And my guest, Amy,
looked magnificent.

"Your room, madam," I said in my best impersonation of a bellhop, as we got off on the eighth floor.

"You shouldn't have," she politely protested, clearly not meaning it.

"Thanks to Mr. Larosse. It's good to have connections."

Near the center of the bed we saw a bottle of Moet & Chandon champagne with a letter.

"Dear Dawson, here is a little token of appreciation. Please treat yourself to something special at Art Miami. And remember to have fun! Many thanks," Charley.

Inside the envelope was a check, for one hundred thousand dollars.

To Charley Weisberg, this was just a pittance. But to me this would be much more than a pittance. This would fund my new fresh start, especially at a trying time like this. You know, with no job, and any remaining assets of mine likely go to Shari and the kids. That was my own pre-drawn conclusion. And poor Charley Weisberg not only had to deal with the aftermath of Sandy, he lost his wife, God damn it! But I just couldn't do it. I felt too guilty about taking this large sum of money! It was a principle thing. I made this argument to Amy over a glass of champagne. She gave a cogent and practical counter argument, and then acquiesced. Very un-Amy like!

"A toast, to our new adventure," I laughed.

"A toast to us," Amy smiled.

Amy, however, was more practical, and put her two cents into the pot.

"Matt, you could really use the money. You should feel comfortable with all you have been through. Your neighbor understood, even with his own loss." she cajoled.

It just didn't feel right. I picked up the check and looked at Amy, and she looked at me. And as I looked at her, I ripped it apart and threw the pieces in the air. We both laughed and then embraced and kissed. Like Rodin's *The Kiss*.

The next morning, I awoke to a room-service breakfast orchestrated by Amy: fresh-squeezed orange juice, scrambled eggs, and whole-wheat toast with black coffee. The view was magnificent, on a terrace overlooking beautiful, serene Miami Beach. Amy brought out the DHL envelope.

"Aren't you going to open it?" she asked.

"Sure, I just needed a clear head." I took the hard, cardboard, legal-sized shipping envelope and pulled the opening tab, then pulled out the letter:

> *Dear Drs. Dawson and Shaw,*
>
> *Morgan Capital Associates (MCA) is pleased to offer MATAL, Inc., funding on the following terms: 1) $50 million upon signing for a 17 percent stake in MATAL; 2) MCA will fund your FDA trial and when completed will invest another $50 million for an additional 17 percent stake in MATAL; 3) $50 million after FDA approval in which MCA will receive another 17-percent stake in MATAL; and 4) MCA will receive an 8-percent royalty for each and every MATAL system sold.*
>
> *I hope that you find these terms acceptable.*
> *Sincerely,*
> *Frederick Morgan*

"Not bad!" Amy said as she smiled broadly.

"Not a bad start," I widely grinned back matching her excitement. "But Shaw will have an issue with the specifics of the terms. I guess its what you call negotiating." I knew that Shaw would multiply the seventeen percent times three and come up with fifty one percent, which would give MCA majority interest in our company; anything else was a nonstarter from his vantage point. Second, the eight percent royalty would be a little hard to swallow in perpetuity. Lastly, Shaw was looking for more up-front capital. But, all in all, it was a very positive opener, especially in my jobless position. But, as Dr. Shaw always said, it's not over till the fat lady sings. And for the present time, I was still unemployed.

"Another toast!" Amy proclaimed. "To your offer."

"Well, it's only an offer," I surmised.

"Yes, but that offer will help to pay the bills." Amy was my one and only true salvation. And even though it was warm in Miami, I knew that with Amy there would never be a better *winter*!

Chapter 97

The first day I was back and forth with Alex over the agreement. We were arguing points. I was too involved. But, on the plus side, I was able to partition my time. I spent only one hour on the phone with Alex. I kept my word!

But even that distraction was too much. I called him on day two. "Alex, your point is well taken, I will let you handle our counter offer with Morgan. The ball is in your court."

All my focus was back to what mattered the most—Amy Winter! After three days of a beach paradise and great nightlife, and sex for that matter, in South Beach, we flew back to New York and arrived back at my place after midnight. Amy had to get back to work, and I had to get on with my life. The next day when I woke, it was cold and crisp, but clear and sunny over the bay. I could see a crystal-clear reflection of the Seafield Estate in Westhampton Beach overlooking Quantuck Bay. Amy was gone. She was not there to enjoy the view. She had left a note. Her firm had lots of business waiting for her, though mostly white-collar stuff.

The note read:

Dear MD,

I had to get back to work. I knew it would happen sooner rather than later. The last few weeks have been unbelievable to me. You are really something special. Call me after 4 p.m.

Love,

Amy

My place was a mess. I had to clean it up, showered, and then threw on my winter coat and went for a drive. Not to Mount Sinai, or to Hampton Bays but to the ocean. The Beach Bakery was open and I grabbed a cup of their new Gevalia coffee, an improvement from their old Green Mountain Stuff. I sat down in the bakery at one of their small tables and felt the vibration of my phone from my pocket. I guess I had turned off the ringtone sound.

Pulling out my iPhone, I saw the photo of my daughter. Bridgette, while the phone persistently continued to ring. I looked up at the date and it was December 15. It was the date that Bridge was supposed to hear from Hopkins regarding her early decision application. This was going to be either a very good or a very bad phone call.

I slid the accept-call button, and Bridgette started talking.

"Dad, guess what?" She didn't wait. "I got into Johns Hopkins."

"Congratulations," I said as I burst into tears. "I cannot believe it! That is so amazing!" I knew how hard it was to get into that place these days, and I was so proud of her. "Hey, how are Jason and Mom?"

"They're okay, Dad. Jason, well, is still at home, and Mom is Mom—she's okay too."

"Thanks for the call, Bridge. I've been a little preoccupied, but everything is turning out okay." I felt a big sense of relief and pride, now that Bridgette was accepted to JHU. No need to hustle back to Port Washington and help her file her other college applications. What a relief!

I looked back at the phone and saw that there was one voicemail message from Alex. I hit the play button.

"Hey, MD, got my package from Morgan! Have meeting on Monday with Lippert to discuss. Will be setting up phone conference. Keep you posted."

I turned off the phone and then turned my attention back to my Bimmer, which was headed south over the bridge toward 105 Dune Road to the parking lot of Rogers Beach. The lot was completely empty. Rogers, the main Westhampton beach, consisted of—besides a large parking lot—a light-grey pavilion with a big deck and a closed concession stand, plus some benches. During the summer, this place was too crowded to park, but not today. Must have been in the thirties outside, temperature wise, so who would go to the beach? Not the surfers. Just someone like me to clear my head.

The ocean surf was rough and strong, a few seagulls were still there. The piping plovers and other sea creatures must have migrated south by now. A lot of beach had eroded during Sandy, but the remaining sand was clean. It looked like half the beach had washed away, sure to return, like it always had.

I walked down to the water and glanced at the swell. I then walked eastward towards Quogue, past the Surf Club, and past magnificent ocean front homes. And when I reached the Quogue Village Beach, or what was left of it, I just sat and cried. I cried for everything that had happened: the loss of my job and family. But then I stopped sobbing. I still and always will have my kids. Jason was not back at school, and now Bridgette will be going to my Alma Matter. And how about Amy? This was no fly-by-night romance.

I stopped crying and started to break into a grin. When I returned to Rogers and exited the pavilion, I saw a police car in the lot. I looked closer as I approached and glanced in the driver-side window. It was McElroy, eating an egg sandwich and sipping a coffee, with his engine still running. He didn't even notice me. I banged on the window, and eventually he rolled it down.

"Dawson, get in," he said.

I sat in the passenger seat, and while he finished his sandwich and enjoyed his coffee, I recounted my recent trials and tribulations. The loss of my job and the divorce papers filed by my wife were just events of life. But then he turned to me and gave me these words of advice.

"Dawson, I know that you feel like you've been screwed. But, Doc, let me tell you. You got your health. You are still a doctor, and you have a bright future."

He proceeded to tell me about his life. McElroy had a son born with a rare type of leukemia, who had been through all sorts of chemotherapy and two bone transplants. He also had a wife who was battered and abused, as a child, and was in and out of mental institutions. Lastly, he had himself, the only breadwinner in the family, barely making enough money to pay their medical bills and survive on the other side of the highway in a small trailer park in East Quogue. He told me that the WBPD medical coverage was good enough to help his seven-year-old son survive and receive his cancer treatments, but the mental-health stuff was not covered at all. His mom had tried to help out while his wife was institutionalized. But she was now back at home, heavily medicated and undergoing therapy weekly.

"We each have our cross to bear," he said as he turned to me. "But if you ever need to talk, Dawson, I'm here for you, man. I'm sorry for how I treated you when I first found you at the Weisberg's place. I was just doing my job."

"I knew that. I would have done the same in your shoes. Appreciate the advice. I am here for you as well. Here is my number if you need me." I handed him my old Mount Sinai Medical Center business card, with my office number scratched out and my cell phone number written on top of it. And he handed me a Suffolk PBA card from the Westhampton Police Department, he wrote his name on the back, along with his cell number.

"You ever need anything, Dawson, you know how to get me." McElroy just smiled at me.

"Always good to have a friend in the police department," I said as I left his vehicle and smiled back.

"Bye, Dawson. And stay out of trouble," he said.

And then I thought about the line I used for years and years at Mount Sinai—as I've always tried to practice conservative medicine and follow the Hippocratic Oath—namely, "Do no harm." But that was not my line—that was somebody else's line, namely, Hippocrates. My classic remark is and always has been:

"I don't have to look for trouble—trouble will find me."

This is what my colleagues, fellows, and students refer to as a *Dawsonism*, and for me, no statement has ever been more truthful!

Chapter 98

The rest of the day I called my kids to tell them again that I love them. First, I wanted to congratulate Bridgette again about Hopkins. I told her I loved her and made a date this week to take her out for Chinese food at her favorite place, Hunan Taste, in Greenvale.

I then called Jason and found out that Bridgette was correct. He was not going back to college. What was I thinking? He had struggled at school and needed time off. Had I been still at Mount Sinai, I could have found volunteer office work for him or some other job, perhaps even as an orderly in the operating room. I made a date to take him to the Barclay Center and see the Brooklyn Nets. "I love you Jason," I said fervently.

I called my local attorney and found out that it was official. Shari and I were formally separated and divorce papers had been filed. He was trying to get us into mediation with a matrimonial attorney in Garden City, Alex Weiss. Alex was very good at cutting through the bullshit and getting a fair settlement for both parties. Shari apparently had agreed to our settlement in principle, as long as she got almost everything. All of our savings, or what's left of it, the house in Port Washington, and our entire art collection. She also wanted to remain the beneficiary of my whole life-insurance policy. I had to commit to pay for the kids' college and living expenses, provided I could find a job, and I got to keep the "shed."

"I guess things could be worse," I thought.

And then I remembered. Amy had told me to call her after four p.m. It was a quarter past already. I picked up my cell and dialed.

"Amy Winter, who is calling?"

"It's MD. How's it going?"

"Inundated at work. Can you meet me at seven p.m. in Riverhead? Just go past the circle and make a left on Main Street towards Tanger. You'll pass the Riverhead Public Library on your right and then see a gas station. When you reach the gas station, stop, and go across the road to park in front of a little white barn. Oh, and bring a bottle of wine."

I wrote down her directions, and at six forty-five, I grabbed a bottle of Ponzi Pinot Noir and drove north on 104 towards Riverhead. When I saw the gas station, I looked across the street towards the white barn. There were no signs, only a little handwritten chalkboard sign and an old white house from the 1800s. I walked down a little stone path and went inside to the restaurant.

"What kind of restaurant doesn't have a sign?" I said as I met Amy.

"This one," she said. "Farm Country Kitchen! It is my favorite restaurant."

We sat at an old wooden table, just the two of us. After the hostess opened my bottle and poured two glasses, Amy made a toast.

Chapter 99

To us," she said. "To my newfound soul mate."

We shared a fried artichoke appetizer with horse-radish sauce and then a Caesar salad. Amy ordered their scallop entrée with guacamole on top. And I ordered a sandwich called the Maria Panini—a blend of chicken, mozzarella, pesto, red pepper, and some more fried artichoke.

We were so full we wanted to pass on desert, but Tom, the owner, insisted we try their bread pudding.

"On the house," said Tom.

We shared a single order and then left to go back to the south shore.

"Amy, thanks for being there for me."

"MD, you don't have to thank me. I feel like I have a new lease on life, and I can't wait to have more time with my MD!"

Right then I looked down at my phone. It was a new text from Cath Lab Gene!

"Call me ASAP—M-2-da-D!"

Up to eight years ago everybody in the Mount Sinai Cath Lab used to call me MD. But Cath Lab Gene started changing that. With his own brand of funk, he began to call me M-2-da-D. I texted him back, using my usual M-2-da-D retort: "U-2-da-Me!" Then pressed send.

Within one minute I had Cath Lab Gene on the line.

"M-2-da-D, I heard what happened. But I also heard that Columbia just canned their Cath Lab director. Their lab is in an uproar. Dr. Myra's team left en masse and went crosstown to Lenox Hill. The lab is up for grabs, and I just got a call from Braxton that he's been looking for you. Our crew wants you to apply. We'd be happy to go with you and screw those Mount Sinai motherfuckers!"

I wasn't even thinking about going back to work. That was the furthest thing from my mind, but probably the best thing I could do. I knew their Chief of Cardiology over the years—even had his number on my speed dial—Professor Joseph Braxton. He was a clinical cardiologist and cell biologist. Always very sociable at the American College of Cardiology and American Heart Association meetings. I knew him well enough to give a call, even though it was after nine p.m.

Chapter 100

Hello, Joe. I heard from my old Chief Tech what happened in your Cath Lab. I guess you heard what happened to me at Mount Sinai. Is it true?" I was trying to conceal how interested I was in the position.

"Yes, MD, Myra's gone. Bought out by Lenox Hill, and he took his entire team with him. I was just going to call you and see if you were interested. We've got lots of positions to fill. We'll need to rebuild," he said.

"Do you want to meet me?" I didn't want to seem too eager, but I knew the uniqueness of this opportunity.

"Yes, how about tonight," he shot back interestedly.

"Tonight? I'm in Riverhead."

"Yes, tonight!" I felt the urgency in this response! His sharp intonation said everything. "This is an emergency for our hospital. Our team is gone! One night we have one of the best interventional cardiology teams and the next day they're all gone. And we are one of the Top Cardiology Hospitals in *US News and World Report*. This is an embarrassment. What it really is is an emergency for our Board of Directors. Can you please meet me tonight? Anytime, anywhere."

"It will take me at least an hour and a half to get there," I punted.

"I have a better idea. You hop in your car and drive west, and I will drive east and let's meet halfway in Huntington. We could be chatting together before ten p.m."

"No problem. Let's keep in touch." As I hung up, I thought to myself, so much for my evening of fun and frolic with Ms. Winter. I did not want to get into my old pattern of putting work first over relationships. That got me in trouble in the past. I was hesitant to broach the subject but I had to, and time was of the essence. On the flip side, I was proud and overjoyed by this new opportunity. Cath Lab Director at Columbia would not be too shabby. At least, it would pay the bills.

I knew it was not okay to leave the dinner table without explaining the importance of this meeting and profusely apologizing to Amy. I was very concerned about her reaction, which was one in which she was very understanding. I gave her a big kiss and a hug and thanked her for the dinner. Believe it or not, she had to get back to work as well. She had several briefs to prepare, and I was really hoping she would prepare my "briefs."

I hopped in my Bimmer—BMW, by the way—and flipped on Sirius XM 67 Real Jazz! David Brubeck's Quartet, "Take Five." I just learned that Brubeck had recently died. December 5, to be precise, when I was at Art Miami with Amy. And now his most notable song was "bebopping" on the radio. "Take Five" was one of my favorite upbeat tunes, and how appropriate after all my adventures. I really felt I needed to "take five," and chill. But when opportunity strikes, you just have to strike back.

Within a half an hour Dr. Braxton and I met a Starbucks right off the LIE. Imagine, deals going down in Starbucks—not Star Boggs. I chuckled. Star Boggs was that chichi place in Westhampton Beach where many a real estate or business deal went down. And there I was with Dr.

Braxton, Chief of Cardiology at Columbia, at a dumpy
Starbucks, located in a crappy strip mall, just off the highway.

"MD, bring whomever you want: nurses, techs, re-
searchers, the works. I'll even give you an endowed chair
to work on your inventions. We're planning to be part of
the New York Technion Institute in 2017, and I want you
on board. I'll even pay you nearly double what Mount Sinai was offering."

That was too much to handle, but not too much to say,
"Done!" Which was exactly what I did.

With one handshake I asked, "When do I start?"

He responded, "Tomorrow."

Chapter 101

Tomorrow was only a little over two hours away. But for most big hospital bureaucracies it would take days if not weeks to expedite one's hospital privileges. Not for me. Braxton worked out temporary medical and cardiology privileges for me immediately. I placed one text to CLG, short for Cath Lab Gene, and by six a.m. was standing next to him, wearing scrubs, in the empty Columbia Cath Lab.

"Gene, we have work to do. No joking around, who do think will come with me?" I picked his brain.

"Like—everyone," he responded. "You built the best cath lab in New York, and we've all had a blast. Everyone, and I mean everyone! We are all with you. Even 'Ms. Every Patient, Every Procedure' Ninotchka wants to go. Maybe not Susan Arrowood, but everyone else."

Sue Arrowood's dad was chairman of Mount Sinai's Department of Medicine. And she was a real stick in the mud. Always looking for trouble.

By the next morning, just about the entire Mount Sinai Cath Lab staff had defected to Columbia. "Tough luck, Mr. Anderson," I thought. And several of the doctors also came with me. By the end of the week, Columbia's Cath Lab [or Center for Interventional Vascular Therapy] was cranking.

Ah, to be busy and back at work.

I did not have a place to stay as of yet, but was fortunate to have a friend like Alex, and began commuting from Plandome to West Harlem, where Columbia was located. The couch was getting a little stale, but the coffee—or shall I say espresso—was still fresh, and so was our friendship. FYI: he did offer one of several guest rooms, but I always felt that his couch was so inviting and loved crashing on it!

"So, tell me about Amy Winter?" Alex asked as he completed one of his classic espresso pulls. He was kind enough to get up with me at four-thirty in the morning and prepare me some Joe for the road. I filled him in on our relationship, and where I think we were heading.

Alex had helped me with my outside inventions, but with my new appointment at Columbia University, I had the opportunity to bring my inventions in-house. And hire the "Shaw-man" as my New Technologies and Innovations Coordinator!

"Alex, how'd you like to come work with me at Columbia? Gangnam style?"

What I was referring to was PSY's free-style worldwide hit "Gangnam Style," and by analogy that he and I would be given the freedom to build, create, invent, and teach. Without the worry of finding startup money!

"Sure," he replied. "Will I get a window?"

Chapter 102

Now no longer unemployed, I was able to get a studio apartment in the city on Central Park West, on the Upper West Side. The days flew by, with all the heavy work in Columbia's Cath Lab, and lots of playing on the weekend, some with Amy and some with my kids. I carved out enough time, as much as my kids would permit, to show them that I was there for them and always will be there for them.

Even at their age they understood the meaning of *irreconcilable differences*. That's exactly what it was: "irreconcilable." Shari and I were going our separate ways, but I knew my kids would always be an important part of my life. I have learned a lot from my past performance. Specifically, not to ignore my most important relationships, and they are my family and my kids. I was not going to make that mistake twice.

I did take my son, Jason, to the Barclay Center and saw the Nets beat the Knicks. And I took Bridgette out for Chinese—a big Johns Hopkins celebration. Whew, the pressure was off! My divorce moved forward. Any weekend time I could get, I spent with my kids, and the rest with Amy, either in my NYC studio or back home in my "shed."

Time flew by—fast, a lot of hoopla about the Fiscal Cliff, one that just sizzled out. And for me, the Parrish Museum position fell into my lap. I was asked to chair the Arts and Exhibition Committee. A responsibility I felt well suited for, especially since my first task was to firm up the spring art show. It was supposed to be called "Ab-Ex Recon!" But what the hell did that mean? Ab-Ex was short for Abstract Expressionism, and who were the main Abstract Expressionists? Jackson Pollock, Mark Rothko, and Willem de Kooning, to start with. But what the hell was "Recon?" Was this an army *reconnaissance* mission? "Recon" was short for "Reconsidered." But who the hell would figure that out? Did the average Joe in Suffolk County Long Island understand that title? Enough so, that they would take a day drive to the Parrish Museum, and pay the entrance fee to see the show? I doubt it. So, I worked on a catchier title: one that included a big-ticket name right there in the title: "Jackson Pollock and his Friends!"

Any such show needed a couple of big-name draws. Our museum's director was working hard to secure the art. He got a de Kooning from a Bridgehampton gallery and two Rothkos from one of the museum's trustees, but had no luck finding a real Pollock drip painting. The problem was not only to find the Pollock, but also make sure it was available in a little over four months. And even if I could find a Pollock, that would bring the show's insurance budget way out of line for the Parrish to swallow. Most major paintings are allocated to museum shows many, many months in advance—this was just too close for comfort.

I knew that the Board would be disappointed, I had to pull a few strings. So, I picked up the phone to make a call. But to whom?

Chapter 103

Opening night at the Parrish was a spectacle, and to-night was no different. Or was it? More limos, more celebs—big ones—and there was no place to park. At least they had valet service. I pulled up my Bimmer and the valet service opened Amy's door. She looked magnificent. Long black dress, high heels, and diamond necklace with diamond stud earrings. And that Vera Wang smell!

I was wearing my black tux, with a traditional black bowtie. I held her hand as we walked excitedly into the museum. The museum was decked out as well. I could hear a familiar Steve Winwood tune coming through the entry-way, "While You See a Chance." It sounded Oh, so good, and the title was apropos. Steve Winwood had been one of my favorite groups in college, and fell into a genre some-where between rock and roll and jazz. The current title was from his classic album *Arc of a Diver*. As we walked in a little further, I caught a glimpse of the band itself. The lead singer had wavy, longish dark hair, greying on the sides. He wore a dark sport coat with a brown button-down shirt, open at the top. This was not a knockoff of the Steve Win-wood band, but the real thing. The lead singer was *Steve Winwood*, strumming his guitar and finishing his hit song:

"While you see a chance take it
Find romance
While you see a chance take it
Find romance"

"Is he trying to tell me something?" I whispered in Amy's ear.

When I walked a bit further past the band, there was a bartender pouring Moet & Chandon champagne. Amy's favorite! I took two glasses and proceeded into the center and main galleries. There it was, like an old bedfellow. Branded in my mind; the centerpiece of the entire show. It was not one of the Rothkos, or the de Kooning. But the one and only Hamptons painting suitable for "Jackson Pollock and His Friends"—and one, that to my knowledge, had not ever been shown in New York, at least not to the public.

No. 5, 1948 by Jackson Pollock
Courtesy of Anonymous (aka Mr. Charley Weisberg)

"Thanks, Charley!" I said to Amy.
"Thanks, MD," she said to me as we toasted and kissed.

Chapter 104

I went down to the basement of "the shed." There in the corner was an old five-hundred-pound black-and-gold safe with an old-fashioned combination. It would have been very difficult to break through the five-inch-thick steel wall. The bearings and gears that worked the lock were state of-the-art, that's at least the way it was in 1942, the year the safe was built.

I reached into my pocket and pulled out my wallet. Still stuffed into the dollar-bill slot was the letter-sized envelope I retrieved before our cross-country adventure—when I ran out of the white truck in front of Ghost. Now, this was a risk I had to take. Not for the food, or my wallet, which might have been enough, in and of itself. No! It was for this envelope. Inside the envelope was the combination to the safe.

I pulled out the envelope and read a series of numbers:

42 four times to the right
13 two times to the left
23 four times to the right again
37 three times to the left again
Then PULL

I followed the instructions very carefully, to a T, and when I pulled on the door handle, the safe opened. I was thinking about what was inside, but I knew. Before my dad died, he had compiled all his important possessions into an eight-inch square box. In the box were some old Morgan silver dollars, a couple of U.S. coin proof sets from the 1960s, a medallion from the Apollo 11 mission which he bought at NASA in 1969, and a small purple-cased velvet jewelry box. I opened the box to find it. I saw it before, many years ago when it resided on my grandmother's ring finger. It was her engagement ring. I opened the box and saw the sparkling stone, even in the dimly lit basement. It was a two-carat Old European-cut stone resting in a platinum setting.

Someday, maybe I would have a reason to use the ring, I thought.

Epilogue

May 2013

A lot has happened since Sandy. We took down the largest art-forgery network the world has ever known! And in doing so, we rescued my neighbor's priceless Pollock painting. I was the main suspect in Mrs. Weisberg's murder, but thanks to all my friends, we found the real killers, and I got out of that one. Whew! My divorce is finalized, and my daughter is at Hopkins. I am now closer than ever before to both of my kids!

I've been working long but productive sixty-hour weeks in the Cath Lab at Columbia, and, yes, Dr. Shaw and I completed the MATAL deal with Morgan Capital. Thank you, Frederick Morgan! Alex is working next to my office at Columbia. He has about two thousand square feet of research space, three associates, plus lots of Columbia students. And yes, a little corner of his lab has an industrial-grade Nuova Simonelli espresso machine. It brings me joy to see the sign right outside of his office:

Professor Alexiev Shaw
Director of New Technologies and Cardiac Innovations

And also joy, to know that I don't have to go far for a great latte!

Sure, all that is important. I am amazed at everything that occurred over the past year! The most important thing that happened to me personally is with Ms. Amy Winters. Amy and I have been together for nearly six months. I wanted to take her to someplace new. I picked her up in my BMW 650i, and the weather was warm enough to put the top down. The fresh air and "Suite No.1 for Flute and Jazz Piano" from *Bolling's Greatest Hits* provided the perfect background for this trip. Jean-Pierre Rampal's flute added the magical rhapsody. Everything had turned green again, and the flowers were in full bloom. We meandered through the local roads and headed north up Country Route 104. I pulled over past the farm on the right, and stopped briefly at the local farm stand, and grabbed a couple of freshly baked apple muffins and two cream sodas.

"Where are we going?" she asked.

"My surprise," I replied.

With one click of a button, I brought my convertible's top back up, and hit the highway. Montauk Highway that is. We drove down Montauk Highway until it became a one-lane road. Then we snailed along in traffic past Southampton, Bridgehampton, and finally entered the town of East Hampton. We listened to the Claude Bolling Big Band the entire way. In addition to Jean-Pierre Rampal, we heard Pinchas Zuckerman on violin and Yo-Yo Ma on cello.

We eventually hit Springs Fireplace Road. I opened the window further to enjoy the fresh air and heard the birds tweeting. As I did that, my bimmer hit a pothole and the top of my head grazed the soft top. I slowed down, and pulled over to the side of the road, realizing that we were on the same road and near where Jackson Pollock crashed his Oldsmobile!

"Amy you do know where we are?" I said half shaken by the mild graze.

"Haven't the foggiest, other than East Hampton."

"We are on Springs Fireplace Road, near where Pollock crashed his car and died!" I was still shaking from the pot-hole, and proceeded to put the roof back down. I took a deep breath in and replenished myself with the fresh air. The *bump*, gave me a chance not only to reflect on Pollock, but to reflect on life, and how fragile it is. And then I re-membered, my late great Hopkins professor, Doctor Michel Mirowski.

"Amy, it hit me! We are so lucky to be alive. And here we are on the same road where Pollock died. As my mentor Dr. Mirowski's would say: *'The bumps in the road are not bumps, they are the road.'* I know what he means by this!"

"I do too, MD. I do too!" She reached for my hand and gave it a gentle caress. My body started to tingle.

I headed slowly and cautiously back up the winding road with a renewed vigor about life. The road led up to an old wooden house near Accabonac Creek in East Hamp-ton.

The sign out front read:

POLLOCK KRASNER HOUSE & STUDIO

The studio was a simple, aged, cedar-shingled building. In fact, the outside resembled my shed in Quiogue. Further down the path, Alex stood on the front steps. And then we all went inside. On the walls were old photos of Jackson Pollock and his wife, Lee Krasner. Some even showed him splashing paint on a canvas on this exact floor. His boots, mostly covered with white splattered paint, were also on display. The actual coffee and paint cans he had used to mix his paints, with their sticks and brushes, were there on a shelf. The wooden floor was the most impressive. The floor contained the same type of splatter as appeared on the painting that I saw on the Weisbergs' wall.

"Classic Pollock," I affirmed.

"Just like *No. 5!*" exclaimed Amy.

"What's all this about?" asked Alex. Alex thought there might be something unusual happening. When do I drag him all the way out to East Hampton? I needed him for emotional support!

"Amy, there's something I have to ask you." I reached into my front-right pants pocket and felt for the small purple-covered jewelry box. My right hand was feeling the velvet covering, and I began to sweat profusely. My breathing quickened, and I became slightly queasy. I was starting to hyperventilate and did not have a brown paper bag to breathe into. I became very lightheaded and fell down to my knees, lowering my head. As I closed my eyes, I visualized breathing slowly into an imaginary bag. My body followed suit. After a few seconds, I started to become more lucid and felt better. My breathing began to slow down. I wiped the sweat off my forehead and then I looked up at her.

"Amy, I love you!" I could barely get the words out.

Then silence! Not a peep!

I gazed deeply into her eyes, and then she gazed back at mine.

"I love you too, MD!"

We were both ecstatic and then we kissed. A long French kiss!

Alex applauded. "Bravo!"

I pulled the velvet box out of my pocket and opened it. The ring shimmered from the sunlight in the distance, but also sparkled from the myriad of splattered colors emanating from the Pollock Krasner studio. The moment was magical. And then I said it!

"Will you marry me?"

THE END

Here is an excerpt from Dr. Dawson's Next Book!

Chapter 1

W hich way is Grand Street?" I asked two local female hipsters in SoHo. The two lovebirds were staring into the designer window, both holding hands.

"Just a few more blocks down Greene Street and you'll eventually hit Grand," the taller, sleeker hipster replied. She was six feet two inches tall, of Asian descent, with long black hair, wearing a cashmere sweater, skinny jeans, and holstering a Prada shoulder bag. Her shorter partner looked equally hip, with her matching long black hair and a slightly smaller tote that also said, Prada.

"Two peas in a pod," I thought.

I made my way around a black Nissan SUV, climbed under some rolled-up tape, and saw one of my favorite stores, Design Within Reach. And right there in the window was the exact chair that Amy and I had been looking at yesterday at Vintage Thrift on Third Street between Twenty-Second and Twenty-Third. Vintage Thrift had a set of six chairs available for $100 a pop.

Those chairs would look great, around our Knoll kitchen table, in our new apartment in Tribeca. It was the Eames Molded Fiberglass Armchair, a classic in its own right! As I looked through the window, I saw a five hundred dollar price tag hanging from the chair. We could buy all six of those chairs at Vintage Thrift for a little more than the price of the new one in the window.

"What a steal at Vintage Thrift," I thought. Wanting Amy to see the showcased beauty, I quickly pulled out my iPhone and headed right onto the sidewalk in front of the store's window to capture the chair's essence.

SNAP!

"WHAT THE HELL ARE YOU DOING HERE!" shouted the oversized beast of a police officer as he grabbed my elbow. His smaller partner started in on me as well.

"Didn't you see the police tape?" said the other officer with more anger than disdain.

"No, Officer, I was so focused in on taking a photo of the chair I . . . I . . ." I just could not get my words out. Stuttering was a problem I thought I had overcome in elementary school. Three years with a speech pathologist named Mae Parsons. I used to call her Aunt Mae. But stress would bring out those bad memories, and I occasionally regressed and began to stutter again.

I pulled out the iPhone and opened the Photos app, looking for the designer chair. I opened the photo and started to zoom into the chair to show the officer. On the bottom left-hand corner of the window was something I had not seen previously, I was so focused on that stupid chair. The image was of a silhouette or black stencil image of a rat, wearing a beret with a star and holding a spray can spraying the color red. How did I miss this? The image was typical of the mysterious English street artist called Banksy. Nobody has ever seen the artist. "What could it mean?" I thought to myself. I changed gears quickly, zoomed out, and showed the officer the photo of chair.

"Here, Officer. This is the chair," I said.

"Let me see some identification?" demanded the first officer.

I opened my wallet and gave him my license, as well as the Suffolk PBA card given to me by Officer John McElroy of the Westhampton Beach Police Department. McElroy and I had shared a special bond. We both had gone through tough times. But as my mom always said, "Tough times don't last—only tough people do!"

"Why are you giving me a police card?" asked the officer. He looked down at my license and then said, "Matthew Dawson, MD. That name sounds familiar. Now I'm putting two and two together. You were the doctor that was on the front page of the *New York Times*. Killed an heiress and stole a painting!"

With one full swoop, the other officer started in again at me. "Do you know that you entered a crime scene." I looked around and saw a wide taped-off area, with no one within the area. The tape said, POLICE, but was essentially illegible since it spiraled around between each post. Maybe a "P" and a part of an "O," or an "L" and a part of an "E." But the word "Police" was not easily discernable.

"Don't you see the body? You're standing in what's left of the dead man's head! A head blown to smithereens!"

I looked down and saw that I was standing smack in the middle of what may have been confused remotely with tossed-out spaghetti and meatballs. Not an uncommon sight in New York City. But upon closer examination it wasn't spaghetti and meatballs at all. Parts of it resembled the cingulate gyrus of the cerebral cortex that I studied back in med school. And the tomato sauce wasn't tomato sauce at all either, but rather the blood and guts contained within a skull.

I glanced over to what the officer referred to as the body, literally ten feet from where I was standing. But I did not see a body at all, just a pile of blankets.

"Officer, I was trying to meet up with my fiancée. I had no idea that this was a crime scene!"

"Tell me you didn't see the police tape?" the officer asked sarcastically.

"I didn't see it at all; it's rolled up, so you can barely see the writing on the tape. And the body doesn't even look like a body, but just a pile of blankets from some homeless guy in the city. And those brains, that I'm standing on, look like someone's dropped leftovers!"

"I'm afraid, Mr. Dawson, that you are under arrest for violating and photographing a crime scene."

"It's not illegal to take photographs of a crime scene," I muttered to myself. No point in voicing my opinion. The officer wasn't listening to reason. Not after he heard my *notorious* name. The officer grabbed my arm, took my iPhone, and twisted my right arm behind my back, slamming on the handcuffs; he did the same with my other arm and hooked the other cuff to it.

"Can I make one phone call, Officer? Can't I at least make one phone call?"

Chapter 2

I was shoved into the back of the NYPD police car and taken down to headquarters on Twenty-First between Second and Third Avenue. The 13th Precinct, to be precise! I was aggressively pulled up the steps into a dark and dingy room with just a table and two metal chairs, and an old-fashioned pull chain single light bulb hanging from the ceiling. Opening my big fat mouth was not going to help anything! I learned my lesson the last time. I did not make a peep.

Then the questioning started. The officer's badge read, "Detective Jose Lopez." He had dark hair and was five feet eight. There were no introductions.

"Dawson, what the hell were you doing down in SoHo?" Lopez asked.

"Officer, aren't I entitled to one phone call?"

"Answer my question," he snapped.

"No, sir, with all due respect, this is what got me in trouble the last time. I am entitled to one phone call."

"Okay, Dawson, have it your way. You have one phone call and only one phone call! That's all you get." Lopez seemed more frustrated than angry as he pointed to the old-style phone on the table and left the room.

And then I thought to myself, "Just one phone call." I did not have my cell phone anymore. Just the old dial phone that rested on the table. Kind of a throwback to yesteryear. I didn't even know these old things still existed. The officer was kind enough to walk out the door and give me what seemed like privacy. But for all I knew, this dismal room was bugged.

"Just one phone call," I said again to myself. And whom did I call? It was like a reflex. I didn't even think about it. It was instinctual. Did I call my fiancée attorney, who by now must be perplexed why I never showed up near Grand Street? She must be even more perplexed that I didn't even give her a call! No, I didn't call her. I phoned Shaw. He was always my point person in life. My savior. And then I remembered what he always told me:

"You don't need an attorney, you don't need a tax accountant, and you don't need a financial advisor. All you need is me!"

I don't know why I didn't just call my damn fiancée, my wife-to-be, my soul mate, Amy Winter! She must be trying to reach me. If I'd had my iPhone, I would see a half dozen texts and voicemails on it. But no, I didn't call her!

No, I called Shaw, Alexiev Shaw!

About the Author

Dr. Todd J. Cohen is a renowned scientist, inventor, and cardiologist. He is an avid writer and editor, and has published many articles in medical journals including *Circulation, JAMA,* and the *New England Journal of Medicine.* He directed two of the busiest electrophysiology programs on Long Island over two-and-a-half decades, and currently serves as the Chief of Cardiology and Director of Medical Device Innovation at the NYITCOM. He is the Founder and Director of the Long Island Heart Rhythm Center located in Old Westbury, New York on the NYITCOM campus. He is an attending physician within the Catholic Health System on Long Island, and in the Mount Sinai Health System in Manhattan. He is also known for his Johns Hopkins Press 2010 Best Health Book entitled "A Patient's Guide to Heart Rhythm Problems," his book "Practical Electrophysiology," currently in its third edition, as well as his many cardiac inventions including one featured in this book in which CPR is performed using a handheld toilet plunger ("active compression-decompression CPR"). He has a passion for art and has served on the Board of Trustees (and currently Chairs the Art and Exhibition Committee) at the Nassau County Museum of Art, in Roslyn, New York.

CPSIA information can be obtained
at www.ICGtesting.com
Printed in the USA
BVHW081957070621
608952BV00012B/1474